"You're pregnant," Bowie repeated.

Marlowe blew out a frustrated breath. "That's what I just said."

"And it's mine?"

"Yes, it's yours, damn it."

"How can you be sure?"

There was fury in her eyes. But somehow, she managed to keep herself under control.

"Count yourself lucky that the handgun my father gave me is in a lockbox and not in a drawer in my desk because if it was the latter, right now I'd be sorely tempted to use it on you. In the long run, that would be preferable to having you as the father, but there you have it. You are the father of my unborn child and that's a horrible fact we're both stuck with."

Her eyes grew very dark as she added, "And to answer your question as to how I know you're the father of this child, I know because I haven't had the time or the inclination to sleep with anyone in months, so unless this baby is the result of some sort of spontaneous generation, you, Bowie Robertson, are the father. Deal with it!"

* * *

Book one of The Coltons of Mustang Valley

* * *

If you're on Twitter, tell us what you think of Harlequin Romantic Suspense! #harlequinromsuspense

Dear Reader,

Welcome to book one of a brand-new Colton saga. This story has everything: babies switched at birth, attempted murders, not to mention a thrice-married patriarch whose disliked second ex-wife is on the company's board of directors despite the fact that everyone wants her off and out of their lives.

Most important, we have two clashing presidents of rival companies who have just discovered that their one night of indiscretion six weeks ago has yielded a significant dividend. Marlowe Colton, the president of Colton Oil, is carrying the baby of the president of Robertson Energy Company, Bowie Robertson. Talk about an unexpected merger.

While they deal with trying to figure out how to tell the two families and where to go from there, the entire Colton clan is reeling from the impact of an anonymous email they have just received claiming that eldest son Asa "Ace" Colton was switched in the hospital at birth and isn't a Colton at all. Thrown into this is a mysterious stalker following either Marlowe or Bowie (or both). And the action only escalates from there. Have I got your attention yet? Good. Then come read and, hopefully, be entertained.

As always, I thank you for reading, and from the bottom of my heart, I wish you someone to love who loves you back.

All the best,

Marie Ferrarella

COLTON BABY CONSPIRACY

Marie Ferrarella

HARLEQUIN® ROMANTIC SUSPENSE

Special thanks and acknowledgment are given to
Marie Ferrarella for her contribution to
The Coltons of Mustang Valley miniseries.

ISBN-13: 978-1-335-62636-3
ISBN-13: 978-1-335-08180-3 (DTC Edition)

Colton Baby Conspiracy

Copyright © 2020 by Harlequin Books S.A.

Recycling programs
for this product may
not exist in your area.

HARLEQUIN®

www.Harlequin.com

Printed in U.S.A.

USA TODAY bestselling and RITA® Award–winning author **Marie Ferrarella** has written more than two hundred and fifty books for Harlequin, some under the name Marie Nicole. Her romances are beloved by fans worldwide. Visit her website, marieferrarella.com.

Books by Marie Ferrarella

Harlequin Romantic Suspense

The Coltons of Mustang Valley

Colton Baby Conspiracy

Cavanaugh Justice

Mission: Cavanaugh Baby
Cavanaugh on Duty
A Widow's Guilty Secret
Cavanaugh's Surrender
Cavanaugh Rules
Cavanaugh's Bodyguard
Cavanaugh Fortune
How to Seduce a Cavanaugh
Cavanaugh or Death
Cavanaugh Cold Case
Cavanaugh in the Rough
Cavanaugh on Call
Cavanaugh Encounter
Cavanaugh Vanguard
Cavanaugh Cowboy
Cavanaugh's Missing Person

Visit the Author Profile page at
Harlequin.com for more titles.

This 300th book is dedicated with love

To my wonderful readers,
Without whom I would still be working as
a health insurance claims adjuster,
Dreaming of becoming a writer;

To
My fabulous editors, especially Patience Bloom,
Whose fear of being buried alive in stacks of
Proposals had them finally deciding to take a
chance on me;

And
To
Charlie,
Who was, and is, my inspiration for every single hero
I have ever written about.
I couldn't have done it without you, honey.

From the bottom of my heart,
Thank you!

Prologue

They enjoyed being in control; they always had. Even back in the early days, alone and struggling to make ends meet, a day-to-day world nothing if not hopeless and bleak, they'd *dreamed* of being in a position when they would finally be in control.

Slowly but surely, they had worked relentlessly toward reaching that goal, moving from stepping-stone to small stepping-stone until finally, *finally* arriving at a place of authority. When they finally controlled people who didn't even realize they were being controlled.

I am that good, they thought with a self-congratulating smile.

And this, *this*, they thought, looking at the email draft on their laptop, was going to be the ultimate achievement, the crowning glory. Because when this email went out and at long last set this greatest plan in motion, they were going to be in control of not just a person or a small group of people but of a large, thriving company.

An entire, billion-dollar company.

It would be, they thought with a smug, self-satisfied smile, like going from presiding over a tiny cottage in the forest to ruling over a giant kingdom.

My giant kingdom.

Oh, there would be a figurehead to front the company, but *they* would be the one who told that figurehead what to do, what to think. *They* would be the one in charge of everything.

As it should be. After all, who better to control all those employees? Who was more deserving to reap all those rewards?

They laughed to themselves.

"Why, *me* of course. I'm the most deserving person I know," they announced to the surrounding darkness of the small office where they presently oversaw the organization they had created and molded out of nothing.

Taking a deep breath, they pulled back their shoulders and focused on the task at hand. The shadowy figure reread the words that had been typed and then retyped so many times since this idea had begun to take its final shape.

This had to be perfect.

The email had to sound coherent. To read as if it was written by an intelligent person—but not by someone who was overly intellectual. Or that some delusional, misguided person had written it.

Above all, it could not come across as if it was a

hoax. It had to read as if every word was nothing but the absolute truth.

They wanted the message to read as if the person who wrote it was cool, calm and just a touch superior. *Because I am*, they thought. *Superior to the lot of them. And more than just by a touch.* Because once they acted on this knowledge, it would be the beginning of their downfall.

It might take a week, or a month or even a year—although they doubted it would take that long—but they *would* definitely fall.

A smug smile curved their lips as they relished the thought and looked forward to the day all of this would come together.

For what felt like the hundredth time, they scanned the words on the computer screen. Words they had been tweaking and tinkering with for what felt like an eternity now.

They would really love to sign a name to the email, but in order for this to work, to avoid intense scrutiny and questioning, the source generating this had to be thought of as anonymous.

One last time, they read each word very slowly.

To: Colton Oil Board Members Listserv
From: Classified
Subject: Colton Oil CEO Ace Colton is NOT a real Colton

Ace Colton, born 40 years ago on Christmas Day in Mustang Valley General Hospital, was switched at birth with another newborn baby boy in the nursery. This shocking truth can be confirmed with a simple DNA

test that will prove Ace is not a Colton by blood. Since the Colton Oil bylaws state the CEO must be a biological Colton, Ace must be ousted. I will provide you with no further information, but rest assured this bombshell is the tip of the iceberg.
Good Day

As their eyes rested on the last word, they felt their smile widen, even more smug and far more self-satisfied than it had ever been.

"Perfect."

Now there was nothing left to do but send this email to all six members of the Colton Oil board—and then sit back, calmly waiting for the fireworks to start going off.

With a mixed surge that was composed of equal parts excitement and confidence, they handed the computer over to their tech expert. This trusted employee had organized the logistics of this mission and would continue to monitor it. They pressed Send.

"And now it begins!"

Chapter 1

Marlowe Colton had always thought that one of the perks of being the president of Colton Oil was having her very own private, luxurious en suite bathroom installed within her rather cavernous office.

An en suite bathroom where she was currently having her very own private nervous breakdown as she stared at a small white stick that had the audacity to mock her with a glaring pink plus sign.

Her breathing grew shorter and more erratic as she continued to stare at the awful, incriminating stick. Her stomach kept tightening until it had twisted itself into a hard, painful knot.

Marlowe realized that she was sweating even as she felt a cold chill shooting down her spine and passing over every part of her body.

And the nausea was back. In spades. Any second now, she was going to throw up.

Again.

"No, you're a Colton," she told the unusually pale blonde looking back at her in the mirror. "You're not going to throw up. You're not!" she insisted.

Marlowe blinked back tears. They weren't tears of joy, or tears of sorrow. What she felt stinging her eyes were angry tears. Angry tears that were aimed at no one but herself.

How *could* she have let this happen? One stupid moment of intoxicated but entirely willing weakness and longing and now here she was, in the throes of morning sickness.

It wasn't possible.

It *wasn't*.

And yet the stick in her hand told her it was all too possible.

It was a reality.

The white stick had come out of the discarded white box that was now haphazardly sitting on the edge of the sink. The pharmacist had assured her that this product was supposed to be the best, the most accurate pregnancy test on the market. She truly doubted that it had made a mistake.

Besides, if she was being completely honest with herself, the thought that she was pregnant had been in the back of her mind for the last six weeks. Ever since she had lost her head and her iron grip on her emotions by succumbing to the sexy, dark good looks and charms that she had been all but bred to hate. Because the man on the other side of that bed six weeks ago had a father who hated her father, and that feeling was very, very mutual.

What in the name of all that was good and proper had she been thinking? Marlowe silently demanded of her reflection.

That was just it—she *hadn't* been thinking. For once in her career-driven life, she hadn't been thinking at all, just feeling. Or at least *telling* herself that she'd been feeling. Feeling an overwhelming attraction to a man she had viewed as the enemy for as far back as she could remember.

This was what came of trying to behave civilly toward someone who she had been taught did not deserve to be treated with any sort of respect.

All of her life, Marlowe had done exactly what was expected of her—and then some. She was a Colton, and Coltons were supposed to behave a certain way. At least Payne Colton's daughter was supposed to behave in a certain way.

She closed her eyes, fighting another strong, rising wave of stomach-lining-destroying nausea as it tried to claw its way up her throat.

If only she hadn't gone to that stupid energy conference...

Or, at the very least, if she hadn't spent so much time arguing with Bowie Robertson, president of Robertson Renewable Energy Company, over proposed pipelines and the environmental consequences they could have. The argument went on and on relentlessly until everyone else at the conference had withdrawn for the night. That left just the two of them to continue the argument on their own.

How heated words had somehow given way to

splitting a bottle of champagne—or had that been *two* bottles?—she still really wasn't clear about. But somewhere along the line, their different philosophies and the eternal ongoing rivalries that defined their lives had just somehow managed to melt away, leaving nothing to get in the way of a very real and exceedingly strong attraction that had mysteriously taken root and been growing between them for who knew how long.

Marlowe could remember only bits and pieces of their night together after that. One of those bits and pieces had included a very strong desire to be, for once in her life, swept away, for the space of at least that one isolated evening.

An evening that became free of thoughts about rivalries, corporate profits and even the ever-increasing concerns about green energy being a threat to her family's oil company.

Just one carefree evening, that was all she had wanted, Marlowe thought.

And now this stick and its menacing, mocking pink cross were exacting a price for those frivolous few hours of passion she had spent.

A price she had never, even in her wildest dreams, been prepared to face up to and pay.

That wasn't to say that she didn't want children. She did, Marlowe thought. She *did* want children. But just not *now*.

And definitely not with *him*.

They hadn't even spoken a single word to each other since that fateful night, as if silence was actually an acceptable way of denying that those few hours of unabashed passionate consorting—of wild, consensual *lovemaking*—had ever happened.

But not talking about it, not acknowledging that it took place, was *not* a way of wiping that night's existence out of the annals of time. The pregnancy test clearly testified that it had happened, she thought ruefully, frowning at the offending mark on the white stick. And that, in turn, had most definitely produced a consequence. A very big consequence.

Marlowe felt her throat closing up. What the hell was she going to do now?

The question throbbed insistently over and over again in her brain. But no matter how many times she asked herself, she came up with the same answer.

She didn't know.

She had absolutely not even a *glimmer* of an idea what she was going to do about this.

The only thing that she *did* know was that her father was going to see this pregnancy—and how it came about—as nothing short of a personal betrayal of him of the first order.

"I wasn't thinking of you at the time, Dad," Marlowe whispered to the man who wasn't there in person but was somehow always around Colton Oil headquarters in spirit. Payne Colton was the reason behind everything she did.

The truth of the matter was that her father had always been a very strong presence in her life, influencing, in one way or another, her every move, practically her every thought.

But not that night.

That night the intrusive spirit of Payne Colton had been utterly absent. At least, he had been by the time she and Bowie Robertson, drunk on champagne and each other, had gone up to her suite at the Dales Inn.

The Dales Inn was the only hotel in town, and coincidentally it was also where the green energy conference was being held.

To someone viewing this from the outside, with everything that was going against them—feuding fathers, rival companies—that night she and Bowie might have come across as a modern-day Romeo and Juliet. Except, once the dust had settled again, they were much more like the Hatfields and the McCoys, but with the Coltons focusing on drilling oil wells and the Robertsons worrying about environmental impact.

She sighed, holding her head with one hand. There was no happy ending in sight here.

But then, she remembered, there hadn't been one for Romeo and Juliet, either.

Her head was really beginning to hurt, Marlowe thought. And it didn't exactly help her condition any to have both her desk phone and the cell phone she had left next to it when she'd walked into the bathroom ringing like crazy now. The phones sounded as if they were jointly heralding the end of the world and doing so just slightly out of sync.

Maybe they were, she thought darkly, still staring at the offending stick.

"Why don't they shut up?" she cried, helplessly putting her hands over her ears.

As if that would stop the noise, Marlowe thought angrily.

She rose to her feet—her legs felt oddly shaky, she realized, holding on to the wall for a moment to get her balance—and opened the bathroom door and glared accusingly at the offending phones.

If they were *both* ringing like that, something had to be very, very wrong, she thought.

Something other than an offending white stick with its glaring pink cross.

Taking a deep breath, Marlowe made her way over to her wide custom-built desk. Part of her was hoping that the ringing would abruptly stop by the time she reached the phones.

No such luck.

Braced for almost anything—after all, the worst possible thing had already happened, she reasoned—Marlowe picked up her multiline desk phone. Thinking it was one of the company's many administrative assistants on the other end, she said tersely, "Okay, this had better be good."

"On the contrary," she heard her father's deep voice rumbling against her ear, "this is very bad. And where the hell have you been? Why aren't you answering your phone?" Payne Colton, chairman of the board of Colton Oil, demanded angrily. "Your damn phone's been ringing off the hook. Why were you just ignoring it?"

"Dad?" Marlowe said shakily, still looking at the stick she was clutching in her hand.

Payne snorted. "Well, at least you still know who I am," he retorted in disgust. "Did you forget your way to the boardroom?"

"What?" What was he talking about? It was after five o'clock. There was no meeting scheduled this late, at least none that she recalled. "No," she responded after a beat.

"Well, that's good, because that's where the rest of us are, sitting around that big old table and twiddling our thumbs, waiting for you to make an appearance." His voice hardened. "I sent you a text," he snapped, the fury he was feeling now more than evident in his voice. "Didn't you see your email?"

No, Dad, I didn't see my email. All I see is this big, ugly white stick that's about to topple my whole world, Marlowe thought numbly.

"Well, Your Highness, we're still all waiting for you to deign to put in an appearance," her father was saying while she was having her crisis. "So read that email I forwarded to you and get that skinny behind of yours in here. Pronto! Do you hear me?"

Hovering over her laptop, Marlowe hit a key. The screen that was currently there gave way to another one that contained her corporate email. She scrolled up the page to the latest message to see what had set her father off like this.

Her mouth dropped open when she got to the subject line.

She reread the words twice.

"Oh my Lord!"

Her father took her shocked response to mean she had looked at the email. Or at least she had seen enough of the email to shake her up, which was good enough for his purpose.

"All right, get in here *now*, Marlowe!" Payne screeched. "I'm not going to ask you again."

Marlowe's knees were shaking so badly, she had to sink down into her chair. This had happened to her twice in the last fifteen minutes, she thought, feeling as if she was completely losing her grip on the immediate world.

Despite her father's voice reverberating in her ear with his loudly shouted demands, Marlowe opened her email, hoping that maybe the contents weren't as bad as it initially seemed.

It was worse. Marlowe's head was suddenly filled with a swirling kaleidoscope of memories, all grounded in her childhood. Adventures and events that she and Asa, whom everyone called Ace, had shared as children. Ace was her big brother. He was a big brother to *all* of them, even to her adopted brother, Rafe. Ace didn't care. He treated Rafe just like he was a *real* brother.

That was just the way that Ace was.

Marlowe looked back down at the email's subject line.

That was absolutely absurd, she thought. Who would *say* such a crazy thing? Who would even come up with such an idiotic idea, she silently demanded, stunned beyond words. Maybe this was the work of some competitor in an attempt to disrupt the company.

"Marlowe? Marlowe, are you there?" Payne Colton's deep voice thundered, bringing her back to the moment and her suddenly cold and incredibly inhospitable-feeling office.

It took her a second to focus and come around. Thinking took another second. "Yes," she said, breathing heavily, "I'm here, Dad."

"No," her father corrected her sharply, "you're *there*. I need you to *come here. Now!*" he declared. "Can you do that for me?" he asked his daughter sarcastically. "Can you hightail it out of your overdecorated office and get yourself to the boardroom *five minutes ago*?" Payne shouted.

It wasn't just Marlowe's knees that were shaking now—it was all of her.

With effort, she gripped the armrests of her chair and literally hauled herself up to her feet. Testing the strength of her legs for a second to make sure that she wouldn't just fall flat on her face with the first step she took, Marlowe slowly moved her hands away from the armrests. By now her heart was pounding against her chest like a drumroll.

"I'm coming," she told her father in what seemed like a whisper.

"What did you just say?" Payne demanded angrily. "I can't hear you!" he declared like the marine drill sergeant that all his children, at one time or another, had felt he was.

Marlowe took a deep breath, filling her lungs with air before she repeated the words. "I said I was coming."

"Then get here already!" Payne snapped.

The next moment, the connection was abruptly terminated. Only her father's disapproval and anger lingered in the air around her like a dark, malevolent cloud.

This wasn't happening, Marlowe silently insisted as she closed down her laptop.

That done, she raced out of her office. None of it, she tried to console herself. None of this terrible stuff was happening. Not this hateful email and not that positive pregnancy test.

It was all just a bad dream, and any second now, she was going to wake up, Marlowe promised herself.

And when she did, all of this was just going to be an awful, fading memory.

Her high heels resounded, clicking rhythmically against the highly polished marble floor as she ran down the corridor to the Colton Oil boardroom. The staccato sound seemed to mock what she had just told herself.

Her heart fell with a thud as she reached the open boardroom door.

It didn't look as if she was going to wake up from this one after all.

Chapter 2

It was almost surreal that after all these years of being on the opposing side of every argument, Bowie Robertson couldn't seem to be able to get thoughts of Marlowe Colton out of his head. The simple truth of it was that he hadn't been able to stop thinking about the Colton Oil president for the last six weeks.

At first, it had been because the woman was single-handedly responsible for what was admittedly the greatest night, bar none, of his thirty-two-year-old life.

Granted that, for years now, he had been very aware of the fact that Marlowe Colton, with her shoulder-length mane of whitish-blond hair and a figure that wouldn't quit, was drop-dead gorgeous. But he had also viewed the woman as the personification of an ice queen. An ice queen with nothing but cutthroat ambition running in her pretty veins.

He had been completely blown away to find out that the total opposite was really the case.

Yes, he had had a great deal of champagne to drink that night, but even an entire river of alcohol wouldn't have been able to drown his brain to the point that would get him to believe something that wasn't really true. He would have to have been beyond utterly drunk to believe that what had actually been a sow's ear had transformed into the proverbial silk purse.

No, he wasn't suffering from some sort of delusion; that had actually happened.

But as enchanted as he'd been by the slightly vulnerable, passionate, warm, funny woman he had made love with in her oversize hotel bed, the cold reality was that it had turned out to be just another illusion, a sleight of hand with no staying power once it was viewed in the light of day.

In fact, he had discovered that Marlowe actually *did* care about the environment and that she had set up awards for Colton Oil employees who created sustainable technologies and were working to make the family business more eco-friendly. That notably went against her father's narrow-minded view, but once he had left her room and was on his way back to his own world, Bowie quickly found out just how cold and vicious Marlowe Colton could really be.

A few short hours after they had spent what he had viewed at the time as an exceptionally passionate night together, Bowie found himself to be a marked man.

Marked for death.

There had been two attempts made on his life in breathtakingly short order. Right after he had left the hotel, someone driving a black SUV tried to run him over. When that attempt hadn't been successful because he had managed to get out of the way just in time, someone tried to shoot him.

The sound of a gunshot had been so benign that at first he thought it was a car backfiring—and then he saw the hole a bullet had made right through the car window that was less than a foot away from where he'd been standing.

The two incidents, so close together, were just too much of a coincidence for Bowie to merely shrug off. It *had* to have been because of Marlowe—or someone acting on that she-devil's orders. It was too much of a coincidence that, right after he'd slept with the enemy, someone tried to kill him…right?

He speculated that the reason for the attempts on his life—the *failed* attempts, he gratefully amended—were twofold. One, the woman had obviously let her guard down that night, and since he was the one who had witnessed this drop and been on the receiving end of the consequences of that action, she undoubtedly didn't want him telling anyone about it. The only way to ensure that didn't happen was to have him eliminated.

Why had she gone to such drastic lengths? She had also shared something with him that, in hindsight, would probably be considered a company secret. She was going behind her father's back and looking into ways to make Colton Oil more eco-friendly. She hadn't told Payne yet because she had nothing tangible to present to him, but it wouldn't be long. All this was told to Bowie in strictest confidence. And even though he had promised to take that to his grave,

Marlowe had obviously decided to hasten that scenario along and kill him. While he didn't think her so-called "secret" was a big deal, she obviously did.

Maybe, given time, he might have just chalked up these feelings as unnecessarily paranoid. After the second failed attempt on his life, he had deliberately kept his distance from Marlowe, avoiding all forms of contact and definitely not calling her. He even made sure to have a security detail around him at all times.

But now, six weeks after their one wildly insatiable night of passion—as well as the two subsequent attempts on his life that had occurred—a third attempt had been made just that morning.

This attempt had borne fruit. It hadn't wounded him, but the bullet that had been fired killed his security guard.

A second bullet had narrowly missed hitting Bowie himself.

It was now painfully obvious to Bowie that lying low and avoiding contact with Marlowe wasn't working. And ignoring the source of the problem was *not* making the problem go away.

So, focusing on that, he decided that it was time for him to confront Marlowe before another attempt was made on his life. Or before anyone else wound up paying the ultimate price by being on the receiving end of a bullet that was meant for him.

Out of respect for the night they had shared, he'd wound up behaving like a coward, not confronting Marlowe about their time together and the subsequent attempts on his life. That in itself was something that, to Bowie, was even worse than death.

Death was quick and final, but the label of being a

coward carried with it a stigma that could haunt him until the end of his days. He was *not* about to allow that to happen.

It was time, Bowie decided, to confront the lioness in her den and get this whole thing out in the open.

Marlowe entered the boardroom, crossing the threshold on legs that still didn't quite feel as if they belonged to her.

She was no longer clinging to the hope that this was all just a bad dream, but she had to admit that the scenario still didn't feel as if it was real.

Marlowe took in the immediate scene within the room. Her father was right. The rest of board was already there, and they were obviously waiting for her.

Looking around, she quickly scanned all their faces. Her father; Ace; her half sister, company attorney Ainsley; and CFO Rafe all looked to be stricken to varying degrees. The only member of the board who did not look stricken was Selina Barnes Colton, the company VP and director of public relations, and coincidentally, her father's second—and mercifully *ex*—wife.

Not only was Selina *not* stricken looking, but if Marlowe hadn't known any better, the auburn-haired viper seemed to be almost gleeful about this potentially dire situation threatening to unravel right before them.

Marlowe had never liked Selina. None of her siblings ever really had, she'd discovered years ago. But truthfully she had never disliked the snide, smug woman more than she did right at this very moment. Why her father insisted on keeping his ex-wife not just with the company but actually serving on the board, giving her an equal voice when it came to decisions, was totally beyond her.

The air in the boardroom was exceedingly tense. Out of the corner of her eye, Marlowe could see that her father was waiting for her to take her seat, so she did.

Only then did Payne speak. The anger vibrating in his voice was impossible to miss.

"Now that we're all here, let me take this opportunity to say that this email, sent by a quivering coward who didn't even have the nerve to sign his own name, is a complete and utter fabricated lie. It's obviously a pathetic stunt pulled by some spineless, sniveling jackass who is trying to derail our company in any possible way that he can."

Listening, Rafe could clearly barely contain himself. "Of course it's a lie," he cried, agreeing. "But how can it possibly be able to derail a billion-dollar company? Even if what this jerk is claiming *was* true—which it isn't—who cares?" he demanded. Rafe glanced at the man who was the center of this ridiculous email. "Ace is a Colton, blood or not. Right?" he said, looking at Payne.

To Rafe, it was a rhetorical question that didn't even need or expect an answer.

But the opportunity was far too good to waste, so Selina was more than happy to offer an answer to her former stepson's question.

"Not to throw water on your theory," Payne's ex-wife murmured in a just barely audible voice. "But you, Rafe, of all people, being adopted the way you were by Payne and his kind late first wife," Selina continued, her voice fairly dripping with a false sweetness as she circled back to her point, "should know that blood is *everything* when it comes to being a Colton."

Although there was a smile on the woman's face, her eyes were cruel and ice-cold, looking not unlike those belonging to a cobra just before its fatal strike.

"What are you talking about?" Rafe asked. "What is she talking about?" he repeated, turning toward the other people on the board for an answer.

When his gaze landed on Ainsley, the woman shifted uncomfortably. Marlowe knew the last thing Ainsley would want to do was side with Selina, especially against someone she actually considered family. In this particular case, however, as odious as it seemed, apparently the law was on the woman's side.

Clearing her throat and avoiding looking at either Ace or Selina, Ainsley told the others, "The reason it would derail the company is because on page one, paragraph two of the Colton Oil bylaws, it clearly states that the company CEO must be a Colton by blood only."

Okay, enough was enough. Incensed, Ace shot to his feet.

"This is crazy," he declared, using, Marlowe thought, the exact same phrasing she had when she'd seen the results of her pregnancy test.

This was crazy. They couldn't oust Ace from the board, Marlowe thought. He belonged on it.

And yet...

"This ridiculous email is a lie," Ace was saying. "A total fabrication meant to send shock waves through our entire company and undermine its very structure.

I'm a Colton! I was born a Colton and I'll always *be* a Colton." He looked at his father. Though it wasn't in his nature to ask for any sort of help or backup, this one time he made an exception. "Tell them, Dad."

It wasn't a plea, it was a request for the older man's verification about his birthright.

Payne nodded so hard, his thick silver-gray hair shook and fell into his eyes.

"Of course it's a lie!" he declared with a fierceness that defied opposition. "Ace is my son. I was right there, in the delivery room, the day that he was born," Payne said, looking directly at his oldest son. "Of course, he wasn't quite this big at the time," he added with a small, dry chuckle. "As a matter of fact," Payne recalled, "he was pretty frail. Everyone in the hospital, myself included, thought it was a Christmas miracle that he even survived. But he *did* survive. Not just survive—he managed to *thrive* almost overnight," Payne recalled with a nearly tangible wave of nostalgia. "And now just look at him!" the family patriarch cried.

It took Marlowe a moment to realize that his small trip down memory lane had been received with surprise by the others around the conference table.

This was part of the narrative that hadn't been previously broadcast. This was the first she'd heard that Payne and Tessa's big, robust firstborn had been born a sickly infant whose chances of making it through the night had been regarded as slim to none.

Despite their obvious surprise, only Selina picked up the thread that had been dropped.

"A Christmas miracle?" she asked in a slightly mocking tone. "Really? Or did you or your first wife at the time deliberately decide to switch that sickly, frail baby with a healthy newborn?"

Payne's face immediately turned a vivid shade of red.

"How *dare* you insinuate," Payne screeched, "that either I or Ace's mother could do something so reprehensible as—"

He couldn't even bring himself to finish his sentence, he was so incensed.

Everyone suddenly started talking at once, their raised voices drowning one another out as each tried to make his or her point.

Despite the turmoil going on in her head and her life, Marlowe's inner instincts took hold. Before she even realized what she was doing, she was on her feet, her raised voice louder than anyone else's as she attempted to calm them down.

"People. People!" she cried even louder. "Calm down!" she ordered in a semi friendly, albeit very authoritative, voice. "Of course this is all a huge mistake. My big brother is a Colton. He always has been—in his heart as well as in his blood. You know that," she insisted. "And, like this awful email said, one simple DNA test will prove that."

"You're right," Ainsley said, adding her voice to back up her younger half sister. She glanced at Ace. "I'll go with Ace to make sure he gets a test fast and have that test expedited as quickly as humanly possible. It'll cost a fortune," she said before Selina had the opportunity to raise an objection concerning the cost of having the test results delivered so quickly, "but it will definitely be worth it. Especially when you think of it how it will prevent certain chaos if the press ever got hold of this."

Selina raised and lowered her shoulders in a careless, dismissive shrug. "It's only money, right?" the woman said scornfully.

"Yes, it is," Marlowe replied. "And it's not *your* money," she deliberately added, knowing that was the sort of thing that would really irritate the hateful woman.

Selina's eyes narrowed, her pupils like two laser pointers as she glared at Marlowe. "To prevent anyone from contesting the results and saying that they were deliberately manipulated to give the results *we* were all after—" her tone placed quotation marks around the word *we* "—shouldn't there be a disinterested third party present to act as a witness—just to keep everything honest?" she concluded sweetly.

"You're absolutely right," Payne said. It was obvious that agreeing with his ex-wife was costing him. "Any suggestions?" he asked the others, deliberately ignoring Selina as he looked around the table.

But Selina refused to be ignored. "How about—" the woman began, only to be drowned out by Ainsley, who spoke over her.

"I can ask Chief Barco to come along and serve as a witness to the whole procedure, from the initial taking of Ace's blood to every single step taken in order to get to the end result." Only then did Ainsley look at Selina. "Will that satisfy you, Selina?" she asked the woman.

"Absolutely," Selina replied smugly. "I'm just trying to make sure that everything's aboveboard so that no one can say the results were manipulated or doctored," she told the rest of the board.

Marlowe kept her expression neutral even as she glared at Selina. They all knew that the only one who would claim that the results were "doctored" was Selina. Selina was clearly the enemy in their midst, but they were going to have to deal with that if the company was going to continue to survive the way it had all along.

Marlowe made a silent pledge that it would, if she had anything to say about it.

For the time being, focused on fighting for the company—and her brother—all thoughts of the earth-shaking test in her office were temporarily pushed into the background.

Chapter 3

Marlowe quickly made her way back to her office. She was a woman with a mission. The crisis surrounding Ace and whether or not he was truly a Colton—a ridiculous question at best—had, however temporarily, displaced her own personal drama. After all, it wasn't as if *that* problem was going anywhere, at least not without some sort of intervention on her part.

And besides, there was still a chance, albeit an increasingly slim one, that it was some sort of mistake, or glitch, and she really was *not* pregnant. But pregnant or not, she would tackle that problem later. Right now, she had to join the rest of her family and *do* something about this terrible, unfounded rumor before it made the rounds. It needed to be disproved and stopped at its source.

Which meant finding out just who this so-called

"anonymous" sender was who had emailed that hateful message to all six of them. Getting to the bottom of this was going to require some expert online sleuthing by someone who was far savvier than she was when it came to technology.

And Marlowe knew just whom to turn to. The reigning expert, as far as she was concerned, was an IT specialist who was already employed by Colton Oil and was currently working right here in the company's headquarters.

If *anyone* could get to the bottom of all this and track down just where this heinous email had originated, it was Daniel Okowski. Not only was Daniel good at his job, but he was also decent and loyal. Marlowe knew that she could trust the IT director to keep the subject matter he was going to be investigating quiet, just as she was confident that once he *did* find out who was responsible for sending this email, he wouldn't make that information public, either.

Picking up the telephone receiver, Marlowe was about to call Daniel when the cell phone that she'd left on the side of her desk beeped, informing her that she had a text.

Her first inclination was to ignore it. She just didn't have time to handle yet another new crisis. One more thing and she was in danger of having a real breakdown.

Her deeply imbedded work ethic trumped her survival instinct, and Marlowe looked down at her phone screen, bracing herself.

The text was from her administrative assistant, Karen. Marlowe didn't even bother reading it. Karen was not the type to bother her unless it involved something important.

Taking a deep breath, Marlowe pressed the number that directly connected her to Karen. The second her assistant picked up, she told the woman, "I'm kind of busy right now, Karen. Can this wait?"

"I don't think he wants to wait, Ms. Colton," the assistant whispered nervously into her phone.

"He?" Marlowe questioned. But even as she asked, her sixth sense, ever alert for the next pending disaster, caused her stomach to suddenly plummet to her knees.

Still, she told herself that she could be wrong, which was why she asked, "Just what 'he' are you referring to, Karen?"

The next second, rather than hearing Karen's voice giving her an answer, Marlowe saw her door being slammed open. Bowie Robertson came barging into her office, loaded for bear. He had no sooner entered than the door banged shut behind him, the sound reverberating throughout the office and echoing menacingly in her head.

"*Me*, Marlowe. Your assistant is referring to me," Bowie declared angrily.

A beat behind, Karen appeared directly behind the man who was currently behaving like a raging bull. Her normally efficient assistant looked extremely fearful and was all but quaking in her shoes.

"Do you want me to call Security, Ms. Colton?" she asked, her eyes furtively glancing in Bowie's direction, then looking away again.

Yes, I want you to call Security, Marlowe silently answered her assistant. But saying that out loud would make Bowie think that she was afraid of him, and she would rather die than have him believe that. She wasn't afraid of anyone, she thought fiercely.

So instead Marlowe tossed back her head, sending her blond hair flying over her shoulder. Her brown eyes, shooting daggers, met Bowie's green gaze dead-on.

"No, not yet, Karen," she told her assistant. "You can go. But stay close to your phone," she cautioned the young woman.

Looking somewhat uneasy, Karen never took her eyes off the back of the intruder's dark head as she slipped out Marlowe's office. She eased the door closed behind her.

The second her assistant had left, Marlowe turned her attention back to the man she regarded as a detestable, unwanted invader. She was now all but shooting bullets at him.

"What the hell do you think you're doing, barging into my office like this? Who the hell do you think you are?" Marlowe demanded hotly of the man she held responsible for the personal minidrama she was going through.

Bowie clearly was in absolutely no mood to back away, no matter how much she yelled. "I'm a man who's done hiding!" he shouted right back at her.

Marlowe stared at him. That made absolutely no sense to her. Bowie was just tossing about meaningless words. Why would he be in hiding?

"Hiding?" she repeated. "Hiding from what?" Marlowe demanded, both confused and enraged.

Bowie's eyes narrowed. "Don't play dumb with me, Marlowe. It doesn't suit you," he said bitingly. Then, because she continued to look like she didn't understand what he was saying, he snapped, "Hiding from your goons." Like she didn't know that, he thought.

"Goons?" she repeated, still just as lost as she had been a moment ago. "What goons? Did you fall on your head, Robertson? What are you *talking* about?" she asked, growing angrier by the second.

So she was going to play it dumb, was she? Okay, he'd spell it out for her, even though he was certain that she wasn't ignorant of the reason that he had come looking for her.

"The goons that tried to run me over and who shot at me—*twice*," he emphasized. "The second time they went target shooting, they killed my bodyguard and, incidentally, just narrowly missed me. *Now* do you know what I'm talking about?"

This had to be an act, Marlowe thought. Nothing more than an attempt to throw up a smoke screen for some unknown reason. The man was crazy.

Furious, she shouted at him, "You are totally delusional!"

"Yeah, well, there's a body lying on a slab at the morgue who begs to differ with you," Bowie told her in disgust. "Why don't you have one of your minions call up the medical examiner at the morgue and ask if he just did an autopsy on a Miles Patterson?" he suggested. "I bet the answer's going to be yes."

He looked absolutely serious, Marlowe realized, beginning to feel uncertain. But how in heaven's name *could* he be? She hadn't sent anyone to shoot at him or threaten him in any way.

Marlowe glared at the impertinent man. If *anyone*

was going to do something to this raving lunatic, it would be her, she promised herself.

And she'd do it with her fists, Marlowe thought.

"*You* are insane," she accused.

"No," he contradicted, "I *was* insane to ever allow what happened between us to go as far as it did. But what's done is done," he snapped. "It's in the past, and I'll be regretting it for the rest of my natural life.

"But I'm here to tell you that you don't have to worry. I don't know what kind of people you're used to dealing with, but I'm not about to take something that was told to me in confidence and spill it to anyone willing to listen. You said it was a secret when you told me, and unlike you people," he said, encompassing her entire family, "when I make a promise, I *keep* it. So call off your hired guns, Marlowe, and just let me go on with my life in peace."

She looked at him as if he were babbling in some foreign language she couldn't begin to identify.

"What the hell are you *talking* about?" she demanded, growing steadily angrier and more frustrated with every second that went by.

Bowie stared at her, incredulous. How far did she intend to carry this charade?

"So what?" he asked. "You're telling me that you're going to continue playing dumb?"

"I am *telling* you that I don't have the faintest idea what you are carrying on about," Marlowe informed him, exasperated. She was *not* buying into this act of his, and she was insulted that Bowie would even *think* that she would.

His eyes pinned her where she sat. "You mean to tell me that you don't know that someone's been trying to kill me ever since I left your hotel room at the Dales Inn six weeks ago?" Bowie questioned angrily.

Marlowe looked at him, stunned and momentarily speechless that Bowie could actually believe she was some sort of black widow, femme fatale capable of "mating" and then killing the man she'd just had sex with.

That was totally bizarre.

Of all the images she'd ever had of herself, that wasn't one she'd even remotely *ever* entertained. She'd never thought herself capable of doing something like that. She *knew* she wasn't glamorous enough to pull it off.

Nor would she want to. Behavior like that was vapid and empty, and completely devoid of any sort of moral scruples. None of that would ever come even close to describing her.

Pulling herself together, Marlowe found her tongue. "Again, I have no idea what you're talking about. *None*," she emphasized. "I don't even remember what this 'secret' was that I was supposed to have told you."

The second the words were out of her mouth, Marlowe's eyes grew large as it occurred to her that she had another problem on top of the one she was already aware of. Oh God, what was this secret she'd told him, and how was this going to blow up in her face?

The suspense and anticipation threatened to eat away at her stomach lining in record time.

"You don't remember telling me anything," Bowie said in a mocking tone. "You honestly expect me to believe that?"

"I can't help what you believe or don't believe, but that's the truth," she insisted angrily.

"No, you're lying," he accused, standing firm. "It's too much of a coincidence that right after you told me your precious secret, people started aiming their cars at me and shooting at me." His eyes darkened. "Our families have been rivals practically since the beginning of time, and I should have had my head examined for going against everything that made sense and thinking that I could have misjudged you. I should have kept my distance from a viper like you the way I always have."

Marlowe glared at him, furious at what Bowie was insinuating. Furious with herself for ever letting her own guard down and allowing him to get close enough to really complicate her world.

Furious with herself for *ever* thinking that he could be capable of being a decent human being...even though he was the father of her child.

Staring at the ruggedly good-looking man now, Marlowe couldn't help wondering if he—or maybe someone in his family, if not the entire lot of them—could be behind that awful email that had thrown her own family into such turmoil.

"Well, you didn't keep your damn distance, did you?" she all but spat out. "And pretty soon everyone's going to know that."

He stared at her, completely at a loss as to what she was saying to him. The woman certainly spent a lot of time babbling, he thought, irritated.

"*Now* what are *you* talking about?" he demanded. "I don't speak gibberish."

Marlowe glared at him. "Neither do I," she shot back at this interloper.

"Then what the hell are you *saying*?" he asked.

He wanted it spelled out? All right, she'd spell it out for him. She was through being patient. "I'm saying that our families are going to have to find a way to tolerate one another."

"And why, pray tell, would they want to do that?" he asked, really wishing that in the middle of all these hot words that were flying back and forth between them he didn't find this woman so damn attractive that his toes all but curled.

Why couldn't he find her the least little bit repulsive, or ugly or even off-putting? Hell, he'd really settle for off-putting.

Instead, while shouting at this woman he was convinced was trying to have him killed, all he could think of was the way her mouth had tasted that fateful night. How soft her skin had felt beneath his hands and how much he *still* wanted to make love with her.

He had to be out of his mind, Bowie thought. That was the only explanation he could come up with. Maybe she had slipped him something that night, something that was now making him behave like a mindless, lovesick loon.

At least he was managing to cover that part up, he thought thankfully.

His question rang in Marlowe's ears. If she had an iota of sense, she would have just let the subject drop, or answered him with some mindless bit of trivia that said nothing. She could just accuse his family for being underhanded and causing all this havoc in her own family.

She could say *anything* but what she knew she'd wind up saying in response to his question.

"Our families are going to have to figure things out, because in seven and a half months there's going to be a little human being with both Colton and Robertson blood running through his or her veins," she said from between gritted teeth.

Dumbstruck, Bowie stared at Marlowe. When he finally recovered the use of his tongue, he could only inanely echo, "What are you saying?"

"What I'm saying, Einstein," she answered sarcastically, "is that our temporary truce that night resulted in a permanent baby. I'm pregnant, you idiot!" she shouted at him.

She felt angry that she was trapped in this situation. Angry that it had ever happened. And most of all, angry that out of all the men in the world who could have been the father of her child, it had to be this Neanderthal.

"You're lying," Bowie accused numbly. She *had* to be lying, he told himself. She *couldn't* be telling him the truth.

But the expression on Marlowe's face gave him very little hope.

"I really, really wish I was," she told him, meaning her words from the bottom of her heart.

Bowie's stomach twisted in a knot, coming perilously close to making him throw up.

"You're pregnant," he repeated.

She blew out a frustrated breath. "That's what I just said."

It wasn't sinking in. He felt like a drowning man

fighting like crazy to keep his head above water. "And it's mine?"

"Yes, it's yours, damn it."

He didn't remember forming the words until they finally emerged. "How can you be sure?"

There was fury in her eyes, and for a moment, he was certain she was going to *really* blow up. But somehow, she managed to keep herself under control.

"Count yourself lucky that the handgun my father gave me for my fourteenth birthday is in a lockbox and not in a drawer in my desk because I have a license to use it and if it was the latter, right now I would be sorely tempted to use it on you. In the long run that would be preferable to having you as the father of my baby, but there you have it. You *are* the father of my unborn child, and that's a horrible fact we're both stuck with."

Her eyes grew very, very dark as she added, "And to answer your question as to how I know you're the father of this child, I know because I haven't had the time or the inclination to sleep with anyone in months, so unless this baby is the result of some sort of spontaneous generation, you, Bowie Robertson, are the father." Her eyes narrowed as she concluded, "Deal with it!"

Chapter 4

Marlowe looked at the silent man sitting directly opposite her.

Tall, dark and handsome by anyone's standards, Bowie Robertson's complexion had suddenly turned very, very pale right before her eyes. If it hadn't been for the change in his color, she would have thought she was witnessing, up close and personal, one of the finest acting performances of her life. But to her knowledge, no one could turn that pale at will. Which meant that her news had caught Bowie totally by surprise.

Well, that makes two of us, Robertson, Marlowe thought.

She almost felt sorry for him, considering what he was probably going through—the key word here being *almost*, Marlowe thought, because *she* was the one who was pregnant, not him. "Wow," Bowie murmured, more to himself than to Marlowe. The thought of having fathered a child left him numb. He had no idea how to deal with it. He had never even thought of himself as a father. Unable to deal with it, he pushed the thought into the background for the time being.

"I believe that sums it up as good as any word." She agreed sarcastically, then switched gears as she demanded, "Now what was that secret I told you?"

Bowie blinked, scrutinizing her more closely. She was being serious, he realized. "You mean you really don't remember what you told me?"

Marlowe liked to think of herself as a patient woman, but after all the things that had happened today, she was utterly out of patience and dangerously close to another out-and-out display of pure, unadulterated anger.

"No, I *really* don't know what I told you," she snapped, enunciating each syllable.

Bowie continued to stare at her. If what Marlowe was saying was true—and she really didn't know what secret she had shared with him or that she had even disclosed *any* company secret while in the throes of their lovemaking—then she couldn't be the one who was trying to have him killed. She would have no reason to want to eliminate him.

So who the hell was trying to kill him?

The attacks had started shortly after he had slipped out of her room at the Dales Inn. Had someone—either there or just outside the hotel—seen him leaving the bar with her?

Or maybe these attempts on his life didn't even have anything to do with him spending the night with

Marlowe. All right, then what? Why would someone be trying to kill him?

His mind was a total blank.

Marlowe noted that Bowie's brow was completely furrowed and he had a very strange expression on his face. So strange, in fact, that she couldn't even begin to fathom what was behind it.

"What is it?" she asked.

Her almost melodious voice broke through the fog around his brain. For a second, he thought she sounded genuinely concerned. So much so that he forgot to keep his guard up against a woman he had been indoctrinated his entire life to regard as someone who came from the enemy camp.

His guard down, he said aloud the words that were currently buzzing around in his head. "If you're not the one who hired someone to kill me, then who the hell did?" he said, totally exasperated.

She had no idea, nor the will, at this moment, to figure it out. Maybe she hadn't even told him anything of importance that night and he was just yanking her chain.

"Well, it's not that I wouldn't love to help you find an answer as to why someone is supposedly using you for target practice," she said flippantly, "but I'm kind of in the middle of a crisis of my own right now."

"You mean something else besides suddenly finding yourself pregnant with the enemy's child?" he asked her cryptically.

Marlowe raised her chin defiantly. "Yes, other than finding myself pregnant." She bit off the words, skipping the rest of his description. The fact that it was his baby only added to her feelings of being overwhelmed.

"So what's this other big crisis of yours?" It seemed to be the right question to ask, Bowie thought, given the situation.

"I can't tell you," Marlowe said. When she saw him raise a quizzical eyebrow, she did offer one piece of information. "It's not just a company crisis…it's a family crisis, as well."

The moment she said the last words, she suddenly covered her mouth with her hands, horrified, as she rolled her eyes. That was too much. Annoyed with herself, she dropped her hands from her face and blew out a ragged breath.

"What is it about you that keeps making me blurt things out like that?" she demanded accusingly, glaring at Bowie.

"Then you *do* remember what you said to me?" he asked her.

"No, I don't," she answered, frustrated, "but apparently you seem to have that kind of effect on me." Marlowe was angrier with herself than she was with him. She should have never had that champagne that night at the inn. Then none of this would be happening.

Belatedly, she thought of where she had been about to go when Bowie had suddenly come storming into her office. Nothing had changed. She still needed to see Daniel and talk to him about trying to track down the person who had sent this email that was causing such shock waves to go ripping through her family's lives.

"Look," she told Bowie as she rose to her feet, "I really have to go right now—"

Bowie followed suit, standing up, as well. He followed her to the door. "To handle that company-slash-family crisis, right?" he assumed.

"Something like that," she replied noncommittally. "But I'll be in touch later to arrange a meeting between us. Somewhere private," she added, "so then we'll be able to talk."

"All right," he agreed. "I'll wait for your call." His tone made it clear that if it didn't come, he would be back to see her.

By now they had walked out of her inner office. Karen looked apprehensively at the heads of the two most influential energy companies in Arizona. "Is everything all right, Ms. Colton?" she asked nervously, her eyes darting toward Bowie and then back again.

Marlowe wasn't in the habit of wearing her emotions on her sleeve, but just for a second, she was tempted to say "No, Karen, it's not. It's so far from being all right, it might never be right again." But she managed to suppress the urge as well as the words. Instead, she said, "Yes, Karen, everything's fine. Thank you for your concern." She swept past her and headed toward the elevator.

Because his legs were longer, Bowie easily matched her quick stride step for step until they reached the elevator. He was going out while she was going up, so he paused for a moment before leaving the building.

Whispering into her ear, he told her, "You lie like a pro."

Stunned, she demanded, "Excuse me?"

"Just now," Bowie explained, nodding his head toward the office she'd just vacated. "When you answered your assistant's inquiry, you told her that everything was all right, but you told me that you were in the middle of a crisis."

"There's no reason for Karen to know about that." Her eyes narrowed as she looked at him just as the elevator arrived. "There's no reason for you to know that, either, but you seem to have this strange power to make me lower my defenses and say all manner of things to you that I shouldn't."

"I'll do my best to use that power wisely," he told Marlowe with just the faintest hint of a smile curving his lips. "Don't forget to call and tell me the time and place that we'll be meeting," he reminded her as the elevator doors shut, removing her from his view. "Or I'll be back," he called out, raising his voice, although he doubted that she could hear.

Marlowe uttered a few choice words in response to his parting ones, but the doors had closed by then, sealing her off from him.

It was just as well, she thought. Why had she ever even *bothered* to talk to the man at the conference? Yes, what came afterward could easily be described as the best, the most remarkable night she had ever spent in her life. But at what price? Marlowe asked herself. And could she really say that it had been worth it?

In view of the present situation, she couldn't honestly say yes. But then, she couldn't really say no, either.

With all these diametrically opposed thoughts going on in her mind, Marlowe felt as if her head was liable to explode at any moment.

She knew she was dangerously close to being on

overload, with just too many shocking pieces of un-settling information bouncing around in her brain, all accumulated in such a short amount of time. She didn't feel able to sort them all out without drowning in words and feelings.

C'mon, Marlowe, get a grip. If you fall to pieces, everyone else will, too. You have got to get it together! For everyone's sake, she admonished herself.

Marlowe realized as she quickly walked down the long corridor that she was consciously or uncon-sciously pinning all her hopes on Daniel, fervently trusting that somehow he would come up with some-thing, preferably the name of the person who had sent them that unnerving email. She was convinced that he had it in him to save the day.

The boyish, studious-looking IT director was only six years older than she was, but in her opinion, he looked younger. Despite his looks, however, he pos-sessed a razor-sharp mind, and if there was *anyone* who could unearth the name of the person sending them this awful email, it was Daniel.

His door was wide-open, and she knocked on the door frame as she crossed the threshold into the of-fice. It looked like the other two people who were part of his department had already left for the night and that Daniel was just about to leave the office himself.

"Daniel?" she said, walking toward his desk. "Do you have a minute to talk?"

Whatever humorous retort he was about to offer instantly faded without a single syllable even partially emerging when he saw who was approaching him.

"For you, always," the tall, thin man told her. Rather than just paying lip service for the effect it had, she knew Daniel truly meant what he had just said. He felt boundless loyalty to the family that had taken a wet-behind-the-ears computer science graduate and placed him in a department where he worked in positions of respect and power, something he had never experienced before.

In return, Daniel had gone to great lengths to show them that he was worthy of the faith and trust they had placed in him. Even so, he never took anything for granted. She knew for a fact that there were a lot of other people in his graduating class who were still struggling to pay off their school loans, while he was able to move around completely debt free because the Coltons had been willing to take a chance on him.

"Something's come up," Marlowe began, trying to find just the right words to use in order to present and explain the dilemma that they all—especially Ace— found themselves currently facing.

"Please, have a seat," Daniel said, gesturing toward a chair that was facing his desk.

At first, Marlowe looked almost hesitant to sit down. But then she finally did, sinking into the chair almost in slow motion.

"Go on," he urged.

After a beat, Marlowe took a deep breath. "Maybe it would be easier if I just showed you, Daniel," she said, because saying the words just might have made her choke, she thought.

"Whatever works for you," Daniel responded amicably. He waited for Marlowe to make the next move or say the next thing.

He watched in silence as Marlowe dug into her skirt pocket and pulled out her phone.

Marlowe forwarded the anonymous email and looked at the explosive piece on the screen in front of Daniel.

"This was sent to all six board members a few hours ago," she told the IT director. At least she assumed that was the timeline, although for all she knew, her father had been aware of this email's contents longer than that. She had no idea how she knew, but she just had a feeling.

She fell silent as she allowed Daniel several seconds to read the words.

Once he had finished reading and then rereading the email, Daniel raised his eyes to meet hers. "Is this on the level?"

"Whoever sent it seems to think so," she answered grimly.

"Do you know who sent it?" Daniel asked next.

Marlowe shook her head. "No. That's where you come in, Daniel," she told him. "I was hoping that you could track down whoever sent this to the board and find him for me."

"You said him—we're sure it's a he?" Daniel questioned.

Sighing, she shook her head again. "Daniel, at this point we're not sure of *anything*."

"Okay," Daniel said, taking the information in stride. He approached the problem from another direction. "You said this just came in?"

This time Marlowe nodded. "From all indications, late this afternoon. My father was the one who notified me," she added. "Do you think you'll be able to track this email back to its source and find out who sent this abomination out?"

"And you have no idea who might have sent it?" he questioned.

"Not even a clue," she answered him flatly. "Daniel, it's extremely important that you get us a name as fast as possible. This needs to be nipped in the bud before it somehow gets leaked to the press." She caught herself gripping the armrests and forced herself to make her hands go lax. "I don't have to tell you that we don't need that sort of publicity getting out."

Daniel nodded, his unruly dark brown hair falling into his eyes. He combed his fingers through it, absently brushing it aside from his black-framed glasses. His attention was completely focused on his boss. "Understood," he replied.

She was struggling to project the picture of confidence, but at the moment, given everything that had toppled down onto her shoulders, that was definitely not easy.

"Do you think you can do it, Daniel?" she pressed.

"I can certainly try," he answered cautiously. She knew he didn't like making promises unless he was 100 percent certain that he could successfully deliver.

"But can you do it?" Marlowe asked again, *needing* an affirmative promise from him. "You're the best in the business, Daniel, and if you can't do this…" A note of hopelessness filtered through her voice as it trailed off.

"Ms. Colton, you have to understand that a search for something this heinous could very well involve the dark web, and that's a great deal trickier to navigate than the regular web. They don't call it the dark web just to create an aura of mystery. The transactions carried out on *this* part of the internet are way more difficult to pin down. I would be remiss if I wasn't being honest with you, Ms. Colton," he confided. "The truth of it is that you might never find out who sent this email."

"But you *will* try to, right?" She was aware that she was practically imploring Daniel at this point.

"That goes without saying, Ms. Colton," he told her. "I will use every trick in the book and lean on everyone I know to help me uncover just who sent out this piece of unfounded propaganda."

She knew he was doing his best to comfort her, but she had one more request. "Can you do all that without telling them why?"

Daniel smiled at her. "The people I deal with are accustomed to these sorts of nefarious transactions. Don't worry, Ms. Colton. If it can be done, I'll do it," he promised, "and no one will be the wiser."

"That's good enough for me," she told him, rising to her feet. "And when you do find out, call me, Daniel. Night or day, call me," she repeated.

"I'll be sure to do that, Ms. Colton," he promised solemnly.

Chapter 5

Well, that didn't exactly go as planned, Marlowe thought as she left the IT director's office.

She supposed that part of her disappointment was tied to the fact that she had begun to expect nothing short of miracles from Daniel. Marlowe had always had a great deal of respect for the man's abilities. The problem was that she had gotten those impressive abilities confused with his ability to do *anything* when it came to the internet.

Truthfully, until he had mentioned it, she hadn't even thought about the dark web. To her, the internet was the internet, whether it was "dark" or not.

If anyone *could* make some notable headway there, it was Daniel. Especially since she had made him realize how important finding whoever had sent out that email was to her. To the family.

Still, Marlowe was definitely not looking forward to telling her father that, rather than "mission accomplished," there was a chance, albeit it a slim one, that it might turn into "mission impossible."

She sighed. There was nothing to be gained by putting this off, so she went back down to the boardroom on the off chance that her father was still there. This was the kind of message that she preferred delivering in person rather than over the phone.

As she made her way down the corridors, the area felt oddly empty at this time of the late afternoon. Unless faced with a deadline that necessitated working overtime, most of the Colton Oil employees had gone home for the day. Even the lights seemed dimmer than usual, somehow, although none had been turned off yet.

Drawing closer to the boardroom, Marlowe heard the sound of raised voices. Or at least one raised voice. It didn't take much for her to recognize that the one she could clearly make out belonged to her father.

There was no doubt about it. No one could project his voice—or his emotions—the way that her bombastic father could.

Knocking on the door, Marlowe didn't wait for a response but opened it and walked right in.

Payne Colton immediately swung around. "What?" he demanded, abruptly curtailing the supposedly encouraging words he was imparting to his firstborn, Ace. However, coming from Payne's mouth, even encouragement came out sounding like he was venting his anger.

Ace Colton wasn't the target or the cause of that anger, but given the scope of his father's displeasure,

Marlowe could imagine he felt as if he might as well have been.

All of his children had decided long ago that Payne Colton's ways took a lifetime to get used to—and even then it wasn't always easy.

Marlowe mustered the best smile she could at the moment and told her father, "I just thought you'd want to know that I put Daniel Okowski on the trail of our anonymous emailer."

The silver-gray mane bobbed up and down in approval. "Good. What did Okowski say? How long before he has some answers for me?"

The fact that her father had placed himself rather than her as the key player in this wasn't lost on Marlowe, but then, he did own the company, and anything that affected the company affected Payne Colton directly, so she wasn't about to quibble. It was a given, she thought, resigned to the fact.

"That's just it, Dad…" she began slowly, attempting to hedge her bets, only to have him break in and interrupt her.

"*What's* 'just it'?" her father demanded. "C'mon, girl, speak plainly. It's way too late in the evening to be playing riddles," he thundered.

"Let her talk, Dad," Ace requested patiently.

Payne glared at his oldest son. He'd never liked being interrupted. "I *am* letting her talk," Payne retorted. "It's not my fault that she doesn't talk fast enough, and when she does talk, it comes out in circles." His eyes shifted back toward his daughter. "Well, go ahead. What is it you're trying to tell me?"

Marlowe picked her words slowly, never taking her eyes off her father's face. "Daniel said that navigating the message might have links to the dark web. That is tricky, and there's a chance that we might never find out who's responsible for sending that email to us."

"What do you mean by never?" Payne demanded, exasperated.

"Exactly that," she responded. "Those were Daniel's words, Dad. Not mine. I guess he means that it's a lot more complicated than any of us might think," she began, only to be cut off again.

Payne laughed. It was a nasty sound with no mirth attached to it.

"Don't be so naive, little girl. Money can buy anything. It can damn sure get us those answers we're looking for, so we can fight even dirtier than this guy who's hiding behind his anonymous email. I'll just give Okowski a bunch of money to wave around, and you'll be surprised how fast those 'dark web' doors will fly open for us," he informed Marlowe and Ace with utterly unshakable confidence.

"I certainly hope you're right, Dad," Marlowe said. Her eyes darted toward her half brother. "For everyone's sake."

"Of course I'm right," Payne retorted. Marlowe saw that her father was dead serious as he added, "I'm always right."

Marlowe only wished that she had even half of her father's confidence.

"I'm going to go back to my office and talk to Okowski about that added incentive I'm giving him," Payne told his children. He held up the cell phone he had in his hand. "Keep these close in case I have to call you about any further developments." And with that, he walked out of the boardroom.

"Why don't you go home, Marlowe, and get some rest," Ace suggested kindly.

She looked at him sharply. "Why would you say that?" she demanded. Did her brother suspect something?

"Well, I hate to put it this way, but to be honest," he said in a kind voice, "you look terrible."

She was instantly defensive, but the feeling quickly subsided. Ace was just watching out for her the way he always did. "Funny you should say that. I *feel* terrible," she admitted.

"Are you sick, Marlowe?" he asked, concerned.

No, I'm pregnant.

But Marlowe didn't feel up to sharing this news with her family just yet, so she merely said, "Just about this situation." Then, because it was in her nature to be the family cheerleader, she said, "Don't worry, Ace. None of us are buying into that ridiculously fabricated claim in that email, and Dad's behind you a hundred percent. We're going to get to the bottom of all this," she promised him with feeling.

"I'm not worried," Ace told her. "Just mad that this is taking away precious time from the work we *should* be doing." He looked at her more closely. "Now go home and get some rest," he repeated, kissing the top of Marlowe's head. "That's an order."

Though it was strong, she resisted the urge to wrap her arms around Ace and cling to him the way she used to when she was little and felt as if the whole world was closing in on her.

Ace would never judge her, never indicate that he thought it was a sign of weakness for her to display a need for comfort. But she knew that if she did that now, Ace would sense that there was something wrong other than the fatigue she was claiming. He would start asking her questions, and she wouldn't be able to lie to him. She never had, but she couldn't burden him with this, either. He had more than enough to deal with without taking on her problem, as well.

So instead, Marlowe flashed a smile at him. "Sounds like good advice, although I really am fine," she assured him.

He nodded, clearly glad she wasn't fighting him on this. Seemingly as an afterthought, he told her, "Call me if you hear anything."

"You, too," she told him.

Ace grinned at her, that same warm grin that he usually flashed. She knew he was doing it for her benefit, and she appreciated it.

"Count on it," he said.

Somewhat heartened, Marlowe left the building and got into her car. But instead of going home—a home she shared with all of her siblings as well as her parents, as the house was large enough to accommodate all of them without having *any* of them running into the other members—she made the decision to go to her *other* dwelling.

She had purchased a condominium in downtown Mustang Valley. It was located at the very base of the mountain. She used it only whenever she found herself working late and didn't feel up to undertaking the drive home.

No one would bother Bowie and her there, Marlowe thought. That meant they could talk in private, although very honestly, aside from asking him a few questions about the allegations he had initially made, she didn't know what she was going to say to the man who had turned her entire world upside down by impregnating her.

She wasn't even sure at this point just what she planned to do about that pregnancy.

Turning on the car's overhead light, she took out her phone and sent a text to Bowie.

If you still want to talk, I'll be at my condo in half an hour. She then texted Bowie the address. Finished, she tucked away her phone and started up her car.

She'd lied about when she expected to arrive home. The condo was only ten minutes away from Colton Oil's headquarters. But she wanted the extra time to change her clothes and try to unwind from this overly stressful day before she had to face Bowie again.

The traffic was light. She arrived at the condo in eight minutes rather than ten.

Parking her car in the underground parking structure, she took the elevator up to her condo. The moment she walked inside, she stepped out of her high heels. The entire trip from her door to her bedroom, she shed one article of clothing after another.

By the time she had slipped into her jeans and her oversize, baggy sweater, Marlowe felt like an entirely different person.

Her stylish high heels were replaced by fuzzy socks with corgis pictured on the front of each. She did *not* look like the high-powered president of a major oil company. Instead, with her perfectly styled hair now pulled back into a jaunty ponytail and all of her carefully applied makeup completely wiped away, she knew she looked more like a teenage version of herself.

Marlowe looked into the mirror, doing a quick survey of herself. For at least the rest of the evening, she had effectively gotten rid of "corporate Marlowe." Or at least the aura of that persona. She had transformed into just a young woman who had unfortunately made a very bad misstep in the heat of passion.

She'd completed her transformation just in time. The condo doorbell rang.

Habit had Marlowe glancing at her watch. Apparently Bowie Robertson had a thing about punctuality. She had said thirty minutes, and damn if he wasn't here exactly thirty minutes after she'd sent her text to him.

Leaving her bedroom, she went to answer her door. She supposed there was something to be said about punctuality, Marlowe thought.

Still, mindful of the fact that she *was* home alone and there was someone out there sending an anonymous email meant to throw her family's life into total chaos, Marlowe took her small, unloaded handgun out of its lockbox and brought it with her as she went to answer the door.

"Who is it?" she asked a second before she looked through the peephole.

Bowie Robertson was standing on the other side of the door, suddenly feeling tenser than he could remember feeling in a very long time. He had no idea what he was going to say to Marlowe, or even why he was actually here. Everything seemed as if it was completely jumbled up.

"Guess."

Marlowe couldn't decide whether or not the voice she heard was friendly or ominous. Had Bowie come here to talk to her or to threaten her? She wasn't sure, but she squared her shoulders, determined to meet this challenge head-on. She was a Colton, and Coltons were never afraid.

Her hand closed over the small weapon in her pocket.

"Well, it's too damn early for Santa Claus, so I'm guessing that this is *not* the answer to my prayer," she said, flipping the two locks on her door and pulling it open with her free hand.

She saw Bowie's gaze land on the handgun she had removed from her pocket.

"Did you invite me over to shoot me?" he asked her, staying exactly where he was.

"No," she answered. After a beat, she lowered the weapon in her hand. "After what you said about someone trying to shoot you, I thought it wasn't a bad idea to keep my gun handy when I opened the door to my condo." She nodded over her shoulder, silently inviting him in before telling him, "Come on in, Robertson."

Bowie stepped over the threshold cautiously. "You know how to use that thing?" he asked, nodding at her lowered weapon.

"My father took me to the shooting range the day he gave me this gun for my fourteenth birthday. I can shoot the top feathers off the head of a turkey at twenty paces," she informed him proudly. "I could give you a demonstration if you'd like," she offered.

"Sorry," he quipped, "I left the turkey at home."

"You could do in a pinch," she told him. "All you'd have to do is hold up a few feathers in your hand and I can shoot those."

"Tempting, but I'll pass," Bowie told her. "My luck

can only hold out for so long," he added, doing a quick survey of her immediate living space. "I don't intend to push it."

Once inside her condo, and with her weapon tucked away back in its place, Bowie sighed audibly.

"You look different," he told her.

"Nothing gets by you, does it?" Marlowe quipped. "Do you want something to drink?" she asked. "I've got a fully stocked bar."

Marlowe was still waiting for him to answer her. "Robertson, you're staring," she said.

"Sorry. I've never seen you look like a civilian before," he told her. His face softened a little. "You look nice."

That surprised her. She had never been complimented before when she looked like this, and she had no idea how to respond, so she didn't. Instead, she went back to her original question.

"I asked you if you wanted something to drink."

He shrugged. "Sure. I'll have whatever you're having."

"I'm not having anything," she told him. "I'm pregnant, remember?"

And the reason he was here, the attempts on his life and all that entailed—including an unknown source, now that Marlowe denied having anything to do with it—instantly came crowding back into his brain.

"Oh, right," Bowie murmured. "For a second, I just forgot." And was trying to forget, despite everything, just how much he still wanted her.

Chapter 6

"All right, let's get down to business," Marlowe said, sitting down on her sofa and approaching this new problem logically. "Who would want you dead?"

Her blunt question threw Bowie. He'd thought that she had asked him here to talk about what they were going to do about the condition she suddenly found herself in. That and perhaps even touch on the night they had spent together, when he had gotten to see a completely different Marlowe Colton than the one the rest of the world—including him, up until then—was acquainted with.

But since she was asking about the attempts on his life, he was willing to address that first. Bowie sat down on the other end of the sofa. He had been giving his own dilemma a great deal of thought since he had confronted Marlowe in her office earlier. As a result, he had come to a new conclusion about it, a totally different one from the one that Marlowe was suggesting.

He started out treading lightly. "While it's true that I have made some enemies in my energy dealings, so have you," he pointed out.

"No argument there," Marlowe acknowledged.

But before she could continue, Bowie advanced his theory a little further, getting to the heart of what he believed.

"I think that this would-be killer is somehow connected to you or maybe to Colton Oil."

Marlowe's face clouded up. "So we're back to you thinking I hired someone to kill you? Is that what you're saying?" she asked incredulously.

"No," he corrected her, "what I'm saying is that these attempts on my life somehow have something to do with you, because someone started targeting *me* only after I spent the night with *you*."

"You mean you think that someone's watching me?" Marlowe demanded, clearly doing her best not to show Bowie how much the very idea of what he was suggesting unnerved her.

Bowie shrugged. "I honestly don't know," he admitted. "But it does make sense in a way. All I do know is that no one took a shot at me or tried to run me over before you and I spent the night together."

Marlowe thought of the anonymous email that had been sent to all six members of the board. Was that somehow connected to these attempts that had been made on Bowie's life?

Maybe Bowie *was* onto something, she thought, although she was not about to tell him about that.

She had absolutely no intention of divulging anything about what was going on in the company unless it turned out to be absolutely necessary.

For now, she just shrugged, doing her best to seem casual. "Maybe you were just lucky before."

"Yeah, maybe," he agreed, although it was obvious from his tone that he didn't really subscribe to that theory. "All right, then why don't we get down to it and talk about the elephant in the room?" he proposed.

Marlowe stiffened, instantly knowing what he was referring to. She felt heat rising up her neck to her face, inevitably turning it to a reddish hue. She was far more comfortable talking about gunmen, hired or crazed, than she was talking about something that was so utterly personal.

But she had been the one to initially blurt out the news to him, so she couldn't very well just fluff Bowie off or shut him down now.

"What about it?" she asked stiffly, her voice devoid of all emotion.

"What do you want to do about…it?" he asked her point-blank.

"You mean you don't have any suggestions?" Marlowe asked sarcastically. After all, she would have thought that an opinionated man, such as he was, would try to impose his will on her, especially since the child was half his. Or at least she *assumed* that was the way he would think of it.

"Oh, I have plenty of suggestions," Bowie assured her.

Big surprise. "I thought so," Marlowe retorted.

She'd pegged him right, she thought. But for some reason, she didn't find that nearly as satisfying as she would have thought she would. As a matter of fact, as she examined her feeling, she was rather disappointed that he was like that.

"But," Bowie went on to say, "it's your body. So ultimately, the decision is yours."

That he was capable of that sort of thinking caught Marlowe totally off guard. Was she actually wrong about him?

"Then you don't care what I do about this baby?" Marlowe asked, trying to get a handle on how he really felt.

"I didn't say that," Bowie pointed out. The fact of the matter was that he clearly did care. Cared a great deal, Bowie thought. "But I'm not the one who has to go through this."

Bowie meant the pregnancy and birthing part, but Marlowe immediately jumped on a different interpretation entirely.

"You're damn right you don't." She couldn't begin to think about everything that was involved, the huge changes that she was going to have to make in her life. Her head began to swirl. "I don't know the first thing about being a mother—" she began in exasperation.

"Most first-time mothers don't," Bowie told her, staying way calmer about this than she could currently appreciate. "From what I hear, it's a learning process that goes on indefinitely." His eyes pinned her down. "You *are* aware of the fact that perfect mothers don't just fall out of the sky, instantly doing the right thing, right?" he asked.

Did he think she was an idiot, or was he just getting his jollies talking down to her? Marlowe fumed, instantly taking offense.

"I'm a workaholic," she reminded him. "How can I possibly juggle those two entirely different roles, being a mother and Colton Oil president, and not doing a horrible job of both?"

Bowie opened his mouth, apparently to answer. Fired up, Marlowe just went on talking.

"I've always been the best at everything," she informed him, not boasting but just stating a fact. "But this…this is something I don't know if I can pull off," she admitted, and that really worried her more than she could express.

Bowie was quick to jump in, making the most of the fact that she was taking a breath. In the handful of run-ins they'd had, he had never seen Marlowe anything but confident. That she was actually having doubts made her all too human in his eyes.

And oddly enough, he liked this version of her. Liked the fact that she was being vulnerable.

And cute as hell, he thought, his eyes once again skimming over what she was wearing.

"Sure you can pull this off," he told her. "You can do anything you set your mind to. Being a mother isn't any different from being the president of Colton Oil—except that there aren't any diaper changes involved in the latter."

"Very funny," she commented, visibly trying very hard not to laugh at the scenario he'd just painted.

His eyes held hers. "And I'll help."

Marlowe suddenly fell silent. She looked at him as if he had just lapsed into a foreign language she was completely unfamiliar with.

"You'll help what?" she questioned.

"With the baby. I'll help," he repeated. He slid in

closer to her on the sofa. "We'll do it together. If you decide to have this baby, then you can count on me being there for you and the baby every step of the way," Bowie assured her, his tone completely serious.

It took her several moments to finally get the words out. "You mean it?" she asked.

Bowie smiled at her. It was a warm, comforting smile. "Cross my heart," he said. And then to get his message across, he did just that. "Scout's honor."

"Since when were you a Boy Scout?" she asked.

But oddly enough, she wasn't belittling him or even scoffing at his answer. She was, Marlowe realized, incredibly touched and unbelievably grateful for his offer.

Bowie's reaction to the news when she had told him had been a complete surprise. So many men would have immediately claimed that the baby wasn't theirs, and yet he had taken the news, once the initial surprise had worn off, in stride.

And unlike what so many partners, especially casual ones, would have said, his response was different. They would have said, "You're on your own, honey." Or just told her to "get rid of it," washing their hands of the whole thing.

But Bowie hadn't. He wasn't behaving at all the way she would have expected that he would. Instead, he was assuring her that he would be there for her, ready to hold her hand, to help in any way she needed. To do anything she asked of him.

Marlowe felt tears filling her eyes. She immediately willed them away. There was nothing she hated more than women who broke down in tears.

And she was strong, Marlowe silently insisted. She *was*.

But strong or not, she felt so grateful for Bowie's closeness, grateful beyond words to have someone to share this completely unexpected, overwhelming responsibility with.

At that moment, she felt not only incredibly thankful to him, but, in addition, she felt closer to Bowie than she ever had to another living soul.

Feeling utterly vulnerable, Marlowe rose to her feet. Bowie rose with her. They were standing inches apart.

Less than inches.

Bowie put his hands on the sides of her shoulders, drawing her closer still. They were all but in each other's shadows.

Marlowe could feel herself leaning into Bowie, and she felt that he was doing the same.

Her breath caught in her throat, and her heart rate suddenly launched into double time as she leaned in even closer to him than she'd been a second ago.

He was going to kiss her, and she desperately wanted him to, she thought. There was absolutely no alcohol involved this time, and she still really, really wanted to kiss him.

To have him kiss her.

And then, without any warning, it happened.

Just as their lips were a fraction away from meeting, a gunshot echoed as a bullet came crashing through her window. It shattered the glass and came so close to Bowie's head that, for one awful, awful moment, she was convinced that he had been shot.

That he had been killed.

Time froze even as he fell on top of her, his body covering hers.

It was the pounding beat of his heart that alerted her he was still alive.

Bowie was apparently trying to shield her with his body the second he'd heard the gun discharge.

The weight of his body on hers had knocked the wind right out of her.

Terror had done the rest.

Bowie stayed exactly where he was, immobile except when he evidently raised his head to conduct an up close inventory of her condition.

"Are you hurt?" he asked, his voice thick with emotion.

"Other than having all this heavy weight on my body, I think I'm fine," she told him, struggling to remain positive. But that immediately gave way to fear. "Someone just shot at you," she cried.

"I know," he told her. "I was there. Except that I think it was at *us*. Or at you." But they could sort that out later. "Are you sure you're all right?" he asked.

"I will be as soon as you get off me," Marlowe told him. "You really are heavy."

Unlike when they had made love and he had taken care to balance his weight on his elbows, she remembered. Today, he'd been too concerned with protecting Marlowe from the shooter to take any other precautions.

"Sorry about that."

Bowie quickly drew himself up to a sitting position. They were both behind the sofa where he had dived, taking her with him.

They were still there, taking care to remain out of range of whoever had done the shooting.

A thought suddenly occurred to him as he looked at her, horrified. "I didn't hurt the baby, did I?"

Despite the situation, she found his concern incredibly sweet. "From what I remember from my high school science class, the baby is currently the size of a pea, if even that big, so I'm guessing she or he is all right."

Bowie blew out a long breath. "Well, that's a relief."

Since there were no more shots, Marlowe ventured out from behind the sofa before he could stop her. "Are you out of your mind?" he demanded, making a grab for her.

"Shooting's stopped," she told him. "I guess he quit while we were ahead," she quipped. Marlowe looked up toward where the bullet had shattered the glass. "Where did that shot come from? It couldn't have been the street," she guessed. The angle was all wrong.

Bowie rose cautiously to his feet. Marlowe was right. Whoever had shot at them was gone.

He took a closer look at the hole the bullet had made. "My guess is that it came from the building across the way."

Marlowe said the first word that came to her mind. "A sniper?"

"As good a term as any for now," Bowie answered. He looked at her again. This time, he frowned. "You sure you're all right?" he asked. "You're shaking."

Embarrassed that he had noticed, Marlowe did what she always did. She took refuge in anger. "Someone just took a shot at one of us. Of course I'm not all right. I want to fillet that SOB."

Despite the seriousness of the situation, Bowie couldn't help laughing. "You really are one tough woman, aren't you?"

"I have to be," she admitted, being more honest with him than she had intended to be. "Otherwise,

I'm going to fall all to pieces." Marlowe realized that he had taken out his cell phone and was calling someone. "Who are you calling?" she asked.

Heaven help her, her suspicions about Bowie were back. Was he calling whoever had fired at them to tell the hired gun that he'd missed his target—her?

"The police," Bowie answered. "Someone just took a shot at one or both of us. Who should I be calling?" he asked her.

But before she could attempt to answer him with an offhanded remark, Bowie held up his hand and put the phone on speaker. Someone picked up on the other end of the line.

"911. What is your emergency?" a woman's voice asked.

"Someone just took a shot at us through the window. Could you send police officers to Ms. Marlowe Colton's residence? No," he told the dispatcher who told him she was taking down the information, "not to the family residence. This happened in her condo right here in town. Yes, that's right," he said, "that's the address." He verified the address that was already registered with the police. "Thank you." Closing his phone, he told Marlowe, "They'll be here in five minutes."

"I really wish you hadn't done that," she told Bowie, less than happy that he had taken this initiative.

"Why?"

"Because now the police are going to notify my father," she told him. "And all hell is going to break loose."

Chapter 7

"Wait, let me understand this," Bowie said, putting his cell phone back into his pocket. "You're Payne's daughter. Wouldn't he want you to be safe?"

"I'm his daughter," Marlowe agreed. Bowie had gotten that much right, but not the rest of it. "That means that, if at all possible, he'd expect me to handle this situation on my own. Quietly."

Bowie shook his head.

"Your father's as bullheaded as mine is," he commented, surprised at how alike two men who professed to be sworn enemies could actually be.

Blowing out a breath, she said, "I guess you're right."

She'd no sooner said that than there was a knock on the door. Marlowe audibly caught her breath as she exchanged looks with Bowie.

"I really doubt that a hit man would knock on the door," he told Marlowe. Still, he knew it didn't hurt to be cautious. Moving her behind him, Bowie made his way to the door. "Who is it?" he asked, one hand on the doorknob.

"It's Chief Barco," the gruff voice on the other side of the door answered. "I just got a 911 alert transmitted to my radio. Are you all right, Ms. Colton?"

Marlowe moved Bowie out of her way and opened the door. A sense of relief went through her as she looked up at the tall, slightly paunchy but commanding fifty-two-year-old police chief. She'd never been so happy to see the bald-headed man before in her life.

"I'm fine, Chief. But the bullet came really close to Bowie over here." Saying that, she turned toward Bowie, and for the first time since the incident occurred, she saw that there was blood at the very top of his ear. He *had* been grazed. "Your ear," she cried, her eyes widening. "You're bleeding."

Bowie ran his finger along the region where she seemed to be looking. There was just the slightest trace of red on his fingertips. He shrugged as if this was no big deal.

"I've done worse shaving," he assured her.

"You shave with bullets?" she asked Bowie sarcastically, attempting to cover up her initial horrified reaction.

"Let me get this straight," the chief said, slightly confused. "You two were together when this shooting happened?"

Like everyone else in Mustang Valley, the chief knew the Coltons and the Robertsons to be sworn enemies. Finding them together must have seemed rather odd.

"Yes," Marlowe answered for the both of them. "I'll show you where the bullet came from." She led the chief to the window.

The chief studied the shattered glass closely. He frowned at the hole and looked around the area for signs of more damage. But for now, the window seemed to be the only casualty.

Barco turned toward Bowie. "Do you have any idea who might have wanted to see you dead, Mr. Robertson?" he asked him.

Marlowe spoke up, interrupting the two men. "Robertson seems to think that I was the target."

The chief's frown deepened. This surely did not fall under the heading of "good news" in his book. "And why is that?" he asked.

"Well, for one thing, it's her condo," Bowie answered before Marlowe could say anything further.

"You do have a point," the chief allowed. "Any other reason for you to suspect that Ms. Colton was the intended target?"

Bowie was forced to shrug, at least for now. "Fresh out of ideas, I'm afraid," he said.

When the chief looked toward her for her input, Marlowe shrugged her shoulders, as well. "Other than the usual crazies who resent my family, I haven't a clue," she confessed.

The chief made a few notes in his battered notebook, then closed it, tucking it back into his jacket pocket.

"I'll have my people ask around, see if anyone saw or heard anything unusual," he told Marlowe. "I can post one of the officers outside your door if that would make you feel safer, Ms. Colton," he offered.

Marlowe smiled. "Thanks for the offer, Chief, but doing that would be cutting down your force by a third," she told him.

The entire Mustang Valley police force was small, but then, considering how quiet the town usually was, only a few law enforcement officers were more than adequate to keep the peace.

As if to contradict the thought, just then the front door, which Marlowe hadn't bothered locking when the chief came in, flew open, rattling the beveled glass in the upper portion of the door so hard, for a moment it seemed in danger of breaking, as well.

"Marlowe, are you all right?" her father demanded as he came storming into the condo. He was closely followed by Callum, his son and Marlowe's twin.

"Are you hurt?" her brother asked at almost the same time.

"I'm fine, really," Marlowe assured both her father and her twin.

Both men stopped dead the next moment as they realized that Marlowe had more than just the chief with her and that the other man standing next to her was *not* part of the police force.

Payne suddenly looked as if thunderbolts were about to come shooting out of his eyes. "What the hell is Franklin's whelp doing here?" the senior Colton demanded, glaring at Bowie. "Is he the one who tried to shoot you?" Payne shouted, pulling himself up to his full height.

"Now, calm down, Mr. Colton," Barco began in a

soothing tone. His words had absolutely no effect on the oil baron.

Marlowe moved in between her father and Bowie, predominantly to keep her father from doing something that they would all wind up regretting rather than to protect Bowie.

Even at sixty-eight, Payne Colton was no one's idea of an old man. On the contrary, her father was still a force to be reckoned with and exceedingly imposing in his own right.

"No, Dad," she insisted, "Bowie didn't try to shoot me."

"Then what the hell is he doing here?" Payne demanded. "Are you spying on us, boy? Doing some recon for your old man because he's just too weak and afraid to do it himself?" With each word, Payne only succeeded in working himself up more and more.

She could tell Bowie was having trouble holding on to his own temper, but losing it would only make a bad situation worse.

"No, sir—" Bowie answered politely, only to have Payne cut him short.

"Well, you can tell that coward who sired you he knows what he can do with his precious company, and I'll thank him not to send his boy sniffing around my daughter, if he knows what's good for him." Drawing back his shoulders, the senior Colton gave the illusion of towering over Bowie, even though they were actually about the same height. "Because if he crosses me, your father's going to get a hell of a lot more than he *ever* bargained for, you hear me?" Payne demanded, all but shouting the question in Bowie's face.

This was going to turn into a really bad situation faster than she had ever bargained on, Marlowe thought. Chief Barco was a nice man, but he was basically afraid of her father. It was up to her to put a stop to it before it got really ugly, Marlowe observed.

"Dad," she said, raising her voice. But her father either didn't hear her or didn't want to hear her, because he went on shouting and threatening Bowie.

"Now you get your sorry butt out of here, boy, if you know what's good for you." Bushy silver eyebrows drew together in an angry wave. "I am *not* going to ask you nicely again," Payne warned in a menacing tone.

"Dad—" Marlowe tried again, raising her voice even louder. She got the same result she had the first time. Her father continued to deliberately ignore her.

Payne turned toward his son. "Callum, get him out of here," the Colton patriarch ordered, "before I do something that I am going to really regret."

"Mr. Colton," Barco said, trying to interrupt Payne, who paid even less attention to the chief than he did to his daughter.

Marlowe was well aware that her father's threats were far from empty. She was also aware of how quickly they could escalate. Sticking two fingers into her mouth, she whistled loudly, which forced all the men in the room to focus their attention on her.

"Nothing you can say right now is going to keep me from throwing this whelp out to teach him some respect for his betters—" Payne began to tell his daughter, not even looking at her.

"Well, you had better learn how to hold on to your temper, Dad," Marlowe informed him, shouting the words at Payne.

"And just why the hell would I do that?" Payne demanded angrily, glaring at Marlowe.

"Because Bowie's the father of your grandchild!" she answered in a voice that all but shook the ceiling tiles loose.

It also stunned the other three men in the room. And even Bowie looked surprised that she was breaking the news this way.

"Say what?" Callum responded, the first one to recover.

Payne blanched. "He's the *what*?" he asked almost at the same time.

"The father of your grandchild," Marlowe repeated, enunciating each word. She saw the shock on her father's face and sincerely wished she could have given him the news a different way. But her father never made anything easy for her. "I'm pregnant, Dad, and you and Franklin Robertson are going to have to find a way to deal with that and learn to stop fighting!" she cried, her voice sounding almost hoarse.

Callum looked at her, wide-eyed. He asked, "Is it true, Mar?"

"Trust me," Marlowe said wearily, "I wouldn't make up something like that."

Chief Barco slanted a look at the Colton men, as if unsure if he should be congratulating the parties involved, or just holding his peace. Instincts apparently had him opting for the latter.

But Payne was not about to willingly accept this situation, not without registering his intense dissatisfaction and contesting the matter.

Glaring at Bowie, Payne angrily demanded, "Did

you force yourself on my daughter? Because I swear if I find out that you did—"

Marlowe blew out an angry breath. As if she didn't have enough to deal with, she had to smooth her father's ruffled feathers. "Nobody forced themselves on anyone, Dad. You know me better than that," she told him. "I would have gutted him before I let that happen." She drew in a fortifying breath, then said, "It was mutual."

Disgust, anger and disappointment all took turns washing over Payne's rugged face. He glared at his daughter. "How could you?" he accused.

Marlowe squared her shoulders. "I'm a grown woman, Dad, as well as your daughter. I think you already know the answer to that," she told him, doing her best to hold it together and not fall apart in light of his heated disapproval.

The disappointment she saw in her father's eyes cut her to the quick, but she wasn't about to show him that by flinching or apologizing. It was already hard enough for her to try to deal with what she had done in the heat of the moment—and the consequences that single action had produced. Attempting to atone for it for her father's sake was out of the question.

Payne turned on his heel and marched over to Bowie. For one tense, horrible moment, Marlowe was afraid that her father was going to punch the other man out—or at least try to.

There did appear to be an inner struggle going on.

But then Payne growled, "If I hear even a hint that you're not treating her exactly the way my daughter deserves to be treated, I will hunt you down no matter what rock you're hiding under and gut you like a pig." Payne then turned toward Callum and issued an order. "Let's go. I'm through here."

But Callum had never acted like his father's lap-dog, and Marlowe knew he was not about to start now. "I'll be there in a minute, Dad," he said.

Payne fumed. "In some places this would be called consorting with the enemy," he angrily informed Marlowe's twin.

"And in some places it's called being a family," Callum countered.

Payne said something that was biting as well as callous under his breath just before he walked out, slamming the door in his wake.

"I'd better go, too," the chief said to nobody in particular. Whenever he was around Payne Colton, he took all his cues from the man.

"Thanks for coming so quickly," Marlowe said.

"Of course," the chief responded, and then he left, as well.

Callum looked at his sister. "He'll come around, Mar," her twin promised.

"You're a lot more optimistic than I am right now," Marlowe told her brother.

Callum turned toward Bowie. "You really think that bullet was meant for my sister?" he asked Bowie.

"I do," Bowie answered, evidently prepared to be peppered with more questions.

Instead, Callum told him, "Then take her up to our cabin in the mountains, but make sure that you're not being followed when you go. If you are followed by someone looking to take either one of you out, the isolated location will only act against you."

She had never taken to having other people make

decisions affecting her. "Callum, I can't go with him to our cabin," she protested. "There's too much to do. That email—" Marlowe began.

But her brother immediately cut her protest short.

"Listen, you have just one major thing to focus on right now—this baby that you're carrying. You need to make that a priority in addition to work. Work will go on whether or not you're there. Maybe not as well," he allowed, "but it will go on. However, there is no question that this baby needs you, and it needs the healthiest version of you that you can possibly provide—because without you, that baby *won't* be able to go on."

Marlowe shook her head. "But, Callum, there *is* a crisis and—"

"And I will handle it for both of us," he assured her. "The rest of the family is all joining forces to try to get to the bottom of this. Now I know you're really good, but you have to admit that even you don't equal the five of us. So go to that cabin with Bowie and take care of my niece or nephew for the next couple of days until things calm down a little—and that's an order," he told her. "Do I make myself clear?" he asked his sister.

"Perfectly," Marlowe answered just before she threw her arms around Callum and hugged him for all she was worth. "You're the best."

"I know," Callum answered with a grin.

"But you will call me if you hit a snag?" she asked, watching her brother's face for her answer.

"I won't hit a snag," Callum told her.

"That's not what I just asked," Marlowe pointed out with a touch of exasperation.

"Yes, I will call you if I hit a snag," Callum told her in a singsong voice.

She still had her doubts, but for now this would have to do. "All right, then, you'd better go and join Dad in the car. You know how surly he gets whenever he's kept waiting."

Callum laughed. "You're preaching to the choir, Mar. That man's picture is in Wikipedia with the word *surly* written right under it." He turned toward Bowie. "I never thought I'd hear myself say this, but if you need anything at all involving my sister, give me a call."

Bowie nodded. "Consider it done."

For a split second, Callum locked eyes with the other man. The silence hung heavily between them. And then Callum said, "I'd better."

Marlowe knew that was as close to a threat as he would allow himself to utter. And then he left.

"Are all you Coltons always this charming, or is it just me, bringing out the worst in you?" he asked Marlowe, following her to her bedroom as she went to pack an overnight case.

"You really want to know the answer to that?" she asked him.

"No, on second thought, maybe I don't," Bowie answered.

"Wise choice," she told him, nodding her head. She closed the lid on the suitcase and snapped the locks shut, secretly marveling at how oddly final that sounded.

Chapter 8

Marlowe found the silence in the car almost deafening. Bowie had insisted that they just take one vehicle to go up to the cabin: his. Marlowe had let him win that argument, even though she didn't like being chauffeured around. Moreover, she liked the control of having and driving her own car. But she could even put up with that if she had to.

What she couldn't put up with was this oppressive quiet that was beginning to burrow its way under her skin. Marlowe had to admit that it was quickly getting to her.

Just as she reached over to turn on some music, Bowie stopped her cold with a question. "So what's this that's going on with your family?"

Marlowe dropped her hand in her lap. The question, coming out of the blue, completely stunned her. She hadn't been prepared to field anything like this.

"What do you mean?" Marlowe asked. Even she had to admit that her voice sounded rather stilted to her own ear, not to mention that her mouth had gone dry.

"I'm not sure if it was Callum or you, but one of you said something about there being a major crisis that needed handling," Bowie said. He glanced in her direction. "*What* major crisis?"

Marlowe's protective barriers immediately fell into place. When unarmed, she had always felt that denial was the best way to go. "I don't know what you're talking about."

Yeah, right, Bowie thought.

"C'mon, Marlowe, you're way too smart to play dumb," he told her, and then he added the crowning touch. "That doesn't look good on you. Why don't you tell me what's wrong, and maybe I can help."

For one moment, Marlowe wavered. She really wanted to be able to tell him. For possibly the first time in her life, she found herself wanting to share her burden with someone rather than just shoulder it on her own the way she always did.

But the truth was she didn't know if she could afford to share it with Bowie—because this could all be just a ploy on his part to get information out of her so he could, in turn, score points with his father.

Despite the fact that she had told her father that he had to find a way to bury the hatchet when it came to Bowie's dad, she herself trusted Franklin Robertson just about as far as she could throw the man—which meant not at all.

Marlowe looked at him, unable to sublimate the

suspicion in her eyes. "Just how do I know that I can trust you?" she asked Bowie bluntly.

Bowie laughed under his breath. "We're totally traveling off what's considered the beaten path in order to get to a cabin hideaway in the mountains. As far as I can see, there isn't a snowball's chance in hell that we're being followed—as per your brother's instruction. If you don't already trust me, then you seem to be willingly setting yourself up for a world of hurt," he told her.

"Now, you don't have to trust me if you don't want to," he continued. "I can respect that. But if you'd like to talk about whatever it is that's clearly bothering you, I just wanted you to know that, at least while we're out here, I'm here for you."

"Oh, you mean like a Boy Scout," Marlowe mocked, worried that she might have made a major mistake in trusting Bowie. Maybe she should just find a way to boot him out of the car and then drive quickly back to the family house.

"No, like the father of that baby you're carrying," Bowie reminded her. "And, to answer your question," he said, "yes, you can trust me."

"No," she replied pointedly, "my question was how do I *know* I can trust you. After all, someone did just try to kill me, thanks to you."

There was nothing on the road up ahead, just as there hadn't been for miles now, so Bowie spared Marlowe a long look. "Because I said so," Bowie answered.

She felt anger crease her forehead. Did he think she was that gullible? "And I'm just supposed to take your word for that, is that it?" Marlowe asked. For all she knew, he might have told people at his company what she had shared with him in confidence. What if her father found out? Would he accuse her of siding with his enemy in this eco-friendly war that was being fought between the two companies?

"Yes, you are," he told her firmly. "Because I don't lie." His eyes met hers before he looked back at the road again. "My word is my bond."

"That all sounds very noble," she told him in a mocking tone, telling him just what she thought of his declaration.

"It also happens to be very true," Bowie replied simply.

The truth was that she wasn't sure if she could trust Bowie or not, but she knew that she really, really wanted to. She had already trusted him with her body. If their relationship was going to progress any further, for the sake of their baby, she was going to have to find a way to trust with the rest of her.

Drawing in a deep breath, Marlowe forced herself to dive into the deep end of the pool. She told him what he wanted to know.

"All six members of the board of Colton Oil—my father, Ace, Ainsley, Rafe, my father's ex-wife, Selina, and I—were all sent identical emails earlier today," she informed him grimly.

"I'm guessing that the email didn't say you were all winners of a clearinghouse lottery," Bowie said.

"You'd be correct," she answered, her tone utterly gloomy. "The email claimed that my brother Ace wasn't really a Colton or my father's son. It went on to claim that Ace was switched the day he was born with another male baby born the same day at Mustang Valley General Hospital."

"Switched at birth?" Bowie repeated. "You're kidding, right?"

Marlowe blew out a frustrated breath. "I only wish that I was."

"Even if he *was* switched at birth, which seems pretty improbable to me, what difference could that possibly make? Unless there's something you're not telling me," Bowie qualified. "Ace was still raised as a Colton, which in my book makes him one." Like Rafe before him, apparently Bowie didn't see what the fuss was about.

"Unfortunately, that's not enough," Marlowe told him, her voice a mixture of sadness and anger. "It clearly states in the company bylaws that the CEO of Colton Oil must be a Colton by blood only. If this crazy claim for some reason turns out to be true and not a hoax, I'm not sure what we're going to do," she confessed.

And therein obviously lay the problem, she thought.

Bowie said, "Changing the bylaws comes to mind."

Marlowe blinked, stunned by Bowie's suggestion. "Excuse me, but have you *met* my father?" she asked. "He'd sooner topple Mount Rushmore than change the company bylaws." Despite herself, she was already picturing the chaos that would result once news that Ace wasn't really a Colton became public. "I don't know what this is going to do to the company, to our family—"

"Aren't you jumping the gun a little here?" Bowie asked. "You're already assuming that this crazy claim is true, and it could just be someone trying to undermine everything that your family's worked so hard to build. You know, there's a simple way to clear all this up," he told her.

She knew what he was going to say. The same thing that had been suggested in the email. "I know, I know. A DNA test," she said flatly. "We've already agreed to have Ainsley take Ace in for one first thing tomorrow when the lab opens. Chief Barco said he's willing to go with them to bear witness to the whole process. Drawing the blood, sealing the vial, everything. That way, he can attest that everything was aboveboard if anyone should contest the results—provided that the test results point to Ace being the genuine article."

"How would you feel about that?" Bowie asked her.

Marlowe shifted uncomfortably in her seat. "Feel about what?"

"What if the test results come back and they point to Ace *not* being an actual Colton," he told her. "Would that change anything?"

"Of course it would change things. It would change everything," she cried. Hadn't Bowie been paying attention? "I already told you, he couldn't be on the board, and—"

"No," Bowie said, cutting her short, "for you. Would it change anything for you? Would you suddenly see Ace differently if the blood running through his veins wasn't that of a genuine Colton?"

"No," Marlowe informed him indignantly. "Of course not. I wouldn't see him any differently than I do right now."

"Then that DNA test really doesn't matter," he told her. "Ace will still be your brother whether or not Colton blood is running through his veins. Besides," he continued, "it's not the blood that makes you family. It's the day-to-day living and what's involved in that day-to-day existence that does it.

"Now, don't buy trouble," Bowie advised. "If something bad is going to find you, that'll happen soon enough. Until it does, just go on with things as if everything's all right."

She was oddly heartened by his words, but she wasn't about to admit it. Instead, she told him, "You sound like a fortune cookie, Robertson."

"It'd have to be a pretty big cookie to accommodate all that writing," Bowie said, visibly amused. "In the meantime, do you or your family have any idea who sent this bundle of enlightening information to all of you?"

Well, she'd already told him this much, so she supposed there was no harm in telling him the rest. "I put our IT expert on it, but he told me not to get my hopes up that we'd get an answer. He feels that it came through the dark web, and some of the dealings there might never be unearthed."

"Maybe I can help," Bowie offered.

Marlowe turned toward him, stunned. "You?" she questioned.

"Don't sound so surprised," he said with a laugh, appearing to take no offense.

Since she was being honest, she told him, "I admit that I am a little." Maybe he had misunderstood her. "This is the dark web I'm talking about." His expression didn't change. Marlowe began to entertain hope. She had to ask, "Do you know your way around the dark web?"

Bowie laughed softly under his breath. "Let's just

say that I know people who know people who might be able to help out in this case."

"You are just full of surprises, aren't you?" Marlowe marveled.

"I'd like to think so. In the meantime, it looks like we've arrived at your designated castle, Your Highness, safe and sound," he added, looking in his rearview mirror for the umpteenth time.

"Time to play house," she said flippantly. The next moment, she realized what that had to sound like. "I mean—" Her voice failed her as she turned a rather bright shade of scarlet.

"I know what you meant," Bowie told her, gallantly taking her off the hook. "You go inside. I'll get your bag," he said.

"I can carry my own bag," she informed him, following him to the trunk of his car.

He popped open the trunk and pulled out the suitcase before she could reach for it. "Will you relax and stop seeing everything as a challenge to your authority, or position or whatever?" he said. "Learning how to accept help is every bit as important as offering help to someone else."

She rolled her eyes impatiently. "You know, you really should start writing down all these golden gems of yours, Robertson. Maybe even put them all into a gift book."

Taking the suitcase, he went toward the cabin. "Please relax a bit, Marlowe. You could probably use the rest. I know I certainly could."

Her eyebrows drew together as she fisted one of her hands at her waist. "Is that an insult?" she asked, her back already going up.

"That's just an observation," Bowie informed her calmly. "I promise you'll know if I'm insulting you. For now, all I'm trying to do is get a truce going—between us, and then, hopefully, between our two families." Opening the front door, he deposited her suitcase just inside the cabin. His mouth curved into a grin. "How'm I doing so far?"

Marlowe sighed. Maybe she was being too touchy. "Apparently a lot better than I am," she answered honestly.

Bowie stood in the doorway, facing out. She could see the cabin was elevated enough to give him a decent panoramic view of the immediate area surrounding it. "I'd say that it's safe to assume nobody followed us," he told her.

Clearly satisfied, he stepped back inside, then closed the door and secured the locks.

"Just in case," he explained, then proceeded to tell her why he had made sure that all the locks were in place.

"Now what?" she asked, looking around the spacious cabin. From where she stood, she could see the entire living space all at once, except for a bedroom that was in the back. But the way she felt right now, having had that bullet come so close to Bowie *and* to her, Marlowe sincerely doubted that she would be able to ever sleep again.

Bowie had a different take on the situation, however. "Now you do what your brother suggested you do," he told her. Bowie evidently knew better than to use the phrase "told you to do."

"Easy for him to say," she commented.

"No, I really doubt that," Bowie contradicted. "I

think he knows that asking you to do something is far from easy and far from a guarantee that you would actually do it."

Her eyes narrowed. "Just what are you saying?" she demanded.

"Only what we both know to be true," he answered. "You're a very strong-willed woman who isn't about to obediently comply with something unless she really wants to."

Marlowe pursed her lips. "Laying it on a little thick, aren't you, Robertson?"

"Maybe," he allowed. He raised his brows as he asked, "You buying any of it?"

He suddenly looked so boyish as he asked her that question that Marlowe found she was having a problem keeping a straight face.

"Maybe," she answered, parroting the word he'd used back to him. It suddenly felt as if it was getting warm in here, she thought. Marlowe changed the subject. "How long do you think we're going to have to be here?"

"Spoken like a prisoner who's ready to fly the coop at any second," he commented.

She raised her chin. "I just like to know what I'm in for and what's ahead of me."

"Maybe what your brother had in mind," Bowie suggested delicately, "is for you just to kick back for a bit and let things unfold naturally."

She shook her head. "Nope, that doesn't sound like Callum," she answered.

"All right, then, how does a couple of days sound to you?" Bowie asked, his eyes on hers.

"Today counts as one day, right?" Marlowe asked.

Bowie glanced at his watch. It was almost ten o'clock in the evening. "If you think that two hours compose a day, then yes," he answered, "today counts as one of those days."

"Good," she pronounced, looking satisfied that she had won.

Chapter 9

"Well, at least we won't be starving anytime soon," Bowie announced, looking into the surprisingly large modern refrigerator in the kitchen. "Looks like it's been restocked recently." He looked over his shoulder toward Marlowe. "There's a pretty good selection of steaks, eggs, a few fruits and some vegetables just waiting to be turned into a home-cooked meal."

He closed the refrigerator door and crossed back to her. "I know it's kind of late, but you probably haven't had anything to eat for hours. Can I interest you in some dinner?"

The second Bowie mentioned food, Marlowe felt her stomach lurching. She pressed her palm against the swirling area, praying she wasn't going to throw up.

"I don't think so," she told him. "The idea of eating

anything right now…" Her voice trailed off. The next second, her eyes widened as she drew in her breath. "Oh no, it can't be."

"Can't be what?" Bowie asked, concerned. The horrified note in her voice had gotten his complete attention.

Marlowe didn't answer. Her stomach was letting her know just how unhappy it was. She could feel herself beginning to perspire, despite the cold temperature outside.

She looked around frantically. She hadn't been here for so long that she'd forgotten where the bathroom was located.

Bowie immediately knew without being told what she was looking for. He had noticed the bathroom while checking out the Colton cabin to make sure no one was already there.

"This way," he said, quickly leading the way to the rear of the cabin. To make sure she was following him, Bowie took hold of her elbow, guiding her in the right direction.

The moment Marlowe sighted the door, she yanked away her elbow and pushed past Bowie, barely slamming the door behind her just in time.

Bowie leaned against the door frame. "Anything I can do to help, Marlowe?" he offered. "Hold your hair out of the way, give you moral support?" he asked, saying the first things that came to his mind because he was worried about her. He thought that she'd looked positively green just as she'd slammed the door.

Marlowe didn't answer him, but he was fairly certain he detected a subdued retching noise coming from the bathroom. Looking at the closed door, Bowie shook his head. Marlowe Colton had to be the only woman he knew who would deliberately try to keep the sounds of her physical misery a secret.

Feeling bad for her, Bowie decided to remain where he was, waiting for her to pull herself together and come out. He was ready to offer assistance any way he could should Marlowe realize that she wanted it.

Or needed it.

When he no longer heard anything coming from inside the bathroom, Bowie put his ear against the door, straining to make out any sound coming from the other side. By no means did he want to invade her privacy, but at the same time he found himself worrying about Marlowe—and the baby she was carrying.

His baby.

Yes, it was early days as far as that was concerned. He'd known about this for only a number of short hours, but being pregnant was obviously creating havoc for Marlowe, and he felt protective toward her and their child.

"Marlowe?" he called to her, knocking on the bathroom door. "Are you all right in there?" When there was no answer, he decided that he had been considerate of her sensibilities long enough. Coddling her wasn't getting him anywhere.

His hand on the doorknob, he turned it. "Marlowe, I'm coming in there," he announced. But as he began to open the door, it was suddenly opened from within and Marlowe emerged, her face slightly damp from what he assumed was the water she had splashed herself with, most likely trying to freshen up.

"What are you getting so excited about?" she asked indignantly. "I'm fine."

He looked at her more closely. "You have morning sickness."

"You have your time confused," she informed him coldly. "It's nighttime, not morning."

"And morning sickness is just a term to describe the nausea that being pregnant sometimes ushers in," he countered, refusing to be baited and get annoyed.

"And you're an expert on that, I take it," she retorted.

It occurred to her, completely out of left field, that she didn't even know if Bowie had a wife stashed away somewhere, or maybe a fiancée. For all she knew, the man had mistresses tucked away everywhere. She knew absolutely nothing about Bowie's private life, nor had she wanted to—until just now.

What if she'd gone to bed with a married man? Or with someone who was just interested in nothing more than a one-night stand?

If it turned out to be the latter, it almost seemed like poetic justice, seeing as how, at the time it had happened, she hadn't exactly been interested in establishing a permanent relationship, either. She had wound up going upstairs with him strictly for pleasure—something she wouldn't have allowed herself to indulge usually.

But there was something about mixing champagne with equal doses of Bowie that had blurred all the lines for her. It had made her behave like someone she didn't even begin to recognize.

"I read a lot," he said in response to her snide question about his being up on the symptoms of morning sickness. "I also read that crackers and soda water sometimes help you feel better."

Marlowe was really skeptical about that. Right now she was feeling miserable, and all she wanted was to retreat and pray that exhaustion would just take over and blanket her.

Bowie answered her glibly, "But the article did say that the prospective mother might react badly to attempts to help her and behave like an angry wet hen."

"A wet hen?" Marlowe echoed indignantly.

"An *angry* wet hen," he deliberately corrected.

For some reason, the fact that they were having this discussion about the condition of a hypothetical chicken managed to hit her funny bone and she began to laugh.

The sound of her laughter coaxed laughter out of Bowie. His laughter fed hers and vice versa. They laughed until her sides literally ached and she couldn't laugh anymore.

When she stopped laughing, allowing an exhausted sigh to escape, she looked at Bowie, feeling contrite.

"I suppose I should apologize for being so short-tempered," she told him.

"You can if you want to, or we could just forget about it and you could go to bed." He clearly had already surmised that she was having a hard time of it, and he apparently wasn't interested in any apologies.

For the first time, she looked around the room and spotted the bed.

She felt a wave of heat wash over her. Did Bowie intend to sleep in it with her, perhaps even have an encore of that night they had spent together six weeks ago?

"What about you?" she heard herself asking nervously, although she tried her best not to show it.

Bowie seemed rather unfazed by the question. He answered her as if it was already a given. "I'm going to take the couch."

She peered out of the bedroom, looking into the living area. "It's not very comfortable," she commented.

"That's okay," he said, unconcerned. "I don't intend to be very comfortable."

Marlowe looked at him, wrinkling her forehead in confusion. What was that supposed to mean? "I don't understand."

"Well," he told her matter-of-factly, "if I get comfortable, I just might wind up falling asleep on the couch."

"And you don't want to?" she asked him, still confused.

He laughed quietly. "It's pretty hard to stand guard if I'm sleeping."

"Wait." He wasn't making any sense, she thought. "You said no one followed us."

"And from what I saw, they didn't," he agreed. "But even so, I don't want to take any unnecessary chances, and I've always been a firm believer in being safe rather than sorry."

Marlowe sighed wearily. "More sayings for that book," she said more to herself than to him.

"Maybe," he allowed with an engaging grin. "But that doesn't make it any less applicable to the situation," Bowie told her. And then he advised, "Get some rest." Before she could protest, as she was so very capable of doing, he winked at her and said, "Remember, you're sleeping for two."

Did he mean she was sleeping for him as well, because he couldn't, or was he referring to the baby as part of that "two"?

Marlowe stood in the bedroom after he closed the door behind him and sighed as she shook her head. She didn't want to be beholden to Bowie, didn't want him making any sacrifices for her.

And yet…

And yet the very fact that Bowie was doing all this created warm and fuzzy feelings inside her.

Feelings she admitted to herself that she had never experienced before. Oh, she'd had her share of boyfriends, and she'd had flings. But none of those boyfriends or the flings could have been termed to be the least bit serious. They certainly never even once came before her job. That was a contest that had never taken place.

None of her so-called relationships ever lasted, and she had never felt as if she was missing anything whenever those relationships had run their exceedingly short courses and quietly faded into history.

She certainly had never, ever felt as if she was falling for someone…

Marlowe blinked as the words startled her, popping up in her head completely unbidden—like a comet streaking across the sky.

She wasn't falling for him; she was just tired, Marlowe told herself.

Tired and imagining things.

Still, she had to admit that part of her stomach's rebellious upheaval was due to something other than strictly this so-called morning sickness that Bowie claimed to be such an expert about.

Falling for Bowie, she thought as she sank down on the bed.

Her.

With him.

No way.

That had to be some sort of a mistake, right? Of course right, she told herself.

Even so, the very idea seemed to waft through her brain, teasing her, whispering insane words.

Would it be so very wrong if you were right about that?

"Damn it, Marlowe, you're just overtired. Get some sleep!" she ordered herself.

That turned out to be a great deal easier said than done.

But somewhere along the line, with all that tossing and turning she did, she must have fallen asleep. Because sometime in the morning she found herself being teased awake by the scent of eggs frying and something she identified as bacon after a moment.

For a split second, the scent was tempting.

And then her stomach kicked in, rebelling and reminding her that food and she were not friends right now.

Instead of going out to the kitchen, she found herself communing with the commode again.

Finished being sick, she got back up on her shaky legs. That made twice in less than twelve hours, she thought wearily.

Marlowe went out of the bathroom and sat down on the edge of the rumpled bed, waiting for her stomach to settle down.

"We're not off to an auspicious start, you and I,

baby," she murmured under her breath, addressing the tiny being within her body.

And that was the moment she suddenly knew— knew that she was going to have this child, keep it and be a mother. As good a mother as humanly possible.

Nothing else seemed remotely imaginable.

Marlowe knew her decision would probably infuriate her father. He undoubtedly expected her to sweep what he viewed, at best, as an "unfortunate circumstance" out of her life. After all, this baby was half Robertson, and Coltons wanted to have nothing to do with Robertsons. Payne had said that so many times over the years that she had lost count.

"Wrong, Dad. We do now," she said, addressing her absent father.

Preoccupied with her thoughts and with this decision she had just made to keep the baby, Marlowe jumped when she heard the knock on her bedroom door.

"Marlowe, can I come in?" Bowie asked, waiting for her permission.

Part of her would have expected Bowie to come barging in, the way he had into her office. That he didn't surprised her—and, she had to admit, pleased her.

Bracing herself, Marlowe said, "Okay. You can come on in."

Bowie opened the door, but rather than walk right in, he peered into the room, checking to see if she was alone. "You had me worried. I thought I heard you talking to someone."

She felt embarrassed that Bowie had overheard her.

Rather than explain what she'd been doing, Marlowe said, "No, just to myself."

She had a defensive look in her eyes, Bowie thought, so he tactfully retreated and changed subjects. "I made breakfast."

That was the last thing she was interested in. Her stomach was knotting up again. "I hope it's something you like to eat, because I'm not hungry."

Bowie frowned. That wasn't what he wanted to hear. "You have to eat," he told her.

"Later," Marlowe answered, putting him off. "I'll eat later," she promised. "I never eat first thing in the morning."

"You didn't eat last night, either," Bowie reminded her.

"So now you're the food police?" she asked with a trace of annoyance.

"No," he answered patiently, "just someone who knows that you need to keep your strength up."

"My strength is fine, thank you," she answered curtly, then immediately felt guilty about the tone she had used. She hadn't meant to lose her temper. He was just trying to be thoughtful, she told herself. "I'm sorry, this whole situation has me on edge. I don't mean to be taking it out on you."

"Well, that's good to know. By 'whole situation,' do you mean this business with the email, the shooter or the pregnancy?" Bowie asked.

"Yes," she answered glibly. When he looked at her quizzically, Marlowe told him, "All of the above."

Bowie sat down on the bed next to her and put his arm around Marlowe's slim shoulders. There was nothing sexual in the gesture. She sensed his only intent was to try to offer her some measure of comfort and support.

"You're not alone in this," he told her quietly. "I intend to be with you on this new journey every step of the way."

She turned her head slightly to look at him. "You mean with the baby?"

"With the baby, with finding out who sent this email to your family and with discovering who the hell is using either of us or both of us for target practice," he concluded.

Hearing him say that made Marlowe feel infinitely better.

And a great deal safer, she realized.

With a relieved sigh, she leaned her head against Bowie's shoulder.

Just having him there beside her like that succeeded in making her feel that all of this would eventually somehow be resolved.

"Thank you," she murmured so quietly that at first he thought that he had imagined it.

She felt Bowie smile against her head.

"Don't mention it." He rose to his feet, extending his hand to her. "Now come into the kitchen and keep me company," he said.

She was glad he refrained from asking her again to have something to eat.

She would do that all in good time. He just had to be patient. It was, she thought as they left the room, a learning process.

Apparently for both of them.

Chapter 10

Bowie watched as Marlowe moved around the kitchen, cleaning up and in general being what to him seemed very domestic. If anyone had asked him, he would have had to admit that he hadn't thought Marlowe had it in her. Maybe once, as a lark, but definitely not twice.

But there she was, cleaning up again, not just after lunch, but after dinner, as well. A dinner she hadn't really bothered to eat because she still wasn't able to keep much down.

When Marlowe caught him watching her, she guessed what was on his mind. "I don't like sitting still, and I don't like leaving a mess."

"Well, it's not like it's exactly your mess," Bowie pointed out. "Seeing as how you didn't really have anything to eat so far, except for a couple of pieces of dry toast."

"And tea," she reminded him as she rinsed off a plate. "Don't forget the tea." Trying to find a way to help her soothe her stomach, Bowie had managed to scrounge up half a box of herbal tea bags from the pantry. He boiled water in a pot and then made her a large mug. "I had no idea you had all these hidden talents."

Joining her at the sink, he took the towel from her and began to dry the dishes she had finished washing. "Dunking a tea bag into a mug of boiled water isn't exactly a hidden talent," he said with a dismissive snort. "It's more of a wrist exercise." He held out his hand to demonstrate. "A very slow wrist exercise," Bowie emphasized before continuing to dry the dishes.

"Still, I do appreciate the effort," Marlowe said.

Bowie laughed. Finished with drying the dishes, he retired the dish towel on the side of the sink. "Yes, now I'll have to rest my wrist for the rest of the evening." His expression turned serious. "Sorry you didn't have any of the steak."

She shrugged his apology off. "I'm not. No reflection on your culinary skills, but the very smell of that steak sizzling tonight was almost enough to send me back communing with the porcelain bowl."

He couldn't picture having to live that way. "I hope for your sake this morning sickness of yours doesn't last too long."

"That makes two of us," she replied, "although I've heard of women feeling like this for the first five months."

Five months of throwing up and the woman would

waste away to nothing, Bowie thought. She was thin to begin with.

"Competitive though you are, that doesn't necessarily have to be you," he told her.

Marlowe gave him a look.

"That's not exactly something I'm aspiring to, either," Marlowe replied.

Several times during that day Bowie had found himself observing Marlowe. Whenever he did, he forced himself to look away, trying his best *not* to watch her. Trying to get his mind on something else. *Anything* else.

He had never been even mildly interested in marriage or in having a family. The idea of having a baby actually unnerved him, and he had always liked to think of himself as fearless. Until this child had suddenly come into the picture, he would have said *nothing* scared him—although having someone out there trying to kill him had come pretty close.

As far as his resistance to having a family went, part of the problem was that he had no model to emulate, nothing to even remotely give him a home base. His own father had hardly ever been home, and even when he was home, he really wasn't. His mind was always elsewhere, calculating and refiguring things that had already been done.

Franklin Robertson was the epitome of a workaholic. Bowie knew that their relationship was tense, and Bowie wanted nothing more than to prove to the demanding man that he had it in him to take over the company when that day came.

A baby didn't figure into any of that. Especially

not a baby whose lineage was half Robertson and half Colton. He was certain that his father would go absolutely ballistic once he found out that little tidbit.

While he wanted Marlowe to know that the baby's future would always be secure, Bowie didn't want her thinking that what the two of them had between them would ever develop into something more than what was there already.

They were outside the cabin at the moment, looking at the peaceful sky and just enjoying, as much as they could, the night air.

But because the stillness was getting to be too much, and he didn't want to risk saying something that might lead them to far more dangerous territory—like the bedroom—Bowie reiterated what he'd already said to her before.

"You know, I meant what I said earlier, about my being there for you and the baby."

"I know, because your word is your bond. Did I get that right?" she asked with a touch of cynicism, parroting what he had told her the day before.

"Yes," he answered, pretending not to notice the shift in her tone. But he really didn't want to take a chance on misleading her. That wouldn't be fair to Marlowe. He needed to be clearer, he decided, so there would be no mistakes made. "Maybe I should also mention that I've always been sort of a lone wolf."

"Are you trying to tell me that you howl whenever there's a full moon out?" she asked sarcastically.

"No," he answered impatiently. "I'm trying to tell you that with my being a lone wolf, well…marriage isn't in the cards for someone like me," he said bluntly, then quickly added, "but that doesn't mean that I would shirk my duty toward the baby."

Her tone grew icy. "That's very nice of you, but you don't have to concern yourself about doing your *duty*," Marlowe told him. "I am more than capable of taking care of and providing for my baby," she concluded flatly.

"You mean *our* baby," Bowie corrected her.

Her eyes narrowed as she looked at him. "The last I heard, possession was nine-tenths of the law," Marlowe informed him, her hand moving to protectively cover her as-of-yet exceptionally flat belly.

She'd clearly had just about enough for one night, she thought. "If you don't mind, I think I'll just turn in early."

She didn't wait for Bowie to respond. Instead, she turned on her heel and walked back into the cabin. Once inside, she went straight to the bedroom in the back, slamming the door in her wake.

Damn it, he hadn't meant to do that, Bowie thought, upbraiding himself. His only intention was to spare her from entertaining any false hopes about their future.

He frowned, looking back toward the cabin door. In getting his message across, he had somehow managed to scare her off altogether. That wasn't what he was trying to do.

This was all damn confusing. He was really attracted to her, probably a great deal more attracted than he had ever been to any other woman before her. But a wife and baby were just not in the cards for him, he silently insisted. RoCo was everything to him, and he had to focus on the company, not on the daughter of his father's archenemy—as melodramatic as that had to sound, he thought, mocking himself. More than likely, she felt the same way about Colton Oil.

With a sigh, Bowie decided to call it a night himself and went into the cabin. Closing the door behind him, he made sure that locks were all secured. Satisfied, he started to go toward the back bedroom, wanting to apologize. But he stopped himself before he got halfway there.

It was better this way.

He couldn't afford to pursue Marlowe, or to allow the attraction he felt for her to get the better of him, beyond being a good dad. For all he knew, if he said anything at all about being attracted to her, she'd laugh at him. Or she might tell him that even though they'd had one good night together, that didn't mean anything in the long run.

Marlowe was married to Colton Oil for the long haul; she had all but told him so. He needed to stop letting his emotions rule his head and get his priorities straight and *keep* them that way once and for all.

Bowie spent an even more restless night this time than he had the previous night when he had intentionally stayed awake.

Come morning, he had made up his mind about what to do next.

"We can't hide here indefinitely," Marlowe told him early the following morning. "I think it's time to go back. I know I have work to do and I'm assuming so do you. If I stay here for another day, I'm going to go stir-crazy."

Bowie smiled, nodding. At least they were in

agreement when it came to this, he thought. "Yeah, me, too."

"Maybe Callum, who's a bodyguard, can help keep an eye out. I guess we have some things in common," Marlowe told him.

Without thinking, his eyes ran over her body. He felt himself reacting before he shut down. "Yes, we do," he responded.

The trip back to Mustang Valley was fairly tense. Bowie kept looking over his shoulder, as if he expected their unknown stalker to pop up at any moment, while Marlowe was very quiet. Her mind was busily trying to figure out just what her connection was to the killer who was after Bowie—and perhaps her, too. Was Bowie right that this had all begun after he left her room that night, or was that all just a terrible coincidence? Or could one of Colton Oil's clients feel that their investment money was being misused because they found out she was looking into making the company green?

She was fervently hoping that she would be able to think more clearly once she was back at work. Back in familiar surroundings.

Going to the cabin had ultimately been a bad idea. She hadn't been able to shake the feeling that she was a sitting duck, waiting for some invisible villain to get off a kill shot. And having Bowie around was just a bitter reminder of the mistake she had made six and a half weeks ago: Bowie thought of himself as a lone wolf. Wolves didn't settle down; they prowled around, she thought.

Well, he was free to do that once they got back to

town. She certainly had no intentions of standing in his way.

As a matter of fact, the way she felt right now, she would be more than happy to *push* him on his way, and good riddance.

As Bowie pulled his vehicle up in front of the Colton Oil building, he noted the rather strange, contemplative expression on her face.

"Everything all right?" he asked her, setting the hand brake and shutting off the engine.

"Just peachy," she replied with what sounded like false cheerfulness. "You don't have to get out," she told him. "I can just get out here."

"No, I'll walk you in," Bowie said firmly. Not giving her a chance to protest, he told her, "I'll carry your suitcase for you."

Her shoulders grew rigid. "I already told you, Robertson," she said, opening the passenger door, "I'm perfectly capable of carrying my own suitcase."

Bowie began to answer, then closed his mouth. Everything was a fight with her ever since he'd said something to make her angry last night. He was tired of fighting.

"Fine," he declared. "Have it your way."

Plucking the suitcase from the back seat, she pulled it out. "I usually do," she replied, sounding deliberately smug.

He should have his head examined, getting mixed up with this bullheaded, stubborn she-devil, Bowie upbraided himself angrily.

Still, rather than pull away, he continued to sit

where he was, watching Marlowe as she walked up to the building entrance and then went inside.

Marlowe was thinking similar, equally critical thoughts about Bowie as she rode up to her office and swept in. Parking her suitcase off to the side, she sank down behind her desk and let loose with a long, deep sigh of relief.

This was more like it.

She was back in her home territory. She knew what was expected of her here, what she needed to accomplish. Being alone in that cabin with Bowie had jumbled up her brain for a little while, made her entertain thoughts she had absolutely no right to entertain.

She— Marlowe froze as she saw the large package that was placed in the middle of her sofa. She didn't remember ordering anything.

Maybe someone had sent her a gift, she decided. Rising from her desk, she crossed over to the sofa. Sitting down beside the package, she picked it up. She turned the box around, examining all six sides of it. There was no return address.

An oversight?

That was odd, she thought. But maybe whoever had sent it didn't want to call attention to him or herself. There was undoubtedly a card inside, probably meant for her eyes only.

Going to her desk to get a letter opener, she used the sharp object to rip through the wrapping paper around the package so she could get to the box underneath. When she did, she still had no clue who had sent it.

Ordinarily, she would have thought the package

had been sent by a secret admirer. But the strange events of the last three days, especially her one inter-action with the mysterious shooter who had fired at both her *and* Bowie, well, that had changed the way she viewed things like a package.

She was being silly, Marlowe told herself. This was probably some harmless gift, or maybe even some promotional gimmick meant to get the attention of the president of Colton Oil.

Having calmed herself down to an extent, Marlowe gingerly opened the cardboard box.

She found a profusion of tissue paper covering a sweet-faced stuffed teddy bear that could easily be placed in any baby's nursery.

Pulling the stuffed bear out, she also managed to pull out a card.

Finally, she thought, wrapping one arm around the bear to hold it in place. Mystery solved, she told her-self, opening the envelope and pulling out the card that was inside.

Congratulations on your baby. Wish it was mine.

The scream that escaped her lips came totally un-bidden. As was her reaction as she threw the stuffed bear to the floor.

Her assistant came running in immediately, look-ing as if she didn't know what to expect when she opened the door. "Is something wrong, Ms. Colton?" Karen asked breathlessly.

Marlowe struggled to get herself under control. The last thing she wanted was to be seen as a hys-terical woman, even though everything inside of her was shaking. Who could have sent this?

"Did you see who left this, Karen?" she asked her assistant.

Seeing that the threat was just a stuffed teddy bear, Karen relaxed and seemed a little calmer as she ventured forward.

"Oh, how adorable," she said, her face softening and forming a smile as she looked at the gift.

"Did you see who left this?" Marlowe repeated, this time more sharply.

Karen shook her head, looking somewhat nervous again. "No, Ms. Colton. Whoever left it must have come in before I did."

Marlowe looked at the teddy bear as if it was the enemy. "So it was already in my office before you got in? What time did you come in?" she asked, her uneasiness growing.

It was obvious that it took Karen a minute to think. "I was here by seven," she remembered. "I had some paperwork to catch up on. Whoever left this for you had to have done it before seven. Is something wrong, Ms. Colton?" she asked.

Marlowe didn't answer the assistant directly. Instead, she instructed the woman in an urgent voice, "Call Security and tell them to come in here, Karen."

Karen blinked, her eyes widening as she looked at her boss. "Security, ma'am?"

"Yes," Marlowe answered, keeping her eyes on the teddy bear. "I want them to examine footage to see who dropped this off and check this thing out completely, just in case it's wired for explosives."

Chapter 11

She had to concentrate to keep her hands from shaking as she stared at the note she had taken out of the package. *Congratulations on your baby. Wish it was mine.*

All sorts of half-formed thoughts were ricocheting around in her head.

Who had sent this?

Why?

Did she have some creepy stalker tracking her after all?

Had someone followed her into the drugstore and watched her buy the pregnancy test? And even if that was true, how could this stalker have possibly known the results of that test?

Or was he just guessing? After all, there was a

fifty-fifty chance of being right. But to what end? And why?

She was back to her first question: Who was doing this to her?

Marlowe could feel herself becoming nauseated again. She closed her eyes and *willed* her stomach to settle down. Willed it to cease its bitter-tasting rise up into her throat and mouth. She pulled her fingers into tight fists. This wasn't the time to let her body dictate to her.

She needed to think, to *do* something, not just be a sitting duck.

Marlowe drew in a deep breath and then let it out slowly, then did it over again.

Security had come in and taken possession of the possibly lethal teddy bear a few minutes ago, so at least she didn't have to worry about the damn thing exploding and harming anyone. That was something, she thought, silently consoling herself.

Marlowe took out her phone. Her hands were still shaking.

She started texting Bowie, wanting to tell him about this newest development in what was quickly becoming a very complicated saga. Before she had gotten to the third word, the company phone on her desk rang, making her jump.

She really needed to get a grip on herself, Marlowe thought.

Blowing out a tense breath, she yanked up the receiver and all but barked, "Hello?"

"Marlowe?" It was Ace's voice on the other end of the line. He sounded as tense as she felt, she thought. "Good," her brother was saying. "You *are* back, then.

I need you to come into the boardroom right now. Ainsley just got the DNA test results back. She wants to tell us the results all at the same time. The rest of the board is already here."

Of course they were, Marlowe thought impatiently. This was getting to be the story of her life. The last one in.

"Did she tell you what the result of the test was?"

She heard her brother laugh, but there was no humor in the sound. "You know Ainsley. If the result is supposed to be a secret until everyone is gathered together to hear it, then she intends to keep it a secret—even from herself—until then," Ace told her. "She hasn't even opened the envelope herself. So hurry up and get here. This suspense is killing me."

"I'm on my way," she promised, quickly hanging up the phone.

With all this craziness going on in her life, the pregnancy, the shooter and now this stalker, she was embarrassed to admit that she had completely forgotten about Ace and the DNA test. Marlowe felt almost guilty that she had.

But it wasn't as if Ace needed her to boost his morale, she silently insisted. Of course the DNA test was going to show that he was a Colton. To think that anything else could possibly happen would be absurd, she told herself, hurrying to the boardroom.

The results were going to be positive. They *had* to be, Marlowe insisted.

Even so, her heart felt like it was racing to the tune of "Flight of the Bumblebee" by the time she walked into the boardroom.

The five other members of the board were already

assembled in the room, just the way they had been when that bombshell of an email had been sent. Looking quickly around, she noted that their expressions all looked just as hopeful as hers did.

All except for Selina, Marlowe thought. Selina's expression was that belonging to a woman who was anticipating *her* version of good news.

"Nice of you to join us," Payne said sarcastically, the moment that Marlowe crossed the boardroom threshold. And then the man shifted his eyes toward Ainsley. "All right, Ainsley, go ahead. Open the envelope and read the results out loud."

Ainsley flashed an encouraging smile at Ace, then ripped open the side of the envelope. She took out the lab results. Pressing her lips together, Ainsley scanned the single sheet of paper in her hand.

"I said out loud, Ainsley," Payne repeated sharply, raising his voice so that it all but thundered through the room.

Ainsley's expression turned grim.

This couldn't be good, Marlowe thought, hoping against hope that her instinct was wrong.

Ainsley read the results out loud. "It says that there is less than zero chance that Ace Colton is a Colton by blood."

"What?" Rafe cried, stunned.

"There has to be some sort of mistake," Marlowe insisted. "It can't say that."

"That can't be right, Ainsley!" Ace declared, looking like someone who just had a land mine explode right in front of him. "There must have been a mix-up at the lab. We need to have the sample retested, this time by another lab."

"Dad," Rafe spoke up, coming to Ace's defense. "Marlowe's right. A mistake has been made."

All their voices were blending together in a cacophony of noise, each voice drowning out the others. Payne himself looked as if he was in a state of shock, and for once in his life, he was speechless.

Of all of them, only Selina looked pleased. *Really* pleased.

"Payne, remember, the bylaws are the bylaws and they have to be obeyed." Her smile deepened, verging on almost malicious. "You know what you have to do," she told him, looking at her ex-husband expectantly. "Go ahead," she urged. "Do it."

"I want no one to speak about this." Payne's dark eyes swept over every face at the table, almost as if he was looking into their very souls. "The public can't get wind of this. This stays in the family. Am I making myself understood?" he demanded, looking at each and every one of them again.

"Payne," Selina said in a patronizing tone.

Payne blew out an angry breath. Marlowe knew that what he was about to say gave him no pleasure. If Ace, or this person who had grown up in front of him with Ace's name, wasn't a Colton, then the man had no business being the CEO of Colton Oil. He needed to step down.

"She's right, boy," Payne said, his voice flat and cold, "you can't be part of the board of directors and you most certainly can't be the CEO now that we know the truth."

Ace stared at the man he had thought of as his father for his entire life. How could some piece of paper, most likely faulty, negate forty years, just like that? As if they had never happened at all?

"Dad, you can't really be serious," Ace protested, stunned, hurt and angry. "I don't care what that paper says, I'm still your son—"

"No, that's just it. You're *not*," Payne retorted, his voice growing in volume. "I don't know who you are, and I certainly don't know who switched you with my son at birth, or why they did, but you are definitely *not* my son, and that means you can't be the CEO of Colton Oil," he repeated, all but shouting the words.

Ace shouted back. "You can't do this!"

Payne's eyes grew cold. "I just did," he informed Ace flatly.

Fury entered Ace's eyes. Visibly stunned and reeling, Marlowe imagined he felt as if the very rug had been pulled out from under his feet and he was struggling to get his bearings. After all, his whole life had just been declared null and void by his own father, a man who was obviously incapable of even an ounce of sympathy or compassion. Surely he had never felt so abandoned and alone before in his entire life.

"You're going to regret doing this, *Dad*!" Ace promised.

Ace stormed out of the room, leaving his disoriented siblings to try to comprehend what all this meant for the company as well as for them.

Marlowe was also wondering why their father had allowed himself to be manipulated to agree with Selina, a woman *none* of them even remotely liked.

Was she behind this somehow? Marlowe couldn't help wondering.

Meanwhile she was also experiencing regrets

again. She regretted having told Bowie about the email and that Ace being related to the rest of them had consequently been in doubt, so a DNA test had been initiated. The bottom line was that the results had caused Ace to be ousted by their father. She could just imagine that this would have the Robertsons beside themselves with joy, although she doubted that Bowie would feel that way. She was beginning to feel that he wasn't such a bad guy, all things considered.

She should have just kept her mouth shut, Marlowe upbraided herself. Desperate to have something to blame, she zeroed in on her condition. If it wasn't for this stupid pregnancy, causing her to be soft as well as weak, she wouldn't have said *anything* to Bowie about Ace.

Well, no more, Marlowe promised herself. From now on, she was going to be as closed off and as tough as she used to be, she vowed.

Marlowe looked at her father, disappointed beyond words at the way he had handled all of this. Disappointed, too, that the man she had looked up to, despite everything, had given in to Selina, of all people, rather than override the witch.

Not for the first time Marlowe wondered if the hateful woman was holding something over her father's head. Something that would make Payne jump through hoops and turn his back on the rest of his family.

There was no other explanation for her father's actions.

It had to be something really big, she decided. Otherwise she was certain that Payne Colton would have sent that woman packing, her tail between her legs, a long time ago—immediately after their divorce, Marlowe thought. Instead, she'd watched her father, never a patient man, keep treating the wretched woman like she was some sort of trusted confidante instead of the hateful, poisonous viper that she was.

Only the look in his eyes, when he occasionally let his guard down, told Marlowe otherwise.

What is it, Dad? What does Selina have on you that keeps you in line like this?

"Okay, everybody, settle down," her father ordered, raising his voice. It wasn't a request, it was a flat-out demand, and they all knew better than not to obey. "With Ace gone, someone is going to have to take over as the company's CEO."

Marlowe stiffened, praying that her father was not about to appoint her to this post. There was just too much going on in her life right now for her to maintain a clear enough head, let alone the entire Colton Oil company. She liked to think that she was up to any challenge, but this would have been just too much for her.

"So, for the time being," her father was saying, "I'll take over the position. It's my old job, anyway," he said with a resigned shrug, as if part of him had always known it would come down to this eventually. "So, unless there are any objections—" his tone indicated that he didn't assume that there would be as he looked around the table again "—meeting's adjourned. Go do your work, people," Payne ordered.

The others filed out of the room, but Marlowe hung back. She and Ace were not as close as they used to be, although they did work together on the board. But she really felt for him because of what he was going through now. That made her feel that she needed to say something to her father about the explosion that had just happened between the two men.

Payne pulled a few papers together, then raised his eyes when he saw that Marlowe hadn't left yet.

"You got something to say, girl?" Payne addressed her gruffly.

He must have assumed that she was going to ask for his forgiveness for the mess she had gotten herself into with the Robertson kid.

"Yes, I do," she told her father. "Ace didn't mean it, Dad."

Payne's forehead furrowed into a mass of wrinkles.

"What?" he demanded.

Her father had a gold medal in intimidation, but Marlowe refused to back down. Instead, she forced herself to push on.

"Ace was just upset," she told Payne. "His whole world has just come crashing down all around him, and he wound up turning all his anger on you. But you have to know that he didn't mean what he just said."

Payne grew angrier.

"What goes on between Ace and me is none of your damn business, missy, so back off, you hear me?" he shouted at her. "And you're in no position to give me any kind of advice!"

Marlowe struggled to hang on to her own temper. She supposed that her father was upset by the news himself and this was his way of dealing with it. But she wasn't in the mood to make excuses for her father or put up with his bad temper or his even worse personality.

"Sorry," she said sarcastically. "I guess I forgot my place."

"Damn straight you did. Well, don't forget it again, you hear me?" he warned. "You might not like the consequences."

Her father was treating everyone as if they were annoying interlopers. There was just no getting through to him today, she thought, annoyed clear down to the bone.

Turning on her heel, Marlowe left the boardroom as quickly as possible, wanting to get away from the man before she said something cutting and surly.

That, she knew, would make her no better than her father—and she didn't have the sort of surly outlook to carry it off.

She was about to return to her office when she caught sight of Ace. He looked both angry and lost at the same time.

Impulsively, she hurried over to the man she had always regarded as her oldest sibling. Because they had two different mothers, Ace was actually her half brother, a fact that her father always emphasized for reasons known only to him, but she had never thought in those terms. Ace was her brother, pure and simple. And the DNA results, along with what had just happened back in the boardroom, didn't change anything.

He was still Ace to her, just as she intended to be still Marlowe to him. She couldn't live with herself if she didn't say something to Ace in an attempt to make him feel better.

"Ace," she called out to him. When he kept walking, she tried again. "Ace!"

Reluctantly, Ace stopped walking and turned

around to face her. The look on his face was defensive and surly, as well as hurt.

"What?" he said bitingly.

"I just wanted to tell you that I don't care what some DNA report says. You're still my brother, Ace Colton, as far as I'm concerned, and I just wanted you to know that you have my full support, no matter what you decide to do. This was a terrible blow, but I know you. You're going to pick yourself up, dust yourself off and find a way to come back from all this."

He looked at her as if she were talking nonsense. "Excuse me, but have you *met* our father? Sorry, I mean *your* father?" He tersely pretended to correct himself. "The man doesn't bend or give."

"Yet. He hasn't bent or given *yet*," Marlowe pointedly insisted. "But there's always a first time, Ace. And I know it's going to happen."

Ace laughed shortly. "I appreciate the Pollyanna pep talk, Marlowe, I really do," he told her. "But right now I think that I just want some space from everything, if you don't mind."

Humoring Ace, she raised her hands as if to symbolically give him that space.

"You've got it, big brother. Just promise me that you won't let that space turn into something that winds up becoming insurmountable."

"Okay, I promise," Ace said in an offhanded manner as he left. There was no conviction in his voice.

With all her heart, Marlowe really wished that she could believe her brother meant what he said.

Chapter 12

"Mr. Robertson, there's a Ms. Colton asking to see you." Bowie's administrative assistant, Gloria Kennedy, who had been with the company since its very beginning, peered into his office. Looking like everyone's kindly grandmother, the woman entered Bowie's office only after knocking first and being told to come in. "Shall I tell her that you're in a meeting?"

"But I'm not," Bowie told Gloria, although he appreciated the fact that she was attempting to guard his privacy.

What was Marlowe doing here? he wondered. He assumed it had to be Marlowe, because why would any of the other Colton women have a reason to come to see him? Something must have happened, he thought. But what?

"I know, sir," Gloria answered patiently. "But it is a Colton, sir, and…"

Gloria's voice trailed off as if that lone fragment was enough to explain why she had kept the woman cooling her heels in the outer office.

Bowie didn't bother debating the matter with his assistant. He normally trusted Gloria's judgment implicitly, but this was an entirely different matter. Without saying another word, he strode into the outer office.

He was just in time to see Marlowe going to the outer door, leaving.

"Marlowe, wait," he called out, crossing quickly over to her.

Visibly annoyed at the way she'd been treated by Bowie's assistant, Marlowe made no effort to stop walking out of the office.

Bowie was quick enough to catch up to her, and he placed himself directly in the way of Marlowe's escape route. He was now convinced that something had to be terribly wrong for her to come into what he knew she considered enemy territory to see him.

Had someone made another attempt on her life? The very idea left him cold.

Catching hold of her arm, Bowie physically stopped her exit. "Marlowe, what's wrong?"

Because he had her arm, she was forced to stop. It was either that or create a scene, and while he knew she had no qualms about doing that if the situation warranted it, for the time being, it didn't.

Tossing her head, Marlowe looked up at him. "You mean other than the fact that your assistant over there could benefit from a crash course in manners?" she asked, casting a disparaging look in the older woman's direction. Gloria stood, looking formidable, frowning at Marlowe.

Right now, his attention was focused on the large box Marlowe was holding. He curbed his immediate desire to ask her about it.

"Yes, other than that," Bowie answered dismissively. He knew without turning to look in Gloria's direction that the woman was taking in every syllable. The assistant was exceedingly protective when it came to him. "Why don't you come into my office?" he suggested. "You can tell me why you've ventured into enemy territory." He expected at least a small smile in response, but when Bowie peered at her face, Marlowe continued to look like the very definition of anger. "Nothing?" he asked. "This is bad, isn't it?"

Rather than answer his question, Marlowe said, "Let's go into your office like you suggested—as long as your fire-breathing protector doesn't object."

Bowie felt like he had to come to the woman's defense. "Gloria was just doing her job, Marlowe," he told her, leading the way back to his office. "There are a lot of people trying to get to talk to me for one reason or another."

"Really?" she said. "That must be really rough on you."

Bowie closed the door behind them. Once it was shut, he turned to look at his unexpected visitor. She really looked upset, and he didn't think that he was the reason for that.

"All right, Marlowe. Let's stop waltzing around. What happened since I dropped you off? Why are you here?" he asked. And, since she hadn't volunteered the information herself, he nodded at the box she was holding. "And what's that?"

She placed it on top of his desk. "That was waiting for me in my office when I got in this morning. When I asked my assistant who left it there, she didn't know. She said it must have been put into my office before she got in. The woman regularly gives roosters their wake-up call, as a sideline."

"So whoever dropped that thing off either came into the office incredibly early, or he knew your assistant's routine," Bowie surmised.

"And if it's the latter, that suggests that whoever did leave this gift works at Colton Oil," she told him. "Otherwise, how could he possibly have known Karen's routine?"

Bowie inclined his head. She had a good point there, he thought. "And just what did this mystery man drop off?" he asked, his curiosity finally getting the better of him.

Marlowe had been doing her best to distance herself from the implications that this "gift" brought with it, not to mention what it indicated about the person who had given it to her. She had just gotten the bear back from Security, which had found the stuffed animal to contain nothing harmful. A lot they knew, she thought.

Telling Bowie about the bear brought those feelings back to her in spades.

Pulling the teddy bear with its note out of the box, she put both on his desk.

"This," she declared.

"A teddy bear?" he asked, as if not quite certain

why she seemed to be so shaken up by the gift. "It's a little strange, but I don't—"

"Read the note that came with it," she insisted. "And then we'll talk."

Picking up the card, Bowie quickly read it. His expression became grave. "I see what you mean."

"It appears that I've got a hostile admirer," she told Bowie. She could all but feel the hostility emanating from the card. Restless, Marlowe began to pace back and forth in front of his desk. She wasn't accustomed to not handling problems, and yet, with no one to focus on, there wasn't anything she could do about this.

Bowie nodded thoughtfully. "That would explain why the attacks on me started after I left your hotel room that morning. It points to the fact that this admirer of yours is jealous."

Marlowe tried not to shiver, but she failed. "My admirer is crazy," she corrected.

"Well, yes, that goes without saying," Bowie agreed. "Can you think of anyone you've turned down recently?"

Marlowe shook her head. "I haven't turned down anyone," she protested. "I've been so busy, nobody's even approached me on a social level. It's been all about work," she told him.

"Okay, have you noticed anyone staring at you lately—worshipfully or otherwise?"

"No to both questions," she told him. She drew herself up. "But I know one thing for sure."

"And what's that?" he asked.

"Whoever this so-called admirer is, it has to be

someone who works at Colton Oil, because I spend *all* my time at Colton Oil," she told him.

Bowie showed just the barest hint of a smile.

"Well, not *all* your time," he told her, his eyes moving down to Marlowe's waist and lingering there for the briefest of moments.

Marlowe sighed audibly. "All right, except for that one anomaly," she allowed. "Which wound up with me getting pregnant, as well as getting my very own creepy stalker—and someone trying to kill both of us," she said in disgust.

"The least I can do is get you a bodyguard," he offered Marlowe as he reached for the phone on his desk, drawing it closer.

Marlowe quickly stopped him from lifting up the receiver. When he looked at her quizzically, she said, "Like that won't be at all conspicuous," she told Bowie, vetoing the idea. "Look, if I wanted a bodyguard, I'm perfectly capable of getting one myself," she informed him.

"But you won't," he guessed. The woman was too stubborn for her own good.

She shrugged off what she knew he was implying. She wasn't being stubborn; she was being practical. "A bodyguard will only get in my way," she informed him.

"Yeah, well, so will a bullet," Bowie countered matter-of-factly. "What if Callum kept an eye out for you?"

But she shook her head. "I really don't think this guy is out to kill me," Marlowe told him. "You, maybe, but not me."

Bowie laughed shortly. "Well, that's reassuring,"

he said sarcastically. "Would you stop pacing?" he asked her. "You're making me dizzy."

"Cold-blooded killers generally don't leave cute teddy bears as their calling cards," Marlowe pointed out, telling him the conclusion she had reached now that she'd had time to think about the situation. "And before you ask, I had Security take this guy apart to see if maybe he'd been wired with explosives or something else equally as lethal. Turns out that the teddy bear was just an ordinary teddy bear. Whoever left this," she lifted up the bear again, "was either just trying to get my attention, or at the very most, to unnerve me."

"You can't take that for granted. If he's playing games like that, it could easily escalate," Bowie told her. "Look, I'm going to get that bodyguard for you, so you might as well stop arguing with me. I can either do it with your permission, or behind your back. It's up to you, but one way or another, you need to wrap your mind around the fact that you *are* going to get extra protection. I am not about to look back at this down the line and regret the fact that I didn't go with my instincts, and because I didn't, you and our child are no longer part of the equation."

"So now we're part of some equation?" Marlowe questioned, clearly trying to goad him into an argument.

"Don't change the subject, Marlowe. I *am* getting you that bodyguard. And don't worry, he'll be totally vetted. His only job will be to look after you and keep you safe. That means that he's not going to give a damn about whatever company secrets you might be harboring and could divulge. He's just going to be there to watch your back—just in case."

He knew Marlowe's suspicions wouldn't be entirely put to rest, but she was going to have to trust someone, and it might as well be him.

"I've got your word on that?" she asked.

He was surprised at her phrasing. If she was being serious, that meant that they were finally making some headway, he thought, pleased.

"Are you willing to take my word?" he questioned, watching her face for any telltale signs that she assented.

She raised her chin and her eyes held his. "Yes," she answered stoically.

"Then yes, you have my word on that," he told her.

When he saw the smile that slowly bloomed on Marlowe's lips, it hit him just how worth it all of this had been. Even though he tried to seal himself off, her smile really got to him.

Marlowe's phone buzzed at that moment. Forced to glance down at the screen, she read the text that had come in for her.

It was from Callum, inviting her to come with him to Mustang Valley General Hospital. He intended to try to find out just who had been on duty that fateful night that the person they had come to know as Ace had been switched with the "real" Ace.

We're going archive hunting, the text told her. Want to come help?

"More bad news?" Bowie asked, looking at Marlowe's expression.

That was when she remembered that she hadn't told Bowie about the results of the DNA test—and the subsequent fallout that bombshell had had.

But that was a story for another day, she decided.

She didn't want to get into it right now, nor did she really have the time to try to field any of his questions, legitimate though they might be.

"No," she answered. "No bad news. Possibly good news," she continued, keeping her response deliberately vague. "I really won't know until I actually get there." She tucked away her cell phone as she started to go for the door. "Oh, Bowie," Marlowe said, turning around to face him just before she opened the door and walked out, "about the bodyguard…"

Because she was standing at the door, he had a feeling that she was going to tell him that she'd changed her mind about having one. Bowie braced himself for an argument. A knock-down, drag-out one if it came to that, because he wasn't about to have her out there, possibly a moving target, without some sort of protection.

"What about it?" he asked.

Her expression softened into a smile. A smile that managed to curl up in the pit of his stomach. "Thanks."

He would have wanted to accept her thanks at face value, but he'd come to know that nothing, when it came to Marlowe, was that easy.

"But?" he asked, waiting for her protest or refusal of the offer.

"No but," she told Bowie. "Just thanks."

Despite her initially trying to tell him that having a bodyguard wasn't in the cards for her, Bowie had remained steadfast and pushed because he was concerned. Marlowe couldn't help but compare that to her father's reaction. Payne Colton knew that she had been the target of an attack at her apartment, but he hadn't said anything about getting her a bodyguard or even acted concerned that the attack had happened.

She knew that her father, by definition, was not a demonstrative man. As far back as she could remember, he had expected his children to take care of themselves, handle their own problems. Time and again, he had said that it "built character." He obviously expected that it would do that for her, as well.

But it was obvious to her that Bowie didn't subscribe to that sort of philosophy. Or, if he did, he still wasn't about to take any chances with the life of the woman who was carrying his child.

There were all sorts of ways to view his insisting on a bodyguard for her in a bad light, but Marlowe chose not to go that route. Instead, she just wanted to enjoy the fact that someone cared enough about her well-being to stand up to her and do what he felt was necessary.

His stock definitely went up, as far as she was concerned.

Bowie grinned then, as if relieved he wasn't going to have to fight her on this after all.

"Don't mention it," he told her.

"Just let me know when your guy starts to do his job," she told him. "Otherwise, his head will end up mounted as a trophy on my father's wall. My father has a way of shooting first and asking questions later," she added.

Bowie laughed dryly. "I'll keep that in mind," he told her.

"You should," Marlowe agreed, nodding. "For your own peace of mind, as well as for my future bodyguard's well-being."

"Hey," Bowie called after her as she opened the door and began to leave. "Aren't you forgetting something?" he asked.

She had no idea what he was referring to. "Like what?" she asked, a trace of suspicion reentering her voice.

In response, Bowie indicated the teddy bear that was still sitting on his desk.

Strangely relieved that this wasn't going to be something that could escalate into an argument between them, Marlowe laughed and shook her head. "I didn't forget. He stays here," she told him. "Think of him as your new little friend." Her mouth curved a little more. "He'll keep you company."

And with that, she walked out.

As was her habit, Marlowe drove back to Colton Oil with a lead foot, stepping hard on the gas to zip through yellow lights that were about to turn red. She admitted to herself that she was not known for her patience, and her patience was in exceedingly short supply when it came to wasting time being stuck in traffic, waiting for lights to turn green.

She calculated that her method enabled her to save both on time and gas, and although saving gas meant nothing to her as a member of Colton Oil, time was something she had always valued a great deal.

Zigzagging through the small, homey streets, she got back to Colton Oil's headquarters even quicker than she had anticipated. Marlowe really hoped it was an omen of how things were going to go in her hunt through the archives.

"You slowing down these days?" Callum asked

when she pulled up. He was down in the parking garage, waiting for her, and she'd arrived later than he'd anticipated.

"Hardly," she retorted, getting out of her vehicle.

Her twin knew better than to continue teasing her.

Chapter 13

Mustang Valley General Hospital was a large, inviting, five-story brick building that had been built back in 1925. It had gone through several renovations by now and could currently boast being a total state-of-the-art hospital. But it had become so only over the last fifteen years, thanks to endowments funded by Colton Oil.

Located at the far end of downtown Mustang Valley on its own well-manicured five-acre plot, the hospital was on the tail end of a winding road down which Callum was currently driving himself and Marlowe. He pulled his car up as close as he could to the front entrance of the building. Because of its large parking lot, finding a spot wasn't an issue.

"Why do I get the feeling that we're about to embark on a wild-goose chase?" Callum said to his twin as he got out from behind the wheel.

"Could be because behind that handsome, rugged exterior, you're a born pessimist," Marlowe answered. "Do what I do. View this in a positive light." She closed the passenger door. "Just think of it as unraveling a mystery for Ace."

"Except that he's not Ace anymore," Callum said as they crossed the parking lot and made their way to the hospital's front entrance.

Almost a foot shorter than her twin, Marlowe hurried to keep up. There was no way she was about to ask him to slow down. "Well, that's the name that he's responded to for the last forty years, and as far as I'm concerned, he'll always be Ace to me."

"Yeah," Callum agreed. "Me, too. But Dad doesn't see it that way," he pointed out as they came up to the entrance.

The hospital's electronic doors drew apart and they walked in.

"So we'll work on Dad until we convince him," Marlowe said. "After all, there's two of us. We outnumber him."

It had been a while since either of them had been here, but the layout was still the same. There was an admission's desk on the left and a desk for outpatients to register on the right. Comfortable love seats were scattered for people to use throughout the lobby.

"Not the last time I checked," Callum answered. "One Payne Colton outnumbers six offspring, especially when one of the biological ones turns out not to be the real deal."

"You're impossible," Marlowe complained. Zeroing in on the woman sitting at the admission's desk, she physically pointed her brother in that direction.

"C'mon, put that gorgeous face of yours to use," she told him in a lowered voice. "Charm the lady behind the desk into giving us the information we need," Marlowe instructed, all but giving him a push in the right direction.

Walking up to the woman's desk, he cleared his throat. "Excuse me," Callum said, speaking up.

"Be with you in a moment," the woman behind the admissions desk, whose name tag read Irene Ryan, said curtly. She continued typing data into the computer that was on her desk, keeping her eyes on the monitor.

Finished, she looked up. The moment she did and saw the man who was looming over her, her features instantly softened. Irene's voice almost sounded melodious as she asked the man, "What can I do for you, sir?"

"This is going to sound a little strange," Callum said, prefacing what he was about to ask. "But we're—" he glanced back at his sister as if for backup "—looking for information about births that took place at the hospital forty years ago. Specifically, births on Christmas morning."

The young admission clerk's smile faded, replaced by a look of confusion. "Is this some kind of joke, or a prank?" she asked Callum. It was obvious that she was growing defensive.

"No, ma'am," Callum politely assured her, "it's not a joke."

Marlowe spoke up, moving closer to her brother. "We're really trying to find any information we can about those births."

Irene paused to think for a moment, then shook her

head. "That's way before the hospital began digitizing its data. My guess is that those records, if they're still around, would have been placed in the batched files stored in the basement. I'm really sorry," the young woman said, addressing her words to Callum rather than to the both of them, "but we don't have the resources or the time to just drop everything and go digging through files that are more than a quarter of a century old." She sat up a little straighter in an attempt to sound more official. "I'm afraid that you're out of luck," she told Callum.

"Are you sure you can't just—" Marlowe began but got no further before the admissions clerk cut her off.

"Yes, I'm sure I can't," Irene said curtly, sparing Marlowe a quick, dismissive look and acting like this was her kingdom and she was the first line of defense.

"Ms.—" Pausing, Callum glanced down at the nameplate sitting on the desk in front of the woman. "—Ryan," he said, attempting to create a bond between them by using her name. "In the heat of the moment, I completely forgot to introduce my sister and myself. I'm Callum Colton and this is my sister, Marlowe Colton."

The woman looked as if she had suddenly been fed a rock and was desperately trying to get it to go down. "Colton?" she repeated uneasily.

"Yes," Marlowe confirmed, abandoning all pretense of attempting to be nice to the woman. "You might have seen it written on some of the dedication plaques scattered around here in the hospital."

It was easy to see that Irene was a mouse, easily intimidated by authority. Placing her palms on her desk, she pushed herself up to her feet. Marlowe noticed that her hands were shaking.

"Um, yes," Irene answered nervously, her eyes now as large as saucers. "Wait right here…let me go get Anne Sewall. She's the hospital's administrator," the young woman told them, stumbling backward as she tried to make a graceful exit—and failed. "I'll be right back," she mumbled under her breath.

Marlowe turned toward her brother, putting a look of satisfaction on her face. "I knew that pretty face of yours would get us results," she told Callum.

"I tend to think that it was hearing our last name that got Miss Would-Be Efficiency moving as if there was a fire lit directly under her," Callum contradicted. Marlowe knew he wasn't the type who needed or wanted to have his ego stroked.

"Hey, I'll settle for whatever works," Marlowe replied with a laugh.

She crossed her fingers, hoping that one way or another, they would wind up getting the information they were after. Forty years *was* a long time, she readily admitted. Who knew what kind of state those old records would be in, once they were found? *If* they could even be found.

"Uh-huh, looks like it's showtime," Callum whispered to his sister as the admissions clerk returned to her desk.

"Mr. Colton, Ms. Sewall will see you now," the young woman told Callum. Her voice had taken on a formal cadence. "You, too, Ms. Colton," she added, as if suddenly remembering that she hadn't addressed the woman standing next to Callum. "Her office is right down the hall. Step that way," Irene added, pointing in the direction she had come from.

"One step closer," Marlowe murmured to her brother as they passed the desk and retraced her steps to an office where Anne Sewall waited.

Anne was a tall, thin woman in her early sixties with a blond bob, wire-rimmed glasses and a heavy-set face. She gave the impression of being overworked even when she was sitting down and not moving a muscle.

The woman rose to her feet the moment that Marlowe and her brother walked into her office.

"Ms. Colton, Mr. Colton, this is a great honor," she gushed, shaking first Marlowe's hand and then Callum's. She made Marlowe think of a lapdog that was desperately trying to gain favor. "Please, sit, sit," she cried, as if repeating the word somehow made the request that much more urgent. She gestured toward the two chairs in front of her antique desk.

Once Callum and Marlowe had both sat down, Anne took her own seat, sliding forward and sitting on the very edge like a bird waiting to take flight at the slightest provocation.

Her brown eyes darted back and forth between her two visitors, as if she didn't know whom to address first.

"What is it I can do for you?" Anne asked eagerly.

Callum took the lead. "We need to take a look at your hospital records, Ms. Sewall. Specifically, we're interested in records about a baby or babies born in the hospital on Christmas morning forty years ago."

The administrator looked somewhat puzzled and

uncertain. "Did you say forty years ago?" the woman asked.

"Yes," Callum answered.

"May I ask why?" Anne asked.

"We'd rather not go into the particulars right now, Ms. Sewall," Marlowe told the other woman.

"But we assure you that there is nothing underhanded going on. The records concern our brother, Ace. He was born here on Christmas morning," Callum explained, then repeated his request again. "May we see those records, please?"

Anne continued to look nervous and uncertain. "I'm afraid that's impossible," she told him.

Marlowe sighed. "We know about the privacy issues," she interjected. "But the records have to do with Ace's birth. If we could just take a look at those records—"

"That's just it. There *are* no records," the woman informed them.

Callum scowled. "How is that possible?" he asked. "My father witnessed his wife giving birth to his first child. All of that has to be documented somewhere—"

"I'm sure what you're saying is all very true. However, I'm afraid that there was a fire in the maternity ward that very morning and it destroyed all the recent records regarding all the births that had taken place in that time frame, not to mention the names of the hospital staff who were on duty the night before as well as that morning. It also destroyed the nearby nurse's station. I'm sure everyone was grateful that the fire was contained and gotten under control before it could do any more damage, and fortunately, the infants were never threatened.

"Like I said," the administrator told them, her voice sounding a little strained, "this was all before records were kept on a computer and archived."

She flashed them a contrite look. "I am really sorry, but I don't have anything to show you." The woman looked almost eager to usher them out of her office. "I will do everything I can to shed some light on how the fire started and if anything at all survived the isolated blaze. But as for the information you're looking for, I'm afraid that it just no longer exists," she told them with finality.

"If I hear of anything, though," she went on, "I promise I'll give you both a call."

That was clearly their signal to leave, Marlowe thought. Callum rose to his feet, as did Marlowe. "I guess we can't ask for more than that," Callum told the administrator. "Thank you for taking the time to see us," he said.

"Of course, of course," Anne said, shaking each of their hands again. "I'm just sorry I couldn't have been of more help," she added, looking genuinely contrite in Callum's opinion.

"Well, that was awfully convenient, don't you think?" Callum asked his twin as they walked out of the hospital. "A fire breaking out just after the real Ace and our Ace were switched?"

"I suppose it could have happened," Marlowe allowed. "But you're right. It just sounds like much too much of a coincidence. If you want my opinion, the person who switched the babies most likely set the fire," she concluded.

"No argument," Callum agreed. The same thing had occurred to him. "Now what?"

The entrance doors closed behind them and they began to walk toward the parking lot and Callum's car.

"Now we keep digging," Marlowe answered. "Maybe we can find out who was working at the hospital around that time. If we're lucky, maybe someone saw something but didn't know what they were seeing at the time. There had to have been a great deal of pandemonium and panic during the fire, what with everyone rushing around, trying to save the babies and their mothers."

"I don't know about that." Callum didn't seem so sure about the scenario she had just verbally sketched.

"What do you mean?" Marlowe asked.

"Dad would have mentioned something like that at some point. Maybe the fire was purposely a very small, isolated one," Callum theorized. "Just big enough to destroy the records, but not big enough to threaten anyone else, including the babies."

"Sounds like a good theory to me," Marlowe agreed. The more she thought about it, the more likely it sounded to her.

"We just need to find someone who worked at the hospital in the maternity ward at the time to confirm that," Callum said. He made it sound simple, but she knew it was anything but that.

Marlowe said it out loud for both of them. "Easier said than done. But then," she reflected, "what fun is easy?"

Callum shook his head. "You do have a very unique way of looking at things."

"I'm a Colton," she said as they got into his car. "I was born unique."

"And humble," he said with a laugh, putting his key into the ignition. "Don't forget humble."

"Never," she replied with a straight face. "I wouldn't forget that." And then Marlowe's expression became serious. "I think we need to call the board together for another meeting so we can tell them what we found out—or didn't find out," she amended. "Maybe one of them has a better idea of what to do next."

"Are you saying my idea wasn't good?" Callum asked, pretending to take offense.

She slanted a look in his direction. "I'm saying that the more ideas we have to work with, the better our chances of resolving all this are. Besides, I think it's time we get everyone involved in searching for any and all hospital personnel who worked at the hospital forty years ago. This isn't a job for just one or two people, not with all of us having our own set of responsibilities when it comes to running Colton Oil."

Callum sighed. "Yes, there is that." Rather than race through a light the way Marlowe was wont to do, he slowed down as it turned yellow, then red. "There's also another factor."

Marlowe shifted in her seat to look at her brother. "Which is?"

Callum took his time in responding. When he did, what he said wasn't anything that she'd expected. "How are you feeling?"

Nauseated as hell, she thought, but since she'd managed to keep everything down, she wasn't about to say anything about it to her brother.

"Okay," Marlowe answered. "Why?"

"Why?" Callum echoed incredulously.

"Yes, that's what I just asked, Callum. Why?" Marlowe repeated.

"Because you're pregnant."

Marlowe rolled her eyes. She was trying to get away from talking about her condition, not dwelling on it. She thought he would have understood that. He was her twin, and there were times when each knew exactly what the other was thinking. "C'mon, Callum, don't you start."

"Hey, I'm just worried about you. I've seen you turn green a couple of times in the last few hours, and green is *not* your natural color. Are you getting enough rest?"

"I am fine, Callum," Marlowe insisted.

He tried again. "Okay, what did the doctor say?"

She kept her face forward, not wanting to make any eye contact. "What doctor?"

"You haven't been to see your doctor yet?" he cried. "Hell, what are you waiting for?"

"Um, in case you haven't noticed, I've been a little busy, with my oldest brother suddenly not being my brother and some crazy person taking a shot at me *inside* my condo. That doesn't exactly leave much time for me to go sashaying off to my ob-gyn's office to read two-year-old magazines while I wait three hours for a consultation with her—*if* she doesn't cancel at the last minute because she's been called away to make a unscheduled delivery."

"Not good enough, Marlowe. You know you're just making up excuses," he told her. "You need to see your doctor."

"Fine," she said from between gritted teeth. "First spare minute I get," she told him.

"Make an appointment or I'll carry you there myself," he told her.

"You need a woman, Callum. Someone you can drive crazy other than me."

"Until that happens," he informed her, "you're stuck with me."

She slid down in her seat, staring through the windshield. "Terrific," she muttered. But deep down, she did appreciate the thought.

Chapter 14

"Looks as if the board meeting has to be post-poned," Marlowe told her brother as they got back to Colton Oil headquarters. Just before they'd left the hospital parking lot, she had sent out messages to all four of the other members on a group chat. It had seemed strange to Marlowe to delete Ace's name from the list of included members, but for the time being, for the sake of peace, she knew it had to be that way.

Three of the texts that she had sent out were answered before Callum pulled up.

"Why?" Callum asked. "Who can't make the meeting?"

She slipped her phone back into her pocket. "Dad, Rafe and Ainsley are all busy for the rest of the day."

"I'm sure one of them is available, right?" Callum said.

"Oh no, we're not having a meeting with just her," Marlowe declared with feeling. "I might be tempted to hold a meeting if the other three are there and dear old Selina wasn't, but there's no way in hell that we're going to have a meeting with *just* her at the table." Taking out her phone, she looked at her schedule for the next day. "Ask them if tomorrow at ten works for them," she said, getting out of the car. "If not, we'll keep pitching different times until we find one that works for everyone."

"Including ex–Stepmommy Dearest?" Callum asked sardonically.

Marlowe sighed. "Yes, her, too," she answered, although not happily.

Marlowe felt her phone buzz. She took it out, paused to look at the screen and saw she had a new text.

"Someone letting us know that they've changed their mind?" Callum guessed.

"No." Marlowe quickly read the message. Several emotions wafted through her simultaneously as she tried to figure out just how she felt about the text from Bowie. "This has nothing to do with the meeting."

Callum tilted his head, peering at his sister's face. "Robertson?" he guessed.

Marlowe looked up sharply. "Since when did clairvoyance become part of your makeup?" she asked.

"I'm not clairvoyant," Callum denied. "But if I were you, I'd really try to work on my poker face," he advised. "Your whole countenance changed when you looked at your phone screen. You lit up."

"You're imagining things," Marlowe insisted dismissively. Getting out of Callum's car, she shut the passenger door.

"No, I'm not," he said. "Hey, do you have feelings for this guy?" He quickly added, "Because it's okay with me if you do—that is, if he's treating you right."

Oh no, she was not about to get into this with her brother. She loved Callum dearly, but this was none of his business—especially since she wasn't 100 percent sure just what she was actually feeling when it came to Bowie.

"Callum," she told him, "the last thing I need right now is to play Twenty Questions with you."

"Okay," Callum said, retreating and raising his hands as if in surrender. "But you're going to have to figure it out sooner or later—for your own sake," he underscored. "Not for Dad, not for Mother or for anyone else, but for your own sake," he insisted firmly.

She knew he meant well and that she was being decidedly far too touchy about the matter. "Yes, O Wise One, I know." Smiling at Callum, she stood up on her tiptoes and brushed her lips against his cheek. "Now go and try to coordinate the troops while I see what this wild card in my life wants."

"You," Callum told her as if there was no question about it. "That would be my guess."

If she were being perfectly honest with herself, Marlowe didn't know if that was what she was afraid of, or what she was hoping for. So she said nothing. Instead, she hurried off, leaving her brother in the lobby. When she called Bowie, she wanted to be able to talk to him in private.

That privacy turned out to be available only in her office.

The minute she walked in, she closed the door. Rather than call Bowie, she crossed to her desk, sat down and proceeded to text him back. The message she sent read: I'm back in my office. What did you want to tell me?

In less than a minute after she had hit Send, her cell phone rang. She didn't have to look at the caller ID.

"Hello?"

"Are you planning on staying put?" Bowie's deep voice rumbled against her ear.

A warm shiver danced through her in response to his voice. She needed to get that under control, she told herself.

Rather than answer Bowie one way or another, she had a question of her own. "Why?"

"Because I need to see you." As if realizing how that had to sound to her, Bowie added, "I've got someone I want you to meet."

Now what? she wondered. She wasn't exactly feeling very social. "Listen, now's not a very good time," she began, getting ready to put him off.

As if he'd anticipated this move on her part, Bowie deftly blocked it. "No time is a very good time with you," he commented. "Stay put," he ordered. "I'll be there in twenty minutes."

She didn't like being told what to do—she never had, not even as a child. She could feel her back instantly going up. "Listen, I—"

"—can stay put for twenty minutes," he informed her, managing to predict what she was about to say.

Marlowe stared at her phone screen. The connection had been terminated. She could feel her temper rising quickly. For a second, she fought against the urge to throw her phone against the wall. Taking in a deep breath to help her get hold of her escalating impatience, Marlowe told herself there was no reason to take her anger out on her phone when she could just as well wait for Bowie and take it out on him in person.

Two more deep breaths later, she buzzed for Karen. The petite assistant was inside her office almost immediately.

"What can I do for you, Ms. Colton?" Karen asked.

"Bowie Robertson will be coming to see me. Bring him in as soon as he gets here," Marlowe instructed.

Although she was obviously surprised, Karen did a good job of hiding her emotion. "Very good, Ms. Colton," the assistant replied. "Anything else?" She stood by the door, awaiting further instructions.

"Not as far as I know."

She knew that it was a vague response to her assistant's question, but at the moment Marlowe wasn't feeling all that focused. On the contrary, her mind felt as if it was spinning around here, there and everywhere. A little like a sparrow caught in a storm, searching for somewhere to land before being helplessly blown completely off course.

About to withdraw from Marlowe's office, Karen looked at her boss over her shoulder.

"May I get you some tea, Ms. Colton?" her assistant offered. "You look a little pale, if you don't mind my saying so."

Mind? Why should she mind having an employee tell her that she looked like death warmed over? Marlowe thought.

She realized that her hands were clenched. She was flying off the handle again, Marlowe thought. What was going on with her, anyway? Her assistant was just trying to be kind, not criticizing her.

"Herbal tea would be very nice, thank you, Karen," she agreed. "Cream, no sugar."

"Cream, no sugar," the young woman repeated. "Got it." Karen said it almost happily, appearing glad to have something specific to focus on.

Marlowe leaned all the way back in her chair and closed her eyes, trying to think.

Why was Bowie actually coming here? They'd just seen each other this morning.

And then she remembered that he had said something about getting her a bodyguard, as well as having someone look into trying to track down the source of that awful email she and the others had all received. Could that be it? Had he found out something important and was coming to tell her in person because he thought the phone lines were being bugged? Was the person who had uncovered all this for her the person he wanted to introduce her to?

Or should she be worrying about something else entirely?

Not for the first time, part of her really regretted ever having gone to that energy conference. If she hadn't gone, then none of this would be happening and she could focus on the drama surrounding Ace's case instead of feeling so scattered right now.

But then, if she hadn't gone to the conference, she wouldn't have spent that spectacular night with Bowie and she wouldn't be...

She wouldn't be wasting her time sifting through possible scenarios and practically talking to herself like some loon, Marlowe thought, completely annoyed with herself.

A light rap on her door had her back snapping into place, rigid and alert. Her eyes immediately darted toward the door. But when it opened, it was only Karen coming in with a large steaming mug of tea.

"Here you go, Ms. Colton," she said, putting the mug down on the desk in front of Marlowe. "Herbal tea, cream and no sugar." The young woman began to withdraw from the office. "I'll let you know when Mr. Robertson arrives."

"You do that," Marlowe murmured.

Almost without thinking, she wrapped her hands around the large mug. The warmth that seeped into her was oddly comforting. Closing her eyes, she let herself drift for a moment.

But the knock on her door a few moments later had her eyes flying open.

"They're here, Ms. Colton," Karen announced, opening the door.

"They?" Marlowe questioned. Who exactly were *they*?

The next moment, Bowie came in, followed by what could have very possibly been the largest man she had ever seen. He wasn't fat, just very, very wide and solid looking. The man had shoulders broad enough to double as a landing field, encased in a navy blue sports jacket that the giant seemed oddly comfortable wearing. But instead of a button-down shirt, he had on a gray turtleneck sweater. Casual, yet refined.

But just who was this man, and why had Bowie brought him into her office?

Turning her chair in his direction, Marlowe began to frame her question. "Bowie...?"

Way ahead of her, Bowie made the introduction. "Marlowe Colton, I'd like you to meet Wallace Bigelow." He smiled. "Your new bodyguard."

It took effort not to have her mouth drop open. She really hadn't expected Bowie to act so fast. "My what?"

"Your bodyguard," Bowie repeated. "We talked about this, remember?"

She had just assumed that Bowie had forgotten about that. Or would at least take his time.

Getting up from her chair, she moved over to the side, indicating that Bowie should move with her. When he did, Marlowe said, "I remember *you* talking. What I don't remember is my agreeing to this."

"Well, you did," he informed her, "and here he is." Bowie moved back to the center of the room, next to the man he had brought with him. "Bigelow, this sunny, smiling woman is Marlowe Colton. I want you to guard her with your life and make sure that absolutely nothing happens to her. Understood?"

"You have my word, sir." Wallace's deep voice seemed to practically rumble through the entire office like thunder.

Okay, this really wasn't going to work, Marlowe thought. "No offense, Wallace, you seem like a very nice man, but I don't need a bodyguard," she told the giant, then turned toward Bowie. "I don't," she insisted.

Bowie's expression didn't change. "Would you like me to drag out exhibit A, that giant teddy bear you brought into my office? Or maybe exhibit B, the card that came with him?"

She knew when she was looking down the sights of defeat. What she needed to do now was gain some concessions.

"All right, all right, you've made your point. But shouldn't a bodyguard be, well, you know, a little more inconspicuous than, say, a skyscraper?" She turned toward the giant of a man in her office. "Again, no offense, Wallace."

For such an intimidating figure, Wallace had a very nice, winning smile. "None taken, ma'am," he assured the woman he had been told to guard.

"Ma'am," Marlowe echoed. She couldn't help wincing. The label made her feel as if she was ancient. "Okay, if this is going to have a prayer of working, he can't call me *ma'am*," she told Bowie.

Bowie grinned. "I think it's in his DNA," he confided. "But Wallace doesn't have to call you anything, do you, Wallace?" The man shook his head in agreement. "He just has to *be*," Bowie told her.

"Don't worry, you won't even know I'm there," Wallace promised her.

That was impossible, she thought. "I highly doubt that," she told Wallace.

"Unless you need me," Wallace added pointedly, his soft blue eyes looking at her.

"He really is very good at his job," Bowie told her. "And besides," he said, getting to what, in his mind, was the important part, "this is nonnegotiable."

Marlowe looked at Bowie. Ordinarily, she would have been spoiling for a fight. But there was something annoyingly endearing about how adamant this man, who hadn't been part of her life a mere two months ago, was about keeping her safe. Not because he wanted something from her, not because he was getting anything out of it, but just because he...cared?

The thought hit her with the force of a six megaton bomb exploding in her brain.

"What?" Bowie asked. "You just got a really strange look on your face. Like something frightened you. Is something wrong?"

She looked at him, not certain how to process this newest thought that had suddenly cropped up in her head. "I'm not really sure," Marlowe told him honestly. "I'll let you know when I figure it out."

"Okay," Bowie agreed, backing away from the subject, "but as long as we're clear, Wallace stays," he told her.

Marlowe pressed her lips together, then nodded her head. Resigned. "Wallace stays," she said. "But he stays restricted."

"Meaning what?" Bowie asked.

To her it was self-explanatory. "He can't venture into any areas that might contain restricted company secrets."

Was that all? He could respect that, Bowie thought. "Fair enough," he agreed. "Wallace is being paid to be your bodyguard, not my spy. Besides, in case you've forgotten, our companies have slightly different approaches toward producing energy."

"No, I didn't forget," she told Bowie. Her mind went back to that evening at the conference, when everyone else had left and they were still talking, at first trying to convince the other of their stands and then...well, then they weren't standing at all. "Yes, I remember. I remember that debate we had at the conference that night."

"Okay," he told her. "I've got to be getting back for a meeting, but Wallace is going to stay with you 24/7. I'll call you later and check in," he told the bodyguard.

"Wait, what?" Marlowe cried, stopping Bowie. "I thought he was only going to be around during working hours."

She should know better than that. "Crazy people don't punch a time clock," he told her. "That includes stalkers who leave oversize gifts in your office. Just because he left this for you at work by no means guarantees that this guy won't pop up anywhere else—and that includes your condo."

"We have security at the house," she informed Bowie. That went without saying.

"Well, now you have a little more," he told her, trying to be reassuring. "It's just until we catch the guy, Marlowe," he promised.

"And when will that be?" she asked.

She expected Bowie to say something, but it was Wallace who answered her question. "Soon, ma'am. Very soon."

"Not soon enough for me," she couldn't help adding.

"I'll call you later," Bowie promised. His eyes took them both in. "Both of you."

Then, before she knew what was happening, he pulled her into his arms and kissed her deeply and thoroughly before releasing her just as abruptly.

And with that, he was gone.

Chapter 15

"I'm sorry, Ms. Colton. She insisted on seeing you," Karen apologized as Selina Barnes Colton pushed her way into Marlowe's office.

"Oh, stop your whining, you useless waste of space. I am part of Colton Oil's board of directors. That gives me a perfect right to see anyone I damn well please in this building, and I don't need permission to do it," Selina informed Marlowe's assistant in her high-handed manner.

To Marlowe, hearing Selina's voice was tantamount to hearing nails being slowly drawn across a chalkboard. It took everything she had not to wince.

"I'll thank you not to talk to my assistant that way, Selina," Marlowe told the woman coldly. "Karen was only doing her job." Her eyes narrowed as she looked at the attractive woman she and the rest of her siblings thought of as a venomous snake. "Now what's so important that you have to come barging into my office like this, disrupting everything?"

But Selina's attention was diverted to the man she saw standing in the background.

"And who is this?" she asked Marlowe. Her eyes slowly appraised everything about the wide, imposing bodyguard. Finished, Selina's eyes shifted back toward Marlowe. There was a smirk on her full lips. "He's a little old for you, isn't he, dear? Has your father met him yet?"

Not waiting for an answer, Selina continued her biting monologue. "I bet Payne hasn't, and when he does, there will be hell to pay, you do realize that, don't you, dear?" Selina laughed to herself, as if enjoying her own private joke. "It's rather ironic. Your father doesn't really take an interest in any of your lives," she said pointedly, "except whenever something one of you does might reflect badly on the company."

Not giving Marlowe a chance to respond, Selina sidled up to Wallace Bigelow and gave him another once-over, doing it up close this time.

"My, but you're a big one, aren't you? But if you think you've got yourself a meal ticket in little Marlowe here, think again," she advised maliciously. "Her father's going to have you out on your—"

She had had just about enough, Marlowe thought. She raised her voice and broke in, wanting to put an end to this and to rescue Wallace from Selina's tongue, as well.

"Not that it's any business of yours, Selina, but Wallace happens to be my bodyguard," she told the infuriating woman.

"Your bodyguard?" Selina repeated in a mocking voice. "Oh, is that what they're calling it these days?" She batted her long lashes at Wallace. "Care to do a little moonlighting on the side, sweetie? You might find it interesting."

"Don't proposition my bodyguard, Selina. It's beneath you, and he hasn't had his antivenom shots yet," Marlowe said, rising to her feet. Wallace was much too polite. In his place, she would have told Selina to get lost a long time ago. But he had merely stood there, enduring the woman's close scrutiny. "Although I'm starting to think that absolutely *nothing* is beneath you," Marlowe told her father's ex.

"What a clever turn of phrase, dear," Selina retorted to her ex-husband's daughter, her tone nothing if not belittling. "Did it take you long to come up with that?" Selina mocked. "Anyway, I came to find out what, if anything, you and that brother of yours learned at the hospital about how your fake brother wound up going home with your father and that mouse of a first wife of his. Anything?" she prodded.

Marlowe instantly took umbrage for the person she had known all of her life as Ace. "You'll find out with the rest of the board when we convene tomorrow," she informed Selina.

"You're planning on drawing this out, are you?" Selina surmised.

Marlowe didn't bother to hide the loathing she felt for the woman. "I don't think it's fair that you know something before the others do," she said, deliberately being vague. She knew that it would get under Selina's skin.

Selina laughed at her. "You're bluffing. You have

nothing. If you did, you'd tell me just to put me in what you deem is my place," she concluded.

Marlowe was up on all of her tricks. She viewed them as rather pitiful. "You're not going to goad me into saying anything, so you might as well just drop this," she told Selina.

Wallace finally spoke up, stepping forward. "Is this woman bothering you, Ms. Colton?"

"Every day of my life, since the first time I ever met her," Marlowe replied with feeling. "But that's all right, Wallace. She was just leaving, weren't you, Selina?" she asked solicitously.

Selina drew herself up. There was pure hatred in her eyes. But she kept her temper. "For now," the woman replied haughtily.

Turning on the heels of her exceedingly expensive designer shoes, Selina walked out.

"Sorry about that," Marlowe apologized to Wallace.

"No need to apologize, ma'am," the bodyguard told her, returning to his initial post. "Almost every family has one of those in their number."

"Doesn't make putting up with her any easier," Marlowe said with a sigh. "I can't shake the feeling that she's like this sleek vulture in a designer suit, waiting for one of us to drop in front of her so she can feast on the carcass."

It suddenly hit Marlowe that she was sharing bottled-up feelings with a man who was, by definition, a virtual stranger to her. It wasn't something she normally did—ever.

"I'm sorry," she began. "I shouldn't have…"

Wallace seemed to understand her discomfort.

"That's all right, ma'am. Talking to me is like talk-ing to a piece of furniture. You don't have to worry. Whatever you say to me won't go anywhere."

Marlowe couldn't help laughing at herself and the entire scenario. "You were right," she told him.

"Ma'am?" he asked.

"You really do blend in," Marlowe said.

"Yes, ma'am," he answered agreeably, smiling broadly at her.

Maybe this wouldn't be so bad after all, Marlowe thought. And she had to admit, having this behemoth around to protect her did make her feel a great deal safer. Finding that teddy bear sitting there in her office this morning had made her exceedingly jumpy. That wasn't a feeling that she welcomed. Though she wasn't about to admit it out loud just yet, she appreciated having Bowie caring for her and their unborn child.

"You know," Marlowe said thoughtfully a few hours later as she finished up the proposal she had been working on, "that woman is always trying to stir up trouble between us."

"Between you and her, ma'am?" Wallace asked, deftly trying to pick up the thread of conversation where it had been dropped earlier.

"No, between all of us. All of my father's off-spring," Marlowe clarified. "Not to mention that there were more than a few times when she subtly tried to get us to turn not just against our father but against each other, as well.

"And," she said, continuing with her thought, "I have no doubt that Selina has whispered in my father's ear and tried to get him to turn against us whole-sale again." She didn't know if it was another wave of morning sickness or thoughts of Selina that were making her stomach suddenly churn, but she was feeling sick again as she shook her head. "I have absolutely no idea why he insists on keeping that woman around." She frowned as she looked at her new confidant. "Dad says she's good at her job, and I have to admit that she is," Marlowe said honestly.

Being honest was almost a curse at times, she thought darkly. But Selina Barnes Colton was not exactly a wizard. If she wasn't there tomorrow, someone else would come along to fill the vacancy and do just as good a job—if not better—without secretly attempting to pit them against one another.

The benevolent giant looked at her thoughtfully. "Perhaps there is something that Mrs. Colton is holding over Mr. Colton's head. Blackmail is a very powerful, dangerous tool in the wrong hands," he told Marlowe.

The point had already crossed her mind more than once. She remembered saying as much to Callum when they had discussed the power Selina seemed to wield over their father.

She closed her eyes. Something else to worry about, Marlowe thought.

True to his word, Bowie called Marlowe to check in on how she was faring with his bodyguard the moment that his own meeting was over.

"Would you mind if I dropped by?" he asked Marlowe.

The very sound of his voice had her brightening. She tried to upbraid herself for her reaction, but it had no dampening effect on the way she responded to him. The plain truth of the matter was that hearing his voice made her smile. She called herself a fool, but it didn't change anything.

"When?" she asked.

"I was thinking now," he answered.

She could feel her heart racing and called herself an idiot. She was acting like a simpering teenager, not the president of a high-powered oil company.

"Sure. I've still got a few things to finish up." It was a lie, but it was all she could come up with on short notice.

"Be right there," he promised. When Bowie arrived at Colton Oil within the half hour, he got right down to business. "So, is everything going all right?" he asked Marlowe, clearly referring to Wallace.

"Well, I hate to admit it," Marlowe told him, "but it's going better than I thought it would."

"Then I was right?" he asked innocently, glancing over toward the bodyguard. "Bigelow is blending in, becoming part of the furniture?"

Deliberately turning her chair away from Wallace's general direction so that her voice didn't carry, she told Bowie, "He's a little too big to be an ottoman, but yes," she said, giving Bowie his due, "you were right. Wallace does seem to have a knack for blending in."

Bowie all but beamed. "Told you."

The man was obviously pleased with himself. That made her a little leery. She didn't want him thinking that she was handing him free rein over her.

"Oh no, you're not going to be one of those men, are you? The ones who say 'I told you so' every chance they get?" she asked. Marlowe was only half kidding.

"Only if the situation calls for it," he told her with

a grin. "All right, I won't say it—this time," he added after a beat.

"You know, I've been thinking," Marlowe went on to say.

"Good thinking or bad thinking?" Bowie asked.

"Well, I don't know how you're going to view this. What I do know is that to implement this I'm going to have to leave Wallace behind," Marlowe told Bowie, warming up to her subject.

He cut her off before she could say any more. "Not doable," Bowie replied.

Marlowe pushed on, curbing her very strong impulse to inform Bowie that he was *not* the boss of her and she was only going along with his providing her with a bodyguard because it suited her purposes. At the moment, however, it didn't, and she wasn't going to allow Bowie to stop her from doing what she felt might be the only course of action available to her.

She talked right over him as if he hadn't said anything. "I want to follow dear old Selina the next time she leaves headquarters, and I can't do that with Wallace shadowing my every move. Selina will see him coming from a mile away, and whatever I'm hoping to catch her doing won't happen. I have to go alone," she insisted.

"No," Bowie contradicted her calmly, "you don't have to go alone."

Marlowe could feel her temper fraying, just like that. "Look, Robertson, I'm not going to argue about this," she informed him.

"Good, because I don't want to argue—and before you get your second wind and launch into another all-out attack, trying to shoot me down, I just want to tell you that you're right."

Marlowe's mouth dropped open, the words she was about to say dying before they ever emerged. He'd caught her completely off guard.

"I'm what?" she asked.

"You're right," Bowie repeated. "From everything you've told me, Selina doesn't have your family's best interests at heart, and I wouldn't be surprised if we found out that she was at least partially behind what's been going on to undermine the company with Ace."

We. He had said *we.* As if they were a set, two parts of a whole. Ordinarily, she would rebel against that, saying something snide because she felt that he was trying to order her around or just take over.

But for some reason she couldn't begin to explain to herself, this time the fact that he thought that way just warmed her.

She could only think that this pregnancy was playing havoc with her mind as well as her emotions. What other reason could there be for her reaction? She wasn't willing to admit that she was falling for the father of her unborn baby, at least, not yet. Even though, deep down in her gut, she already knew the answer to that.

"So you agree with me that I should follow her the next time she leaves the building unexpectedly. See what she might be up to," Marlowe concluded. She didn't expect it to be this easy. He had to be up to something, she reasoned—or did he just really care for her?

"I agree with everything," Bowie told her, "except the part about you following her on your own."

"Robertson," she began, frustrated because they seemed to be going around in circles.

But Bowie pushed on as if she hadn't just said his name. "Which is why I'm going to tag along when the time comes," he told Marlowe, then turned toward the bodyguard. "When that happens, consider yourself relieved, Bigelow."

"Yes, sir."

"Wait, what just happened here?" Marlowe asked, feeling railroaded.

"I just agreed with you," Bowie replied simply.

"The *other* part," Marlowe stipulated from between clenched teeth.

"The other part?" Bowie repeated innocently.

That only managed to fan her anger. "Yes, the other part. The part about you taking Wallace's place and coming with me while I follow Selina to wherever she plans to go."

"Seems to me like you have a clear understanding of that part," he told her. And then he grew serious. "Look, Marlowe, there's someone out there who clearly has it in for Colton Oil in general and maybe you specifically. In either case, I have no intentions of taking a chance on you getting hurt—or worse."

"*You* have no intentions," she echoed.

"Then we understand each other," he concluded, evidently hoping that would be the end of it.

Marlowe drew herself up. "Since when did you get to figure into this equation?" she demanded.

Bowie's eyes looked into hers. "I think you know the answer to that," he informed her in a low voice that was only loud enough for Marlowe to make out.

"Oh, and having you with me won't set off any alarms with Selina?" She laughed at the very idea.

"I thought the idea was to follow the woman discreetly so she could lead you to whoever she's working with—if she *is* working with anyone," he qualified.

Marlowe blew out a breath. She was defeated and she knew it. Bowie had just shot her down, and he was right. She would be safer with him along—not that she'd mind having him by her side. She had no doubts that Selina was vindictive enough to do something drastic if she set her mind to it.

"All right, you win," Marlowe told him. "When I follow Selina, I'll let you know."

He looked at the man he had hired to be Marlowe's bodyguard. "Bigelow?"

The big man knew what was being asked of him. "I'll call you and let you know, sir," he promised.

"My word isn't good enough for you?" Marlowe questioned, looking at Bowie.

"You might get caught up in the moment and forget to call," he explained innocently. "While Bigelow here has only one thing to focus on—your safety," he told her.

"You have an answer for everything, don't you?" Marlowe said curtly.

"That's why they pay me the big bucks at my company," Bowie replied.

Chapter 16

Everyone who filed into the boardroom the next day was aware of the conspicuously empty chair at the conference table.

Ace's chair.

Marlowe could see by the looks on her siblings' faces that they all felt as awful about Ace's absence as she did. Oddly enough, she had the feeling that her father felt the same way that the rest of them did.

All of them except for Selina, of course. Her father's haughty ex looked like the cat that had eaten the canary—and had enjoyed every bite.

Selina leveled her gaze at Marlowe, looking at her expectantly. "Well, go ahead, tell us what you learned, Marlowe," she urged. As if she and that woman had a close relationship, Marlowe thought, rather than the antagonistic one that existed between them.

"We didn't learn anything," Marlowe informed Selina coolly.

"Well, that doesn't sound right," Selina commented. The woman cocked her head, as if trying to understand. "Why not?" she asked.

Marlowe fought the really strong desire to scratch the woman's eyes out. She had a feeling that Selina already knew the answer to that.

Taking a breath, Marlowe managed to get her temper under control. Going down to Selina's level wouldn't accomplish anything or lead anywhere, Marlowe told herself.

Deliberately turning toward the other people who were around the table, she said, "According to the hospital administrator, the day Ace was born, there was a fire in the maternity ward. All the records there at the time were destroyed in that fire."

"A fire?" Ainsley repeated, surprised. "I don't remember ever hearing about a fire breaking out at the hospital before."

Marlowe nodded. "From what Callum and I could piece together, it was just a small fire, and it was quickly gotten under control before any lives were threatened," Marlowe told the group.

"But not before the maternity records were destroyed," Rafe concluded.

"No, not before then," Marlowe said, knowing how suspicious that had to sound to them. It did to her, as well.

"That sounds awfully convenient to me," Selina said to the other board members. There was more than a trace of sarcasm in her voice.

"Yes, it would seem that way," Marlowe was forced

to agree. It was obvious that she was far from satisfied with this outcome. "But I'm not giving up until we get to the bottom of this—and to an explanation of what sounds like a Christmas miracle."

Her siblings exchanged looks. Marlowe had lost them with her last sentence.

"How's that again?" Ainsley asked.

"Dad, didn't you say that when he was born, Ace was very frail and sickly. So frail and sickly, the doctors didn't expect him to live through the night. And yet, he not only lived, but he actually went on to thrive, almost overnight. The night after his birth," Marlowe specified.

Remembering, Payne smiled sadly. "I thought those were just the Colton genes, coming to the forefront and taking over," he told the rest of his children.

"Or," Marlowe suggested, "it could be someone switching babies that night, substituting a healthy son for an unhealthy one."

Marlowe knew that, on the outside, it sounded preposterous. "But why?" Ainsley asked. "Why would someone do that? Who stood to benefit from the switch?"

"Well, from where I'm sitting, *that* sounds like the million-dollar question," Rafe told the others.

"So you all think we should go looking for the real Ace—provided he survived his sickly infancy." The statement came from Payne and surprised everyone. He was not in the habit of asking anyone for advice, least of all his children.

Ainsley put her two cents in. "I think we should look for the real Ace, but we should check him out before we risk telling him who he really is," she told her father. "You don't want to take a chance on bringing in someone who was shortchanged in the morals department. We have no way of knowing what sort of influences the real Ace had in his life while growing up. For all we know, he might have turned into some kind of serial killer."

Payne was shaking his head.

"Blood or not, the Ace we knew was—*is* my son," Payne insisted, clearly upset by the discussion, despite the fact that he had been the one who had ousted Ace from the boardroom to begin with. It was obvious to Marlowe that for the first time in his life—as far as they knew—Payne regretted something that he had done.

"Well, you can always ask our Ace to come back on the board," Ainsley told her father.

"People." Selina raised her voice to get their attention. "You are forgetting about the bylaws. You can't just go against them like that because it suits you to do so," she informed the others sitting around the conference table.

Payne looked as if a gathering storm was about to break. "I can if I want to," he informed his ex-wife angrily.

"Payne," Selina countered, looking at him squarely. There was a warning note in her voice as she told him, "I beg to differ."

Marlowe saw the expression on her father's face. He was struggling to get himself under control. That wasn't his style. He was a volcano that blew on a regular basis.

There was something else going on here, Marlowe thought, not for the first time.

Because it was what she thought he wanted, she decided to try to buy her father a little time. "Why don't we hire a very good, very discreet private investigator to try to locate the so-called real Ace? And while he's at it, maybe the detective can also locate *our* Ace, who as far as I know seems to have taken off. He's not at home, and he's not at any of his regular haunts." Nor was he answering her calls when she tried to check up on him. She had left a total of five messages and received no answers. She hoped that he wasn't doing anything drastic, just giving himself a little space and taking a breather from all of this for now.

Rather than talk over them, Rafe raised his hand to get the others' attention. "Why don't I look into that for us?" Of all of them, he, as an adopted son, surely knew better than any of them what Ace had to be going through at the moment. "I've got a couple of ideas on how to follow up on this," he told the others.

Selina looked as if her interest had been suddenly piqued. "Just how do you plan to proceed?" she asked.

Rafe looked at the woman, unmoved by her question. "I'll let you know when and if I find something," he said her.

Miffed, for once Selina turned toward her ex. "You know, I get the feeling that your children don't trust me, Payne."

Payne's eyes narrowed as he looked at the woman who had been a thorn in his side for years now.

"There's a lot of that going around," he replied cryptically.

That was not what she was expecting. Selina shot her ex a very cold, dark look. Caught in the cross fire, Marlowe could hardly keep from shivering.

Payne drew himself up, looking even more formidable than he usually did. "Well, if there's nothing else, this meeting's adjourned," he declared. "I've got a meeting to get to with some possible investors." He glanced toward Rafe and Marlowe. "Keep me apprised of any progress you make. And definitely call me if you locate Ace—our Ace," he specified. "Tell him he and I need to talk." He took a breath, then added, "I feel bad about the way we left things."

Well, this was new. Marlowe exchanged looks with her siblings.

"Dad?" she said hesitantly. "Are you feeling all right?"

"Why?" Payne challenged gruffly.

On the spot, she knew she had to push on even though she wasn't up to a shouting match. "Because you don't usually feel the need to, well, apologize," she told him.

Payne's complexion went through several changes in color. "Yeah, well, sometimes things need to be shaken up," was all Payne seemed willing to say. "I've got to go," he repeated, removing his all-but-overwhelming presence from the boardroom.

Marlowe exchanged looks with her siblings. "Who was that man?" she quipped, only half in jest.

Rafe raised his broad shoulders in an exaggerated shrug. "Beats me."

Turning to pick up the notepad she'd brought in with her, Marlowe suddenly became aware of another empty seat at the table. She looked around the room to no avail. "Where's Selina?"

Turning to answer Marlowe, Ainsley said, "She's—gone." It was obvious that was *not* what she thought she was going to say when she'd started her sentence. "I didn't see her leave, did you?" she asked Rafe.

Annoyed with herself for not noticing the woman slipping away, Marlowe said, "No, but she probably just slithered out. You know how vipers are."

Marlowe's mind was racing ahead, weighing several possible answers to that question. Possibly Selina had just gone back to her office to lick her wounds. Or perhaps she had slipped out to meet with someone. She still couldn't shake the feeling that her father's ex-wife was somehow involved in sending that anonymous mass email that had started all of this turmoil. For that matter, she could be even further involved in all this. Maybe she had even known about the switched infants and had helped with the switch—but Selina would have been a child herself when Ace was born.

Her head began to hurt.

She needed help with this, she thought. Impartial help. That ruled out her siblings for now. They all viewed Selina in the same light that she did. If her intent was to be fair, she needed someone outside the circle so that she could be sure she wasn't allowing her own intense dislike of the woman to color her outlook or taint her conclusions.

She left the boardroom quickly.

Wallace was waiting for her in the corridor. At her request, he had remained outside the boardroom because, with everything else going on, she didn't feel like having to explain his presence to her father. Wallace had agreed only after he had checked out the boardroom and was satisfied that the large room was accessible only through one set of double doors.

The moment she emerged from the boardroom, he was right at her side.

Marlowe got right to what was on her mind. "Do you think your boss is out of his meeting yet?" she asked the bodyguard.

"You're my boss," he responded in his quiet, authoritative voice.

Marlowe sighed. "Your *other* boss, Wallace," she specified.

Wallace looked at his watch. "Yes. Unless it ran over," he qualified.

That was all she wanted to hear. "Thanks," she murmured.

It amazed her how quickly she recalled Bowie's cell number. She'd started dialing it before she realized that she hadn't had to pull out Bowie's business card this time.

He answered on the second ring. "Hello?"

She felt the hair on the back of her neck curling in response to the sound of his voice. This was getting worse, she thought, not better.

"Are you available?" she asked.

She heard him chuckle softly. "Well, you'll have to buy me dinner first, but, yes, I'm available."

"Very funny," she said dismissively, then got down to the reason for her call. "I really need to follow Selina."

"So you said."

"I know," she said impatiently, "but I think it might be more urgent than I initially thought. I'm fairly sure that she's got something big on my father. Something that has him practically twisting in the wind and jumping to obey her slightest whim." She paused, looking for the right way to phrase this. "I might be totally wrong about this, but I think that it might have something to do with Ace being switched with a healthy baby at birth." She realized how that had to sound to Bowie. "According to my father, when Ace was born, he was really sickly. They didn't think he'd even make it through the night, and suddenly, not only did he make it, but he was thriving."

"And no one noticed?" he questioned.

"From what I gather, my dad and his wife at the time chalked it up to being a Christmas miracle," Marlowe told him.

Bowie was quiet for a moment, thinking. "Well, best guess, Selina might be trying to bring down Colton Oil," he suggested.

"No, that's more your father's style," Marlowe said. Then, suddenly realizing what she had just said, she tried to backtrack and apologize. "Sorry, that just came out. But anyway, Selina would have no reason to bring down Colton Oil. It's far more to her advantage to have the company bringing in money. That way, she gets to continue living in the lifestyle that she's grown accustomed to enjoying. That woman will never have enough money."

That made sense, but blackmail wasn't always about making sense. "It could just be her way of getting revenge," Bowie brought up. "You know, because your father divorced her all those years ago."

"According to the story, the divorce was Selina's idea. And even if it wasn't, wouldn't she have done something to undermine the company long ago, not waited all these years to make a move?" she asked Bowie. That only made sense to her.

"Ah, but revenge is a dish best served cold," he said.

There was that, she supposed, but she wasn't convinced. "Maybe," she agreed. "But right now, I just want to be sure that the viper isn't going to do something awful to foul up Ace's life."

"Which Ace?" Bowie asked.

"The Ace *I* know," Marlowe snapped. The next second, she instantly regretted her reaction. "Sorry. My temper keeps spiking." She blamed it on stress and the pregnancy. The latter was in part Bowie's fault, but she couldn't allow herself to go down that path. There was no future there.

Marlowe heard him chuckle again. The sound all but undulated through her, sending goose bumps all along her body.

"Yes, I noticed," Bowie said. "Okay, I'll be there in the next forty minutes."

She sighed. Forty minutes might be too long to wait. She needed to be ready to take off at a moment's notice. "That's all right, I can just—"

"Okay, hold your horses. How does twenty minutes sound?"

"Better," she told him. "Fifteen would sound even better than that."

He laughed. "Only if I learn how to fly."

"I thought you already had that superpower," she deadpanned.

"Very funny. Look, I just need to wrap something up and I'll be there as quick as I can. Wait for me." It wasn't a request, it was an order.

She didn't like being given orders, even if she was asking him to come. She struggled to make light of it. "Or what, no dessert?" she asked him.

Another one of his chuckles rippled through her. "Okay, if you want to call it that."

Was he talking about sex? She could feel herself responding to the very suggestion and abruptly shut down. That was what had gotten her into this mess to begin with, she reminded herself.

"Robertson, if you don't get down here in the afore-mentioned fifteen minutes, I will be gone by the time you *do* get here," she warned.

"Cool your jets for a few minutes, mama. I'll be there."

Mama.

Marlowe felt her back go up. "Don't call me that," she retorted.

"Don't worry, you're not going to lose your identity. But you are going to be someone's mama—aren't you?" he asked.

"Just get here, Robertson. We can have that other discussion some other time," she informed him.

She had already made up her mind about the baby. But she didn't want Bowie thinking that he could just bend her will and turn her into some obedient, subservient human being.

Maybe she shouldn't have called him, she thought, terminating the call.

She didn't need this further aggravation.

Chapter 17

It had been almost a week that she and Bowie had been conducting their surveillance on Selina. Six days of discreetly sitting in his car near the guest house where Selina resided on the Colton ranch.

It had gotten them no closer to any answers about her former stepmother. Nor had they gotten more information about the attempts on their lives or the mysterious email sent to the board.

Selina was either determined to keep a low profile now that the wheels of her plan had been set in motion, or "she didn't have anything to do with that email about Ace that went out to all of you," Bowie concluded on the sixth evening. After sitting in the car, night after night, he was beginning to feel as if his legs were permanently cramping up. "And this is all just a wild-goose chase."

Bowie had parked his car well in the shadows, confident that Selina couldn't detect them.

From their present location, Marlowe couldn't even see the main house, and after being out here, night after night, she was beginning to get a little antsy, not to mention really stir-crazy.

Added to that, she felt much too close to Bowie, and she didn't need that added stimulus.

Glancing toward Bowie, Marlowe sighed in response to his last comment. "I'd hate to think you were right," she admitted.

"Don't get me wrong," he qualified. "I am perfectly willing to sit in this car with you for as long as you want, but wouldn't you feel more comfortable sitting in a secluded booth in a restaurant?" Bowie asked her. "If nothing else," he shifted, doing his best to get comfortable, "there's more leg room in a booth."

Marlowe looked toward the guest house again.

Nothing.

Selina had gone inside the house a little more than two hours ago, and the lights throughout most of the house had been out for the last forty-five minutes. "She's got to be up to *something*," Marlowe insisted. She felt it in her bones, even as she noted to herself that no further attempts had been made on their lives.

"Oh, no argument there," Bowie agreed. Selina was far too devious a woman to just sit around and do nothing. "But right now I'm not so sure what that something has to do with Ace."

Marlowe sighed. Bowie was right. This was just a waste of time—just as the other five nights of surveillance that had come before tonight had been.

"You're right," she told him. "Drive me back to Colton Oil headquarters and we'll call it a night."

He turned on the ignition and slowly retraced his route, quietly driving away from Selina's home until he got to the main road.

"Why don't we shake things up a little?" he suggested once they were headed away from the ranch. "Instead of you going back to the office so you can pick up your car *and* Bigelow, why don't you give him the night off? You and I can get a late dinner, and then I'll bring you home to the Colton compound afterward. You did say the place had security, right?" he asked, making sure that wasn't something she'd said just to get him to back off when he'd suggested getting her a bodyguard.

"I did and we do," she told him, adding, "but I don't think dinner's such a good idea."

He slanted a look in her direction. "Still afraid to be seen with me out in public?" he guessed.

Marlowe drew herself up. "I am not afraid of anything," she informed him.

"Right. I forgot. You're fearless," he said. "So then why this reluctance to be seen out in public with me?"

"It's not you," she said, "it's dinner. There's no point in paying for a fancy meal when all I can keep down these days are crackers and tea—and I consider even *that* a victory," she added.

"Still getting sick to your stomach?" Bowie asked her. He'd thought that would have passed by now. Obviously not.

Just talking about it made Marlowe feel queasy. "That's putting it mildly, but yes, I am."

There was sympathy in his eyes as he looked at her again. "I'm sorry."

She almost believed he meant that, but then that night they had spent together came back to her like a blaring movie trailer. "It's not your fault. Oh, wait, yes it is—and mine, too," she deliberately corrected herself.

There was no point in arguing over this part of it. He just wanted to take her to get something to eat, whatever she could successfully keep down.

"We can stop at a restaurant and get you tea," he told her.

There weren't that many places to eat in Mustang Valley. She was acquainted with all of them. "No restaurant is going to want to serve their customers just tea," she told him.

"Oh, I don't know about that," Bowie contradicted. "They might be willing if they know that there's a fifty-dollar tip coming."

"A fifty-dollar tip?" she questioned. "For *tea*?" That sounded absurd to her.

The absurdity of that didn't seem to bother Bowie because he said, "That's right."

"For tea," she repeated in disbelief.

He nodded. There weren't many cars out this time of night. They were making good time. "That's what I said."

She shook her head. "It's a wonder you people have any money if you spend it like water."

"Not water—tea," he corrected with a straight face. "So, what do you say? You willing to go out and get some decaf tea and crackers and anything else that you might be able to keep down?"

The man was going to keep hammering away at this, talking her ear off until she agreed, Marlowe thought. With a sigh, she surrendered.

"Oh, all right. Let's go and get some tea," she told Bowie, giving in. Her stomach was really acting up and threatening to give her a hard time. Maybe having some tea would make her feel a little more human.

"Better?" Bowie asked her fifteen minutes later.

They were sitting in a small booth in Lucia's Italian Café, and Marlowe was sipping a cup of tea very slowly. In between the sips, she was taking small bites of the plain crackers that were arranged in a small circle on her otherwise empty plate.

Marlowe nodded in response. She had to give him his due, she thought. "Better. Thank you," she added after a beat.

"Hey, like you pointed out, this was all my fault," he said, glancing toward her waist. "The least I can do is get you tea and crackers to make your stomach feel a little better."

That made her feel guilty. Bowie had put up with her recriminations and her mercurial shifts in mood these last few days when he didn't have to. Anyone else would have told her to get lost and then left. But he hadn't. He was a good man—one worth a woman's time and affection. Even if that woman wouldn't be her…

Marlowe looked at him for a long moment.

"What?" he asked, glancing down at his chest. "Did I spill something on my jacket?"

"No," she answered quietly and then forced herself

to say what she was thinking. "You're not such a bad guy," she acknowledged.

Surprise filtered across his face. And then Bowie said, "Careful. You don't want me to get a swollen head now, do you?"

Marlowe frowned slightly. She was attempting to apologize, and he was making jokes. For a second, she thought about just abandoning the whole thing, but she was too stubborn not to continue. "I'm trying to say I'm sorry," she said, exasperated.

For a moment, Bowie grew serious. "I know," he said. "And I'm trying to let you know that you don't have to," he countered. And then he turned his attention back to the turbulent condition of Marlowe's stomach. "Now, how are the crackers?"

She looked at what was left on the plate. They weren't exactly tempting, but at least she wasn't throwing up. "Flat."

"Are you talking about their shape or their taste?" he asked her, curious.

She didn't even have to think about her answer. "Both."

Bowie found her response encouraging. "Well, at least your sense of humor is alive and well—such as it is."

She wasn't sure if that was a put-down or his idea of a compliment. Most likely the former, she thought. "Sorry I'm not up to your stand-up comedian standards."

"You're forgiven," Bowie deadpanned. And then he decided to get down to business. "Seriously, what does your doctor have to say about this?"

"My doctor?" Marlowe repeated, momentarily confused by the question.

"Yes, about your morning sickness," Bowie stressed.

Finished, he wiped his fingers and put aside the napkin. "Surely he or she must have a better remedy for what you're going through than just tea and crackers. That was the solution of choice back in my grandmother's day. Seeing all the progress medicine has made, they have *got* to have come up with something better than that in this day and age."

In response Marlowe merely shrugged and looked away, avoiding Bowie's eyes.

For once, Bowie evidently decided that he wasn't going to drop the subject. "What's that supposed to mean? They haven't come up with anything better?" he questioned.

Why was he hammering away at her like this? "I have no idea what they've come up with," she retorted.

"You haven't asked the doctor?" he guessed, somewhat surprised.

She sighed. "No, I haven't *gone* to the doctor," she answered, exasperated.

Bowie stared at her, stunned. "You haven't gone to the doctor?" he repeated incredulously.

"Well, there's nothing wrong with your hearing," she retorted.

"Which is more than I can say about your common sense," he informed Marlowe. "Why haven't you gone?" he demanded.

She could feel her temper beginning to spike and had to struggle in order to keep from telling him what he could do with his questions. She knew he was concerned, but it annoyed her that he was treating her as if she didn't have enough sense to think for herself. Why did she have to go to the doctor? She knew what was going on. She was pregnant. As far as she knew, she was healthy, so there was no rush to submit herself to having her doctor poke and prod at her, right?

Why did people keep nagging her about seeing a doctor? First Callum, now Bowie. Didn't anyone have anything better to occupy their lives with than *her* life?

She felt as if she was spoiling for a fight. "Maybe you haven't noticed this, but I've been a little busy lately."

"That's no excuse," Bowie informed her quietly so that they wouldn't attract any undue attention from the handful of other people dining at the café. "You make time for the doctor." His eyes held hers as he went on to tell her, "This is important, and you're not the only one involved here, Marlowe."

"Meaning you?" Marlowe asked, ready to tell him what she thought of his interference in her life.

"Meaning the baby," he told her.

That took the wind out of her sails, effectively deflating them as well as embarrassing her. Damn him, he was right. For the baby's sake she should have already gone to the doctor just to make sure everything was all right. Except for this awful morning sickness, she felt she was healthy. But what if she wasn't? What if she was overlooking something important, or hadn't realized it yet? And even if she herself *was* healthy, she needed to take prenatal vitamins and get checkups—for the child's sake.

Marlowe pressed her lips together. This was not

easy for her. She forced the words out. "You're right," she told him grudgingly.

"Does that mean you're going to make an appointment with your doctor?" He evidently wasn't convinced that she wasn't merely paying lip service, just telling him what he wanted to hear.

"Yes," she fairly hissed.

She wasn't off the hook yet. "When?" he asked.

"Well, I can't very well make it now, can I?" she pointed out. "It's after eight and her office is closed for the day."

Bowie nodded, accepting the excuse. "When?" he repeated, his eyes on hers.

She really wanted to shout at him, but she managed to keep herself under control because there were people around.

"Tomorrow," she told him, gritting her teeth. "I'll call the doctor tomorrow. Is that good enough for you?" she demanded.

He inclined his head. "Ask me again *after* you make the appointment."

Marlowe rolled her eyes. He was really pushing it, she thought. "You are the most infuriating man," she told him.

To her surprise, Bowie flashed an almost blinding smile at her. "But I'm growing on you, aren't I?" he asked her.

She was tempted to tell him a number of things, none of them flattering at the moment. But she refrained. "I reserve the right to remain silent," she answered.

She saw the way he smiled at her and knew he had

her number, no matter *what* she said to the contrary. What he said next confirmed it.

"You don't have to," Bowie told her. "That says it all." He looked at the nearly empty plate and her tea-cup. "If you've had your fill of tea and crackers, I'll take you home."

She rose from the table, surprised when he drew the chair back for her. She had to admit, the man had some very good inherent traits. And he might very well make a good father—or husband…

"Take me to the condo instead," she told him. "I don't feel like answering any questions, and if I go home to the ranch, with a bunch of people wandering around, I'm bound to run into someone, and they'll ask questions. I'd rather just have some solitude."

"All right, I'll just give Bigelow a call," Bowie began to say.

"No, don't," she said as they walked out of the res-taurant and to his car. "Give the poor guy a break. I'll be all right for one night," she assured Bowie.

He rolled over what she'd said in his mind as he got into his vehicle. "I'm not going to take that chance," he informed her.

Anticipating that he was about to take out his cell phone, Marlowe caught hold of his hand. "Wallace has probably made some plans for the evening. Even if he hasn't, let him just enjoy some peace and quiet for a change. I don't need a babysitter. I'll be fine," she assured him.

He left his phone in his pocket and instead started up his car. "Yeah, you will be," he agreed, surpris-ing her. "Because for tonight, I'm going to be your bodyguard."

She thought of the last time they had been together for the duration of an evening and her mouth curved in an ironic smile. "That didn't exactly turn out well the last time, now did it?"

He drove toward her condo a short distance away. "If you recall, I wasn't your bodyguard then," Bowie reminded her.

No, he wasn't. He was something totally different, she thought, remembering that night. The next moment, she shut the memory away.

Walking into her condo a few minutes later, Bowie looked toward her living room. "I see you got the window fixed," he commented.

"It's January, and even though this is Arizona, the temperature can still drop down into the thirties at night," she reminded him. "That's more than a little brisk."

"I was just making an observation," he told Marlowe. "You know, not everything's a criticism. You really have to stop being so defensive."

She opened her mouth to respond, then closed it again. Lord, she hated it when he was right, but she knew she had to admit it.

"Sorry, you're right. This whole situation has me feeling really uptight. Not to mention that I haven't really been myself lately."

"Take a few deep breaths and just focus on calming down," he told her.

"So, now you're a life coach?" she asked, then instantly regretted it.

But Bowie apparently took no offense. "I can be

if you need one," he offered. He sounded so genuine that she regretted being so flippant.

"What I need is a drink to help me unwind." She saw him opening his mouth and beat him to the punch before he could say it. "I know, I know. The baby. I know I can't have one."

She looked so despondent, he wanted to do something for her. And then he thought of something. "Got any cans of chicken soup around?"

Of all the things she might have expected him to say, that was not one of them. "Why?" she asked. What did he want with soup?

"It's comfort food," he told her. "It shouldn't really bother your stomach and it might just help settle it."

"Guess we'll never know. I don't have any cans of chicken soup in the pantry." She saw him taking out his phone. Had he changed his mind about Wallace taking over bodyguard duty? "Who are you calling?"

Bowie held up his hand to stop her flow of words because someone had picked up on the other end of the line. "Yes, this is Bowie Robertson. Let me speak to Lucia, please."

"Lucia? You're calling the owner of the restaurant we were just in?" she asked, surprised.

"You want something, always start at the top," he told her.

Before she could say anything, he was talking to someone on the other end of the line again. It took her a second to realize that he was ordering food to be delivered to the condo.

"I'm fine," he said to the person on the other end. "Yes, I was there earlier tonight. We were discussing your wonderful meals and the lady I was with had a sudden craving for some of your wonderful chicken soup. Would you mind having someone come by and deliver? Oh, about five servings should do it. Wonderful. Here's the address." And then Bowie rattled off the address to the condo for the owner of the café.

Marlowe listened to him, in awe of the way he could make people jump through hoops and still not resent him for it.

She was beginning to understand how he had managed to come as far as he had. And how he might just be the man she'd never known she'd needed in her life.

Chapter 18

Marlowe sat across from Bowie at her dining room table, looking at the overly large container that had just been delivered. There was still steam rising from the soup, and oddly enough, the aroma that rose up to greet her was very tempting. Food hadn't smelled good to her for a very long time now.

She raised her eyes to Bowie. "Am I supposed to eat this or swim in it?" she asked.

"That's up to you. Whatever you feel like doing," he told her. "But personally I think that eating it might be the better way to go. Where are your soup bowls?" he asked, looking around the small, exceptionally neat kitchen.

"In the cabinet above the counter," she answered. She still couldn't believe that Bowie had actually had the soup delivered. That was exceedingly thoughtful, and it didn't match the image she had of him—but that was beginning to change, she realized. Drastically. "I didn't even know that Lucia's Italian Café delivered."

"They don't usually," he said in an offhanded manner, setting the two bowls he had found in the cabinet down on the table.

"But they just did for you," Marlowe pointed out.

"Let's just say that's because I'm a very good tipper," he told her with a wink. Finding a ladle, he brought that over as well, then looked at Marlowe. "We should eat this while it's still hot. What do you think?" he asked.

Marlowe shrugged. "Go ahead," she told him. She watched as Bowie used the ladle and distributed equal measures of the soup into her bowl, then his. A great deal more of the liquid still remained in the container. She picked up her soupspoon, paused and then placed it back down.

"What's wrong?" Bowie asked. She looked as if she was bracing herself for a huge ordeal, not just a bowl of soup.

"I'm still not sure about this," Marlowe confessed.

Bowie realized that he was hungry, but he wasn't about to eat anything until Marlowe did. His spoon remained suspended above his own bowl. "What's the worst thing that can happen?" he asked her.

Well, that was easy enough to answer, Marlowe thought. "I could throw up."

He nodded as if conceding the point while not really thinking much of it.

"If that does happen, I'll hold your hair back so you won't get it dirty while you're purging your stomach," he told her pragmatically.

She looked at Bowie. Most men wouldn't take something like that in stride; they'd do their best to get away from it. She looked at him more closely. "You're serious," she said in surprise.

"People usually know when I'm kidding," he assured her. "I have this telltale smile that gives me away. Go ahead," he urged, nodding at the bowl of soup sitting in front of her. "Take a spoonful." He saw the leery look that came over her face as she stared at the steaming bowl. "It's soup, Marlowe, not poison," Bowie reminded her.

Hoping for the best even as she feared the worst, Marlowe dipped her spoon into the steaming liquid and brought it up to her lips.

To make her feel more confident, Bowie did the same, taking in a spoonful of soup at the same time that she did. He watched her the entire time, probably holding his breath and mentally crossing his fingers—not for himself but for her. In his opinion, Marlowe really needed to get something more solid into her stomach than just the crackers she'd had earlier.

When she realized in surprise that she seemed to be able to hold down the first spoonful, she attempted a second one. And then a third. Her stomach remained in a dormant state.

"Everything okay?" Bowie asked, peering closely at her face.

The smile on her lips bloomed very slowly, hesitantly, then went on to coax out just the tiniest bit of a relief. She looked almost afraid to say anything because if she did, she felt that she might just wind up jinxing everything.

He saw the small battle that was going on within her. "Marlowe, are you okay?" he pressed, concerned.

"I am…very…okay," she told him, sounding out each word and really happy to relate that message. "The soup seems to be…not wanting to come back up," she declared in surprise.

Looking pleased to hear that she *wasn't* experiencing yet another bout of nausea, Bowie nodded.

"That's really good to hear," he told her. "But don't overdo it," he advised. "Your stomach is probably still wondering what all that warm liquid coming in is. From what I've gathered, you and food haven't exactly been on the friendliest of terms, so let yourself get accustomed to this by degrees. That way you won't lose the ground you've gained."

"You don't have to baby me," she told him, feeling he was talking down to her.

"I'm not," he protested. "I'm just in training so that when this little person finally gets here, I'll be ready for her or him."

She frowned. "I didn't think you wanted to hang around for that. You made it clear that commitment wasn't your thing," she reminded him.

"I don't know," he said honestly. "Maybe it is. I'm taking this one step at a time, seeing where it goes," Bowie told her. "But I was serious about being there for you and the baby," he insisted. "I have no intention of running out on you, Marlowe. And," he went on, "I want you to believe that. I might not have a clue how to be a great dad—I was shortchanged when it came to the role model department."

An ironic smile curved his mouth. "My own father was hardly a good model. But the one thing I do know is that I really wanted my father to be there for me, to be around when I wanted him to watch me compete in a sport or beam with pride when I walked across the stage to collect my college diploma. That much I can do for my kid. I figure I can wing it when it comes to the rest of it. The thing I know for certain is that I never want my kid—"

"*Our* kid," she deliberately corrected. Her heart warmed at Bowie's words, though.

"Our kid," Bowie continued without missing a beat, "to feel that his father doesn't care." And then he raised his eyes to hers as another thought hit him. "I don't want you to think that I'm crowding you, or dictating terms regarding this baby, but—"

"Stop talking," Marlowe told him.

That came out of nowhere, and she had managed to completely catch him off guard. He stared at her now. "What?"

Marlowe was on her feet and rounding the table to get closer to him. Everything he had done and said tonight had abruptly knocked down all the walls she had so very carefully constructed around her heart in her effort to keep from getting hurt. Everything he had said had made her heart soften to the point that she had allowed herself to feel what she had been trying so hard *not* to feel: an exceedingly strong affection for this man, which she had allowed to sneak into her heart without truly realizing it.

Now, as she came up to where he was seated, she slipped her fingers into his hair and around both sides of his face. She tilted his head just a little, and brought her mouth down to his, kissing him with all the energy, all the unbridled emotion she could feel pulsating through her veins.

When Marlowe finally drew her lips away from his, Bowie looked at her, making no effort to hide the fact that he was stunned. He looked like it took him a second to regain the use of his brain and another second to remember how to form words. She could feel that heart continuing to beat fast enough to take off on its own.

"Was it something I said?" he asked her.

The breath she released was shaky. "It was *everything* you said," she told him.

There wasn't a drop of alcohol in her system, and yet it felt as if her head was spinning madly like a runaway top.

Lord, she had missed this, she thought. Missed the feeling of being utterly intoxicated, not on alcohol, but on the man who had already made her throw all caution to the winds once and was now making her want to do that all over again.

She desperately wanted to feel that way again. To feel as if the very world was at her fingertips just waiting for her to do something. To feel as if she could soar above the clouds.

She wanted to feel invincible, and she realized that only he could do that for her.

As she kissed him over and over again, she could feel him weakening, feel him giving in to the strong wave of desire that had washed over both of them.

But then, just as surprisingly, just as she had pushed his jacket off his shoulders and down his arms while he had begun to undress her, too, Bowie abruptly stopped.

Stunned, bereft, she looked at him, confused and hurt. Was he rejecting her? Didn't he want her? Marlowe wanted to flee, to hide, but instead, she made herself stand her ground.

"What's wrong?" she asked him in a shaken voice.

He wanted her more than he had ever wanted anything. More than he wanted to breathe, but he couldn't just consider his own needs in this.

His eyes searched her face. "Marlowe, are you sure about this?"

For a moment, she was speechless. And then the sunshine slowly returned.

"Do you want me to fill out an application?" she asked him.

"I just don't want you to regret this in the morning," he told her.

"What I'll regret in the morning," she told him, "is if you stop now."

He searched her face again, looking for the flaw in her statement. He found none. She was being serious, and everything inside of him lit up.

"Then let's make sure you have no regrets," he told her in a low voice that instantly seduced her.

The time for words was over. Now there were just very deep-seated emotions finally rising to the surface, seeking release. Seeking validation after being suppressed for what felt like an eternity.

Within seconds, it felt exactly the way it had that night at the conference. Except this time, there would be no gaps waiting to be filled in, no spaces that needed something to complete them.

This was all happening just the way it was meant to happen.

The hunger seemed to rise up suddenly, coming from his very toes and sweeping over him in a breath-stealing rush. It was making demands that had him all but shaking inside.

He hadn't admitted to himself just how much he had wanted her. How much he wanted to hold her, kiss her and, most of all, make love with her until he was just too tired to breathe.

Bowie hadn't wanted to admit it because something within him felt that admission would somehow undermine him, shackling him to something he didn't want to be shackled to.

But he wanted this.

Wanted her.

The moment he allowed the thought to form in his mind, Bowie suddenly felt as if he was free. Free to finally be himself and to enjoy this all-too-fleeting revelry that was throbbing so hard throughout his entire body.

"Are you all right?" he asked, looming over her and eager to continue. But he wanted to be very sure that he was taking nothing for granted, wasn't allowing his own needs to blind him to any possible discomfort on Marlowe's part.

Marlowe blinked, perplexed. "Why wouldn't I be?" she asked.

"Your stomach, the baby…" he said, letting his voice drift off in case he had left something else out.

Her eyes smiled at him. "My stomach, thanks to the chicken soup from Lucia's, feels wonderfully calm for the first time in a while. As for the baby, it's cheering you on," she told him with a laugh. "So whatever you do," she said, her voice dropping to an enticing whisper, "don't stop."

"Then I won't," Bowie told her, his words gliding along the hollow of her throat.

His smile seemed to burrow right into her, lighting up her very soul.

His lips and hands seemed to be everywhere at once, touching her, pleasing her, making her ache for more. And all the while, she couldn't help wondering how she had managed to go so long without this after having sampled it that very first time the night their baby was conceived. She felt like a giant jigsaw puzzle that had just been put back together after an endless wait.

Although she wanted nothing more than to enjoy this, to absorb every touch, every single nuance of his fingers glancing along her skin, she just couldn't lie back and have this happen without some sort of reciprocation on her part.

Marlowe eagerly slipped her hands beneath Bowie's shirt, opening buttons, moving aside the fabric and all the while yearning for the next exciting moment.

And the next.

A moment filled with reverence, with kissing. With fire.

His breath along her skin excited her beyond all measurable scope, and she desperately wanted to make Bowie feel what she was feeling. Determined to try, Marlowe returned his kisses with a frenzy that she had never experienced before, fueling a fire that burned to unimaginable heights within him.

Bowie felt his heart pounding, and while he wanted

to experience the rush that came with ultimate release, he was determined to prolong what was happening between them for as long as was reasonably possible.

Capturing Marlowe's hands to keep them still as well as from causing him to reach the peak of their experience, Bowie kissed her slowly, deeply, his passion increasing with each passing moment until Marlowe all but melted into a puddle right beside him.

A hot, contented, bubbling puddle.

She bit her lower lip as she felt his mouth branding every inch of her body with hot, achingly slow, arousing kisses.

Unable to remain still, she began to twist and turn beneath him as she tried to absorb each imprint, each arousing pass of his hands gliding along her throbbing skin.

He was making her crazy.

Shifting, she reversed their positions, and suddenly, she was the one who was leaving hot, moist trails along his heaving body; she was the one making him ache for her instead of the other way around.

Marlowe was working him up to the point that he was afraid, any second now, he was going to wind up wanting her *too* much and lose the control he was exercising over his body.

"Who would have ever thought that underneath that beautiful, cool exterior was this churning volcano of molten lava about to erupt and shower its fire all over me?" Bowie said with a laugh.

"That has to be the best-kept secret in Arizona," he added, his eyes shining as he looked at her again.

And then there was no more time for talking, no

more time to continue to keep feeding the fire. The fire they had lit was now hot enough to consume them both.

Bowie shifted his body, moving along hers until he was directly over her. His eyes all but devoured her, holding her prisoner.

Lowering his mouth to hers, he captured her lips and then moved to enter her.

At first he did so slowly and then with more feeling, moving so that the dance that was within their souls suddenly bloomed and became very much a reality.

Marlowe caught her breath as a shower of stars exploded within her. By the way he moved, she knew he'd been captured in the fallout, as well.

With all her heart, she wanted to hold on to this feeling forever, even though she knew that really wasn't possible.

But at least she had now, which meant a great deal to her and made her heart sing. As for the rest of it, she would deal with that later.

Chapter 19

She knew her bed was empty the second she woke up, even before she opened her eyes the next morning.

Marlowe was reluctant to actually open them, because then she would know for sure, and until she did, she could continue to pretend she was wrong. That Bowie was still here beside her.

Oh, grow up, Marlowe. You can't just spend the entire day in bed with your eyes shut, in a state of denial.

That wasn't who she was, she told herself. Denial was not the way she operated, anyway.

Bracing herself, she opened her eyes.

The emptiness hit her harder than she would have ever thought it would.

He was gone.

So what? Marlowe upbraided herself angrily.

After all, she knew what she was getting into,

right? Bowie Robertson had turned out to be an honorable man, saying that he would step up when the time came, but he had made absolutely no promises to her about their future together in the traditional sense. When it came to that, he hadn't said any of the things a woman wanted to hear with the sole goal of getting her into his bed.

As a matter of fact, if she were being honest about it, she thought with a sigh, Bowie hadn't tried to get her into bed at all. *She* was the one who had made the first move. She had kissed him and made it abundantly clear that she wanted to make love with him last night.

If anything, Bowie had even tried to get her to back away, pausing right at the beginning and asking her if everything was all right. If she had suddenly backed away at that point, she knew he would have let her.

He might not have been happy about it, but he would have definitely let her.

No, she thought, tossing off the covers and looking around for her robe, last night had been a wonderful, *singular* experience—well, all right, *two* experiences, she amended with a smile. But right from the beginning she certainly knew that he had no intentions of turning that into their way of life from here on in.

If things wound up working themselves out, there might even be a few repeat performances of last night, but there was nothing on the drawing board to suggest it would turn into something permanent, and the sooner she wrapped her head around that, the better off she would be.

Besides, she had enough complications in her life right now. She certainly didn't need anything more.

The main things on her mind right now should be finding who had targeted her and Bowie previously. And Ace and who had switched him for her so-called real brother that night. Also she needed to find out why they had done it. For all she knew, the person who had switched those two babies could have even been her own father.

The more she thought about it, the more it sounded like it could have been something he would be capable of. After all, the image of a sickly first son was not exactly in keeping with the kind of legend Payne Colton would have liked to project.

C'mon, Marlowe, up and at 'em, she silently ordered, sitting up. Seeing her robe, she pulled it over and put it on.

Last night was in the past—as was Bowie, she insisted. Time to face a new day. All she needed was to grab a quick shower and get dressed, and she could be on her way—that thought stopped her. Her car was still back at Colton Oil's headquarters. Unless she felt up to a long walk—and she didn't—she needed a ride.

Callum, she decided. She'd give her twin a call. He wouldn't mind driving her in to work, and he wouldn't ask her a lot of unwanted, pesky questions while he was doing it. Callum, thank goodness, knew when to mind his own business. He—

Marlowe stopped abruptly. Was she imagining things? Because right now she could have sworn she smelled…chicken soup?

But that was impossible. She was positive that Bowie had put the remainder of the container of soup into the refrigerator before things had heated up between them last night. If it was there, how could she smell it now?

Curious, she went into the kitchen to investigate. Startled, Marlowe stifled a scream. But it was still loud enough to have Bowie almost drop the pot he had just finished warming up and was now about to transfer to the counter.

He put the pot down just in time. "Hell, Marlowe, you just made my heart stop," he told her. "And not in a good way," he added, as if remembering last night.

She glared at him. If there was one thing she hated, it was acting afraid in front of an audience, even an audience of one.

"Well, that makes two of us. I thought you'd left," she accused, taking a deep breath in an attempt to calm down her galloping pulse. "What are you doing here?"

"Not exactly the most welcoming tone of voice I've heard, but I'll answer that I said I was taking Bigelow's place as your bodyguard. That would include this morning until I get you back to the office and under his watchful eye. Don't you remember?" he asked.

Marlowe shrugged. The only thing she had thought of this morning was that he wasn't there. "I just assumed when I woke up and you weren't next to me…"

"That I had folded my tent and disappeared into the night?" Bowie guessed. Had he caught a glimmer of disappointment in her eyes when she'd screamed? Perhaps that thought made him smile, although he clearly did his best to maintain a straight face.

"Something like that," Marlowe admitted, hating just how happy the sight of him made her feel.

His being here didn't change anything. He'd practically told her as much. He was just being honorable and living up to his word, but that didn't mean he was about to turn over an entirely new leaf and become a new man. He was a commitmentphobe, and that wasn't about to change.

"Well, you assumed wrong," he told Marlowe.

So it would seem, she thought. Desperate to change the subject, she nodded at the pot on the counter. "What's with the soup?"

He turned toward the counter, grateful to have something else to focus on. "Since you tolerated it so well last night, I thought maybe you could have some more soup for breakfast, too—until you can eat other food," he explained. Then he looked at her more closely. "How's your stomach this morning?"

"Well, I haven't thrown up yet," she answered, then added philosophically, "but then, the morning's still young."

"Ever the optimist," he commented. And then he smiled encouragingly. "Maybe this is a sign of things to come," he told her.

"Maybe," she allowed, although she wasn't nearly as confident as he was. She was still holding her breath, waiting for her stomach to rebel against her.

"I've got water boiling for herbal tea just in case," he told Marlowe. "But since the soup's all warmed up," he said, taking the ladle and putting just a small serving into a bowl, "why don't you try sipping some of that first?"

"You don't have to do this," she insisted.

Being on the receiving end of all this fussing from someone who wasn't being paid to dance attendance on her made her feel uncomfortable. Having him wait on her like this put her in his debt, and she didn't like the way that felt.

"I know," Bowie answered. "Maybe I'm just trying to explore my domestic side," he told her, a grin twitching his lips.

"Heating up chicken soup and boiling water for tea isn't exactly going to turn you into the next Julia Child," she informed him.

"Another dream shattered," he quipped. And then he indicated the bowl he'd placed in front of her. "Just eat the soup, Marlowe."

She frowned. She didn't want to be beholden to him in any manner, and yet here he was, serving her and keeping her company while she ate.

"I can call a cab, you know," she told him, "or have one of my brothers come and pick me up." She looked at him almost accusingly. "You don't have to hover over me like this."

He patiently refuted her arguments. "Number one, I'm not hovering." He had taken a seat opposite her. "Number two, I already told you, I'm taking Bigelow's place until I get you back to him. And number three, if I didn't have such a thick hide, thanks to my father, I would have said that you trying to get rid of me like this is hurting my feelings. Now eat your breakfast."

He was talking down to her, she thought, leveling an annoyed look at Bowie. But she grudgingly did as he told her to.

Picking up her spoon, she raised it, then dipped it into her soup. "Anyone ever tell you that you're a dictator?"

"Yes," he answered simply. "It's one of my better

leadership qualities." He waved at the bowl. "Now stop stalling and eat. I've got another meeting to get to this morning."

"Then go," she all but ordered him. "No one's keeping you."

Bowie frowned at her. Being with this woman required a great deal of patience, he couldn't help thinking. "Were you always such a slow learner?" he asked. "I just said I wasn't leaving your side until I turn you over to Bigelow. Now stop arguing with me and eat!"

"You know, maybe you should take lessons from Wallace," she informed Bowie.

"I'll be sure to let him know that. It'll make him happy," he said. "Now are you going to eat your soup, or am I going to have to feed you?"

She raised her chin, almost spoiling for a fight. "Go ahead," she challenged.

He'd never been one to back away from a challenge. "All right, I will." Picking up the spoon, he dipped it into the bowl and then proceeded to say, "Open up, Marlowe. Here comes the airplane heading straight for the hangar."

He said it so seriously, she couldn't help but laugh. And once she started, it was hard for her to stop. When she finally did, Bowie picked up the spoon again, filled it and brought it up to her lips once more as if nothing had happened.

What he hadn't counted on was the act of feeding her like this, of keeping his eyes on her as he slipped the spoon in between her lips, aroused him.

As it did her.

Bowie managed to get exactly three spoonfuls into her mouth like that and then the spoon, as well as the

pretense of feeding her, were abandoned. He rose to
his feet, bringing her up with him. And then he took
her into his arms and kissed her.

She felt his smile against her lips. "You know,"
Bowie told her, "at this rate, you're going to wind up
starving to death."

"Well, if that happens, I'll die with a smile on my
face," she told him, her eyes never leaving his.

"Yeah," he agreed. "Me, too."

"Are you going to be late now?" Marlowe asked
Bowie nearly an hour later.

Bowie was finally taking her to Colton Oil headquarters after first calling Wallace to alert the bodyguard that he needed to be there to take over. Bowie
was not about to just leave her at the building and take
off. He took his responsibility very seriously.

"I'm the one conducting the meeting. They can't
very well start without me, although I really wasn't
planning on being late," he told her.

And he hadn't counted on wanting her so much
after they'd already made love twice the night before.
He was beginning to think of Marlowe as an addic-
tion that he couldn't seem to shake.

"That's what you get for trying to be nice," she
told him.

"Trying?" Bowie echoed. "I thought I was pretty
successful in that department."

"I was talking about being nice," she informed him,
"not the other part."

He grinned at her, even as he warned himself not
to get drawn in again. He didn't have time for entan-
glements or for getting caught up with the daughter

of his father's archrival…even though they were now having a baby together.

So why was he having so much trouble convincing himself to leave her alone?

"So was I," he told her, his grin getting under her skin.

It occurred to Marlowe that he was driving awfully slowly for a man who was supposed to be in a hurry. This was a sports car, for heaven's sake.

"Can't this thing go any faster? You're not the only one with meetings to get to," she told him. "I've got one scheduled for half an hour from now, so step on it," she urged.

"Five minutes isn't going to make a difference," he told her. "It's not just your life you'd be risking by speeding. You're going to have to start thinking more like a mother, Marlowe."

She really didn't take well to being lectured to. "I am thinking like a mother," she informed him. "An impatient mother. Now make this car go faster!"

Her eyes widened as she felt the car slowing down, not picking up speed. Looking at the speedometer, she saw that she was right. Bowie *was* slowing down.

"What are you doing?" she demanded.

"Making you take a breath." He wasn't kidding anymore. Bowie was deadly serious. "If you're not careful, you're going to wind up giving yourself pre-eclampsia," he told her.

She stared at him. He was making that up, she thought. "Say what?"

"That's where you wind up with high blood pressure, swollen ankles, and a lot of other unpleasant symptoms and side effects, which in turn will force you to spend the duration of your pregnancy laid up in bed, something I have a feeling that you *really* wouldn't like," he concluded. "So stop being such a rebel and just take it light, all right?"

"How do you know all this?" she asked, still not certain if she believed the man in the driver's seat or not. She wouldn't have put it past Bowie to have made that word up.

"Since you told me about our pending bundle of joy, I've done a lot of reading up on the subject," he told her. "Preeclampsia is also something you would know about if you made that appointment with your doctor." The look on Bowie's face told her just what he expected her to do next.

"Fine," she told him, rolling her eyes. "I'll make that appointment with my ob-gyn. Now can you *please* get me to my office, or do I have to flag down a turtle to get me there?"

"No offense, but I don't think you'd fit on the back of a turtle," he told her, clearly doing his best to keep the smile off his face. "Besides," he said as he slowed down and pulled over to the curb on the next block, "we're here. And here's Bigelow, right on time." He brought his car right up to where the bodyguard was standing and waiting for her.

With a welcoming smile, Wallace leaned in and opened the passenger door for Marlowe.

"Good morning, Ms. Colton," the bodyguard said brightly. He presented his elbow to her, waiting for her to take it.

Marlowe deliberately ignored his elbow as she swung out her legs and rose to her feet. "I can still get out of a car on my own, Wallace," she informed the bodyguard stiffly.

"Never said you couldn't, ma'am," the bodyguard replied politely. He still watched her every move carefully—just in case.

Bowie leaned over inside the car toward the passenger side to get a better look at the bodyguard.

"I'd say you've got your work cut out for you, Bigelow. As you can see," Bowie told the man on his payroll, "Ms. Colton left her sunny disposition at home this morning."

Wallace flashed his employer a smile. "I'm sure everything will be fine, sir," he said, glancing toward Marlowe.

"Just get me away from Mr. Personality here," Marlowe said from between clenched teeth. "Before I say something he won't appreciate."

"As you wish, ma'am," Wallace said, making certain that he was only half a step away from her at all times as he escorted Marlowe toward the building's entrance. Reaching it, he held the door open for her.

Bowie remained where he was until he saw Marlowe walk into the building. Then he gunned his engine and pulled away.

Hearing the sound the car made as it left, Marlowe muttered under her breath, "I *knew* that sports car could go faster."

"Yes, ma'am, it really can," Wallace agreed, following her inside the building.

Chapter 20

Pausing, Marlowe rotated her shoulders and then rubbed the bridge of her nose.

Her head was killing her and her vision was getting really blurry, making the words on her computer screen look as if they were shimmering and moving about as they went in and out of focus.

Marlowe sighed as she looked at her watch. She had been working on this new proposal and telling herself "five more minutes" now for the last hour and a half. Every time she thought she was finally finished, something else would occur to her and she would have to stop and rework what she had written previously to make it jibe with what she had put down a few minutes ago.

She hated to admit it, but maybe she was pushing herself too hard.

It was getting to the point that things were beginning to spin around in her head. Even Wallace had grown completely quiet. He had adjourned to the outer office, leaving her alone. He'd done it undoubtedly in hopes that it might just help usher her along and get her to finally finish what was ultimately going to be a rough draft of the report she was going to be finalizing tomorrow.

The report that she was going to present to the state energy commission.

Marlowe bit her lower lip. This had to be just right, and at the moment, no matter how much she reworked it, she really didn't feel that it was.

Marlowe sighed again.

Where had all this insecurity come from, she asked herself. Ever since she'd gotten pregnant, it was as if up was down, down was up and everything felt as if it was skidding sideways. Her confidence had always been her best asset, and now...

Now she needed to straighten up and fly right, Marlowe sternly told herself.

And that, she realized, was *not* going to happen until she took control of herself, went home and got a decent night's sleep.

Her days of running on fumes were definitely over. She hated to admit this, even to herself, but this, perforce, was going to be a brand-new chapter in her life.

"Okay, Wallace," she announced, raising her voice so that it would carry into the next room, otherwise known as her administrative assistant's office. Wallace would avail himself of that area whenever Karen had gone home and he felt that she needed a little space to finish up whatever she was working on. "Your wish has come true. We're going home."

While her bodyguard wasn't exactly the most talkative man in the world—there were times when he was downright quiet, almost eerily so—he did always answer her when she addressed him. Even if he wasn't in the room, he would come back in and then answer her because he didn't believe in shouting.

But Wallace wasn't answering her now. He wasn't making a sound.

Had he fallen asleep? No, that didn't seem possible, she thought. The man ran on batteries.

"Wallace, did you hear me?" she asked, raising her voice a little louder. "I said I'm packing it in and you can take me home now."

Still no answer.

Curious now, she pushed her chair away from her desk. Maybe Wallace had gone to the men's room, although in all their time together, she couldn't recall the bodyguard having availed himself of that facility even once. It had gotten to the point where she had begun to think of the man as a human camel.

"Wallace, are you there?" she asked, an uneasiness beginning to spread through her. Why wasn't he answering? If he had suddenly started to feel sick, wouldn't he have said something to her? He usually checked in with her if he was going to do anything out of the ordinary.

Marlowe was fairly certain that Wallace wouldn't have just gone off to get a breath of fresh air. The man was the most self-contained person she had ever met. He didn't eat or drink on the job, and she was beginning to think that Wallace was the closest thing to a self-propelled robot she had ever encountered.

Growing a little concerned now, she called out, "Wallace, where are you?" as she walked out into Karen's office.

Still there was no answer.

The outer office was fairly dark, and she didn't see him.

Not at first.

And then, staring into the darkness, Marlowe realized that she could make out a form.

Her knees went weak.

Wallace was over in the corner, lying on the floor, partially hidden behind Karen's desk. Rushing over to him, she saw that there was a bloody crease across his temple. Stunned as well as worried, Marlowe fell to her knees beside the man, feeling for a pulse.

At first, she couldn't find one. Forcing herself to calm down, she tried again and finally detected a faint beat. Wallace was alive.

She almost cried.

"Oh God, Wallace, you gave me such a scare," she told him, addressing the unconscious man as if he could hear her. She had no idea what had happened to the bodyguard. All she could think was that he had to have tripped on something and wound up hitting his head on the corner of the desk when he went down.

But whether that did or didn't happen didn't matter right now. There was a far more immediate problem to be handled.

"We've got to get you to the hospital," she told Wallace as she took her cell phone out of her pocket.

But before she could even hit the number nine, a

voice came out of the darkness and said, "I wouldn't do that if I were you."

Startled, her heart pounding almost wildly, she got up quickly and turned around toward the voice. She saw an average, nondescript man stepping out of the shadows and coming toward her.

As he came into the light, she realized that the man was holding a gun.

It was pointed right at her.

For the last several days now, she had had this strange, uneasy feeling that she was being watched. A feeling she couldn't shake, even though no one had shot at her or Bowie in over a week. With effort, she had managed to convince herself that the only one watching her was Wallace and that she was being paranoid.

But now she saw that she'd been wrong.

There was something definitely wrong with this man, she thought, but she couldn't let fear get the better of her. Wallace needed medical attention, and she was the only one who could get it for him.

"He needs an ambulance," she insisted, beginning to dial her cell phone.

"He doesn't need anything," the stalker told her darkly. When she continued to dial, he barked, "Put the phone down. Now!"

Afraid he would harm Wallace further, Marlowe did as the stalker told her, never taking her eyes away from the man.

"What did you do to him?" Marlowe demanded, doing her best to use an authoritative tone.

"What did you do to him," the stalker parroted, mimicking her voice and making it sound high-pitched and singsong. "It's always someone else who has your attention, isn't it?" he snapped. "Never me. Well, now I have your attention, don't I?" he asked, mocking her. His eyes narrowed, resembling small laser beams. "Now you have to pay attention to me, don't you?" he asked—and then he swung the gun toward Wallace, aiming it at the man's head. "Because you know I can snuff your friend out. Just. Like. That. Right?" he taunted.

"Don't!" she cried before she could get hold of herself. "Please don't. You have my attention, my complete attention. I swear it," Marlowe told the man with feeling. "Just don't shoot him."

The man sneered as he looked at her contemptuously. "You don't even know who I am, do you?" he demanded. He looked familiar, but only in a vague sort of way. For the life of her, Marlowe couldn't recall where she had seen him before, or even *if* she had seen him before or was only imagining it. But she sensed that if she said that to this man, it could send him over the edge or have some other dire consequences. She wasn't ready for either Wallace or her to pay that price.

So she lied.

"Of course I do," Marlowe told him in her warmest, friendliest voice.

For just a split second, she could see that her ruse was working and he believed her. But then his expression transformed into an ugly mask of pure hatred and, his face turning red, he shouted, "Liar! You *don't* remember me. I've been in love with you for over two years now but you never even gave me the time of day. Never even knew I was alive," he shouted, his face growing even redder.

"That's not true," Marlowe insisted, even as she racked her brain trying to remember seeing him somewhere. Desperate, she came up with an idea. "Of course I knew you were alive. But you know how it is, how my father is," she told him. "If I let my father know about you, about how I *felt* about you, he would have made your life a living hell." She lowered her voice, as if confiding information to her stalker. "He doesn't want me paying attention to anything— or anyone—except for the oil company."

Though it sickened her, she drew closer to the man, playing up to him. "I pretended not to notice you so that you could go on working here." She was making it up as she went along, praying that she had guessed right with this wild stab in the dark she was making.

The man's pale, gray face lit up, really pleased. She had guessed right, she thought triumphantly. The stalker *did* work here in some capacity.

But where?

Marlowe thought back, remembering that uneasy, really creepy feeling that would come over her unexpectedly. He had to work somewhere in the company where he could see her with a fair amount of regularity. Maybe even daily.

Whom did she have daily contact with but didn't notice?

She tried to think, but it was almost as if her brain was suddenly paralyzed. Frozen.

Nothing came to her.

His smile faded as the truth came to him. "You *don't* remember me," he shouted. "You only have eyes for that Robertson man. Ever since I saw you two at that conference…"

"Oh, but I do, I do," Marlowe told him with feeling, trying to convince him. "It's just that you're waving that gun around and you're scaring me, so I'm having trouble thinking."

Anger creased his forehead as he glared at her. "You'd like me to put the gun down, is that it?" he asked her.

Her eyes met his, and she did her best to stay calm. More than anything, she needed to get him to listen to her. "Yes, please."

His eyes grew even colder. He raised the gun, aiming it at her. "You must think I'm really stupid," he accused her with a sneer.

"No, no, I don't think you're stupid at all," she denied adamantly. "I think you're smart. You were just biding your time, that's all. That was your plan all along."

Marlowe kept talking, but she could see that she wasn't getting through to this man. She was beginning to think that he was totally crazy. She could feel her heart starting to sink.

Her phone had already gone off once since her stalker had come on the scene, menacing her. And now it rang a second time.

Her stalker cocked his weapon, taking aim at the offending cell phone.

"Turn that damn thing off or I'll turn it off for you with my gun!" he all but shrieked.

"All right," she told him in a soothing voice as she reached for her phone, "I'll turn it off."

"Use your left hand!" he ordered sharply. This time the stalker shifted the gun so that it was pointed at

Wallace. "Or so help me, I'll finish him off right now,"
he threatened.

The last of her hope withered and died within her.
Marlowe drew in a shaky breath. She had no choice
but to do as he said.

Damn it, Bowie thought, Marlowe wasn't picking
up, either. Now he *knew* something was wrong.

It had become his habit to check in once an hour
with Wallace. But the bodyguard hadn't picked up his
cell phone in the last hour, even though he'd called
Wallace a total of three times.

And then he'd called Marlowe, but she wasn't picking up. He'd had his assistant check to see if there
was a dropped signal, but all systems came back up
and running.

Bowie tried again without success.

If the system was up, why weren't Bigelow or Marlowe answering their cell phones?

He could feel a knot tightening in his already
twisted stomach.

Something was very, very wrong.

Racing to his car, he drove over to Colton Oil headquarters at top speed the entire way, thinking that
Marlowe would have enjoyed feeling the rush of cold
air against her skin.

The sports car had barely come to a stop when
Bowie leaped out, running all the way into the building. All he could do was pray he wasn't too late.

The elevator wasn't there. He didn't have time to
wait for it. Instead, he took the stairs, racing up the
steps and taking them two at a time.

His lungs were burning by the time he reached Marlowe's floor.

Running to her office, he nearly came to a stop right then and there when he saw Wallace on the floor, unconscious and bleeding.

Half a dozen scenarios played through his head, each one worse than the one that came before. "Bigelow, where is she?" he demanded.

For one awful moment, he was afraid the big man was dead. But then he heard the bodyguard emit a low moan. Relieved, he knew he couldn't waste any precious time trying to make the man regain consciousness. He had the very sick, uneasy feeling that seconds counted and he might have already gotten there too late to be able to save Marlowe.

"Marlowe!" he shouted, scanning the area. "Where are you? Are you all right?"

There was no answer, only the sound of his own voice echoing back at him.

"Marlowe, say something! Anything!" he pleaded, fear all but closing his throat.

And then Bowie heard it. It sounded like a muffled cry. Like someone, he realized, whose mouth was being covered to keep her from crying out.

Scrambling back up onto his feet again, he called, "Marlowe, I'm coming!" It was more of a promise than a declaration. "Just hang on—I'm coming!" he cried, racing toward the sound of the muffled cry.

Bowie ran into her office and saw someone at the far end of the room brandishing a gun and dragging Marlowe into the stairwell that was located at the very far end of the wide office.

Her private stairwell, he remembered. He wasn't

sure where it led, but he had the awful feeling that if the stalker was able to drag her inside, he could barricade himself and Marlowe in there. The very least that could happen was that the stalker might wind up harming her—and their unborn baby.

Bowie knew he couldn't let the man succeed in getting in there with her.

Exerting practically superhuman effort, he all but flew through the room, cutting the distance between himself and Marlowe and the stalker at an incredible rate. With one giant surge of effort, he leaped up and then *into* the man, tackling him before the man could succeed in making off with Marlowe.

Marlowe tumbled backward, but the shock of the blow he'd sustained when Bowie crashed into him had the stalker dropping her hand.

Backing up, Marlowe watched Bowie battling her would-be kidnapper. Despite his slighter build, incensed with fury, her stalker was able to match Bowie swing for swing. Desperate to help, Marlowe looked around the immediate area, searching for something—*anything*—to use as a weapon so she could knock the other man out.

Feeling half-crazed, she saw the commemorative statue of an oil rig her father had given her. Grabbing it, she intended to swing it at the stalker the very first clear shot she got of the man.

But the stalker and Bowie kept switching positions as they grappled for the weapon.

And then suddenly, the gun went off.

Marlowe screamed, terrified. Her heart froze. Who had shot who?

For one long, horrible moment that seemed all but

suspended in time, she couldn't tell. Both men looked ashen.

And both men, she realized one awful, awful moment later, had blood on them.

Finally, Bowie staggered up to his feet. With a sob, Marlowe threw her arms around him.

"Are you hurt? Did he shoot you?" she cried, running her hands all over his upper torso, searching for the bullet wound. "Tell me he didn't shoot you," she begged Bowie.

But he didn't have to.

At that moment, the man shrieked, and then his body crumpled, falling to the floor. That told Marlowe all she needed to know: he had been the one to catch the bullet, not Bowie.

"I'm all right," Bowie told her, pulling himself together. "What about you?" he asked, quickly scrutinizing every inch of her. "Are you hurt? Did he hurt you?" he cried, searching for some telltale sign of an unseen wound.

"I'm fine," she assured him, leaning her head against Bowie. "He didn't hurt me."

Chapter 21

Once Bowie placed the call to the police station, Chief Barco and one of his people, officer James Donovan, arrived at Colton Oil headquarters within minutes of the call.

When the two men walked into Marlowe's outer office, Wallace was just trying to get to his feet. But Bowie placed his hand on the man's wide shoulder, making the bodyguard stay where he was.

"Don't get up," Bowie ordered him.

Any half-hearted protest Wallace was about to express died on his lips without a sound in deference to Bowie's authority.

"Everybody all right here?" the chief asked, concerned. His kind green eyes swept over the three people he knew in the room.

Bowie spoke up. "I am, but Bigelow here needs an

ambulance to take him to the hospital." He turned toward Marlowe. "And it might be a good idea to have Ms. Colton checked out, as well."

Marlowe immediately vetoed the suggestion. "No, I'm fine, really," she assured the chief, who looked as if he was ready to whisk her off to the hospital himself. "Or I will be as soon as you get that man out of my office and into a jail cell." Her eyes were filled with loathing as she thought of all the harm her stalker could have done if he had fired his weapon.

Barco turned his attention to the bleeding, semiconscious man on the floor. "I take it this is the man who took a shot at you in your condo," the chief said. "Cuff him, Donovan," he ordered.

The officer eagerly produced a set of handcuffs and quickly complied.

"If you check the bullets that were gathered up in front of the hotel when someone took a few shots at me, as well as the bullet that killed my personal bodyguard," Bowie told the chief, "I think you'll find that they all match this man's gun." Hysterical, the stalker had confessed to Marlowe and Bowie after he'd been shot. He nodded at the stalker as Donovan was dragging the man up to his feet. Marlowe had told him all about the man stalking her and it was all he could do to keep from strangling the man with his bare hands.

The chief's eyes narrowed as he glared at the prisoner. "Get this scum out of Ms. Colton's office, Donovan."

The officer nodded. "With pleasure, Chief," he told his boss.

Fully conscious now and in pain, the stalker began

to yell. "You can't get rid of me that easily," he shouted at Marlowe.

"I wouldn't bet on that, you bastard," Bowie said with loathing.

"But we were meant to be together. We were!" the stalker insisted, a frantic look entering his eyes. "Tell them, Marlowe. Tell them we belong together and that they're standing in the way of true love!" He was practically shrieking now.

Seeing the maniacal look on the stalker's face was when it suddenly hit her. She knew who her stalker was. "Edward Jones," she cried, moving forward past Bowie. "You work in the mail room!" Marlowe recalled how uncomfortable the man's intent stare made her feel whenever she had occasion to be anywhere near the mail room.

She could feel her flesh creep now.

Jones took her recognition to be an omen. "See?" he cried, trying to yank away from the officer who was leading him away. "She remembers me. She knows we're supposed to be together! Get these cuffs off me, you stupid ape!" he ordered hysterically.

"Yeah, right. In your dreams," Donovan said. "Keep walking."

Jones was still shouting as Donovan led him outside to where the police car idled, waiting.

Meanwhile, the chief had glimpsed Marlowe's face as her stalker was being led out.

"Don't worry, Ms. Colton," Barco reassured her. "I am personally going to lock that scum up and throw away the key." The chief looked from Marlowe to Bowie. "He won't be bothering either one of you anymore," he promised. "And whenever you're feeling up to it, come by the station and I'll take down your statements." He tucked away his cell phone. "Right now my advice to you is to go home and put all of this behind you."

"That's good advice," Marlowe agreed. "But I'm not about to do that until I see Wallace get the care he needs."

"It's just a scratch, ma'am," Wallace told her. He obviously didn't want to be a burden to her.

But Marlowe frowned as she looked at the man's bloody forehead. "You could have bled to death from that scratch if I hadn't found you when I did," she informed him.

"But, ma'am—" Wallace began to protest.

Bowie stepped in, interrupting the bodyguard. "Just say yes, Bigelow. Trust me, I'm telling you this for your own good. It's a lot easier than trying to win an argument—any argument—with her."

Marlowe pinned Bowie with an almost lethal look. "And when did you *ever* win an argument with me?" she asked.

Bowie laughed under his breath. "The key word here, Ms. Colton," he said, addressing her formally, "was *trying*." Hearing a siren in the distance gradually growing louder, Bowie looked at the man he had hired to keep Marlowe safe. "Sounds like your ride's here, Bigelow."

Minutes later, two attendants came in pushing a gurney between them.

"No need to ask who the patient is," the taller of the two attendants said. "Don't worry," he said to Wallace, "they'll have that stitched up and you'll be good as new in no time."

"Make sure that he is," Marlowe told the attendant.

"Yes, ma'am," the other attendant replied.

Wallace looked at Marlowe after the attendants had helped him get onto the gurney. "I'm sorry, ma'am," he apologized.

"For what?" she asked.

Wallace appeared genuinely distraught. "For not being able to protect you."

Although his hand was far larger than hers, she picked it up and squeezed it. "He got the drop on you. It could have happened to anyone," she insisted. "And it all turned out well in the end, which is all that really matters, don't you think?"

"If you say so, ma'am," Wallace responded.

"You do what the doctor tells you, big guy," Bowie instructed. "I'll be there to check in on you in the morning. Meanwhile, I'm just glad you're all right," he added with sincerity.

The chief had been standing by quietly while all this was taking place. Once the ambulance attendants had left with Wallace for the hospital, Barco turned toward the two people who were still in the room.

"Well, if there's nothing further, I'll be going, too. I've got to book that SOB," he told them. Then he confided, "I'm going to be looking forward to having the judge throw the book at him for all the emotional grief he caused, not to mention that he killed your security guard."

Bowie nodded. "I think that makes three of us," he told the chief.

Bowie waited until the chief had finally left to join Donovan before he slipped his arm around Marlowe's shoulders.

"It looks like it's finally over," he told her. And then he looked at her, surprised. "Marlowe, honey, are you shaking?" She knew he was aware how much she didn't like having attention drawn to any display of weakness, but her reaction had apparently caught him off guard. "What's the matter?" he asked Marlowe. "We got the bastard. He can't hurt you—or anyone else—anymore."

Because she had always come on like gangbusters, he evidently had no idea how to handle this new, vulnerable side of Marlowe.

"I don't know," she cried, upset and self-conscious over her behavior. "I guess it's just a reaction to everything."

She had managed to hold it together while it was happening, but now that it was over, now that she thought of how close she had come to being kidnapped or even killed, how close Bowie and Wallace had both come to the same fate because of her, Marlowe just couldn't get herself to stop shaking. Her baby's life had been in danger, too—and she had nearly lost Bowie forever.

"I'm sorry," she apologized, turning away and waving her hand at the whole thing. "This isn't me."

Bowie put his arms around her, drawing her close as he held her. "Well, until the real you turns up, I'll just hold on to the fake you if you don't mind. Just until she stops shaking."

Marlowe made a disparaging, self-conscious noise. "That may take a while," she confided. She was still avoiding looking into his eyes.

Bowie spun her back around gently and, placing his index finger beneath her chin, forced her to look at him.

"That's okay," he assured Marlowe, stroking her hair. "I don't have any place to be—except the ER while the doctor checks you and the baby out."

"I already told you, I'm fine," she insisted.

"I'd like a professional opinion confirming that," he told her.

"But—"

"Shh," he told her as he ushered her toward the door. "Humor me. That baby is half mine."

Because he felt that Marlowe could benefit from being in familiar surroundings, when they finally left the ER, Bowie took her to her condo in the city rather than to his own place.

Though she tried to disguise it, she still seemed rather shaky to him. He spent the night doing his best to comfort Marlowe and reassure her that at least *this* threat was over, even though the larger, more involved mystery involving Ace was still ongoing.

They talked about a variety of things until, exhausted, she finally fell asleep.

When Marlowe opened her eyes the next morning, the first thing she saw was Bowie's face. He was lying in bed beside her, awake and watching her sleep. She had the impression that he had been like that throughout the whole night.

"Were you able to get any sleep at all?" she asked Bowie, feeling both guilty and yet touched at the same time.

Bowie shrugged off her concern. "I dozed off and on," he told her.

"Mostly off," she guessed.

He smiled at her. "I never needed much sleep, not even as a kid." Peering more closely at her face, he asked, "How do you feel?"

That caused her to stop and think. The first thing Marlowe became aware of was her arm. She realized that it ached and felt as if it were on fire. That was thanks to her stalker, who had twisted her arm behind her back as he tried to drag her into the stairwell.

"Like I've been run over by a truck," she said honestly.

Bowie sat up instantly. That was when she'd realized that he was still dressed, as was she. Nothing had happened between them. Bowie had been serious about guarding her, she thought.

The man had been a total gentleman.

Bowie looked guilty about being remiss. "I knew I should have made you stay at the hospital just in case," he told her, berating himself for failing to do that. "Let's go—I'll take you back now."

Marlowe grabbed hold of his arm, making him stay where he was. "Take it easy," she told him. "My shoulder hurts because that crazy man yanked it. He didn't break it. Besides, we already went to the hospital to make sure the baby was all right. Everything is fine." She took a breath, centering herself as she tried to think. "If you want to take me some place, take me to the police station so I can give my statement and hopefully get that sick SOB locked up until the turn of the next century."

Bowie laughed shortly. "Amen to that. But first," he qualified, "since you seem to be able to keep food down now, you need to have something to eat."

Marlowe rolled her eyes. "You're being a mother

hen again," she complained, trying to redirect his attention. She didn't want to eat; she wanted to go down to the station and give her statement now that she was no longer shaking.

"Mother hen?" Bowie repeated, pretending to be insulted. "I'm just making sure you keep your strength up, that's all," he insisted. "Now get ready, and I'll see about making you some breakfast."

She looked at him, puzzled. Something wasn't jibing. "I thought you said you couldn't cook."

Bowie frowned. "Beating two eggs with a fork and then pouring the results on a hot frying pan isn't cooking," he told her. "It's called survival."

Marlowe laughed to herself as she shook her head. "You have a very unique way of looking at things, Robertson."

In response, Bowie just grinned at her. It was a grin that was really beginning to get to her, Marlowe thought. Rather than becoming immune to it, she found that each time she saw the corners of his mouth curving, the defensive walls that she had spent so many years building up to protect herself from feeling anything just became thinner and weaker.

At this point, they had turned into tissue paper and were close to shredding away.

If she wasn't careful…

Marlowe shut the thought away before it solidified and became reality.

"So?" Bowie asked.

Having changed her clothes, Marlowe had returned less than twenty minutes later, ready to go out and face the day. Bowie had placed a plate in front of her, making her sample his efforts.

Marlowe didn't answer him at first, thinking it prudent to take a second forkful before she said anything. As the second mouthful made its way down her throat and into her stomach, she found her opinion didn't change. She had to give Bowie his due.

"It's good," she pronounced. "Surprisingly good." Marlowe looked up at him as he watched her. "Are you sure you don't cook?"

"On the rare occasions when I don't send out for food or stop off at a local restaurant—wherever I happen to be—I dabble with whatever I have on hand." When she looked at him uncertainly, he explained, "I don't like being helpless in any given situation."

"So you learned how to cook," she concluded. In her opinion, that put him in a class by himself.

"I learned how to wing it," Bowie corrected. "I've seen enough people frying an egg to know what to do with said egg on my own."

Nodding, Marlowe took in another couple of forkfuls. "Well, whatever you did with it," she told him, "this is very good."

She hadn't said it, but he sensed that she was about to say "but." He decided to coax it along. "So, what's wrong?"

"Oddly enough, nothing," she answered. But it was obvious, even to her, that her response wasn't 100 percent the truth.

"But?" he asked, waiting for the rest of her statement.

Looking uncertain, Marlowe laid down her napkin. "I'm still waiting for my stomach to reject the breakfast you made. No offense," she qualified. "It's not a reflection on you. It's just that since this little guy moved in," she said, placing her hand over her abdomen, "a living hell has been going on inside my stomach."

"Maybe you're over the worst of it," Bowie theorized.

She closed her eyes, afraid to allow herself to even begin to entertain that idea because of the disappointment attached to it if she turned out to be wrong.

"Oh, if only that were true," Marlowe responded wistfully.

Bowie seemed determined to have her think positively. "Maybe it will be," he told Marlowe. "Tell me when you're ready to go," he said.

Within five minutes, finished with the meal Bowie had made for her, Marlowe retired her fork and pushed away her empty plate.

A small smile quirked her lips. "I'm ready," she declared.

"And you're sure you want to go in to the police station to give your statement?" Bowie asked.

Marlowe nodded. "To the police station and then to work. You can just drop me off at Colton Oil," she added. "I think it might be better if I face my family alone and tell them what happened." Knowing how her father thought, she didn't want any possible fallout to hit Bowie.

He could guess what was on her mind. "I'm not afraid of your family, Marlowe," Bowie said.

"I didn't say you were, but I think it just might be better giving them the details on my own. Having you there would only be a distraction."

Wanting to lighten the moment, he asked, unable to keep the smile from his lips, "You mean for you, or your father?"

"For now," Marlowe answered, "let's just say both. But you know what will be nice?"

He was game. "I'll bite—what?"

"Going into work and *not* having to look over my shoulder every few minutes." It had taken her the entire length of the night, but she had finally managed to allow Bowie to convince her that her stalker no longer posed a threat to either one of them, that he wouldn't suddenly reappear in her life.

Chapter 22

The moment that Marlowe walked off the elevator and approached her office, members of her family began to appear, converging and surrounding her. They all but swallowed her up as they fired their questions and concerns at her.

Her father outdid them all. He came storming down the hallway as soon as he was alerted that Marlowe was in the building.

Payne Colton's eyes met and held his daughter's. "Where the hell have you been?" he demanded loudly, frowning at her.

Confronted with her father's harsh greeting, it made Marlowe regret that she had turned down Bowie's offer to come with her to her office. He would have definitely been her buffer.

No, she thought, she was a big girl, a mother-to-be. She could fight her own battles.

Marlowe searched her father's face, doing her best to try to read between the lines. Had he heard about the stalker? Did he even care? She didn't have a clue.

"And hello to you, too, Dad," she responded cryptically.

What happened next took her totally by surprise. Her father threw his arms around her, embracing her and giving her what amounted to a bear hug.

"Dad?" she asked uneasily, utterly stunned by his action. She could count on less than five fingers of one hand just how many times her father had demonstrated this sort of affection for her. Holding her breath, she waited for an explanation.

Releasing her, Payne drew back his shoulders. "Chief Barco stopped by the house late last night to notify us that he arrested a lunatic stalker working in the mail room and that lowlife had tried to kidnap you. Barco scared your mother half to death," her father informed her in an accusatory voice. "That poor woman must have called you more than a dozen times." He demanded, "Why didn't you pick up?"

"I turned off the phone," she explained, trying to subdue the wave of guilt she felt. "After what happened, I just wanted to put the whole thing behind me and try to get back to my old self."

Her father frowned. "I understand all that, but you still have an obligation to the family," he reprimanded. "When you didn't answer, we didn't know what to think. You could have saved us all that grief."

"I'm sorry, Dad," Marlowe apologized.

But one of her brothers took offense at the way

their father was badgering Marlowe. "C'mon, Dad, give Marlowe a break," Rafe chided.

She didn't like being defensive, but she liked being blamed for having a normal, understandable reaction even less.

There was no such thing as being cut any slack when it came to her father. "That homicidal maniac almost succeeded in kidnapping me," she stressed, repeating what her father had already acknowledged.

"But he didn't," Payne said, pointing out the obvious. And then normal curiosity got the better of him. "How did you stop him?" he asked.

"I didn't," Marlowe answered, then told her father something she knew he didn't want to hear. "Bowie did."

Payne's salt-and-pepper eyebrows drew together, forming a single squiggle. "The Robertson kid? What was he doing in your office after hours?" he demanded.

"Oh, I don't know," Marlowe answered her father, deliberately sounding nonchalant, "saving my life when he didn't get an answer from the bodyguard he hired to watch over me."

"He did what?" Payne demanded. His face turned a bright shade of red as he tried to come to terms with what his daughter had just told him. "What the hell is Robertson doing hiring bodyguards for you?"

"Bodyguard, Dad, not bodyguards. There was just the one," she emphasized. "And to answer your question, Bowie hired a bodyguard for me because he was *worried* about me. For good reason."

That was clearly not a winning argument in Payne's

estimation. "We Coltons can take care of our own," he said bitingly, throwing back his shoulders.

"Apparently we're not very good at it," Marlowe contradicted, "because if Bowie hadn't come to check on his man, we might not be having this conversation right now. Just admit it, Dad," she retorted, losing her patience. "Bowie did a good thing."

"Yeah, after he did a bad thing," Payne declared, deliberately staring at his daughter's still flat stomach.

Disgusted, Marlowe threw up her hands. "There is just no talking to you!" she cried, completely exasperated.

"Well, you're going to have to, missy," he informed his daughter. When she looked at him quizzically, he explained his comment. "As our new CEO, you'll be reporting directly back to me."

She had been expecting this ever since he'd let Ace go, and it had been weighing heavily on her mind. "About that," she began, since her father had given her an opening. "I don't know if I can handle being a CEO *and* an expecting mother."

The look on Payne's face told her that he harbored no such doubts. "You underestimate yourself, Marlowe," her father said. "I have every confidence that you'll rise to the occasion."

"But," Marlowe began, feeling that her father was not being realistic, "I'm going to be a new mother in a few months," she stressed. And that opened up an entirely new, unknown world for her. A world she knew nothing about and one she felt she needed to focus on, in order not to shortchange the baby, herself—or Bowie.

That argument was not a deterrent for her father,

however. "So, you'll find a good nanny. Hell, I'll even pay for one," Payne told her, then declared, "There, problem solved."

"Not really," Marlowe told him. He was being far too simplistic. "And even if finding a good nanny did solve *my* problem, what about all the other mothers who are working for Colton Oil?"

Her father looked completely lost. It was obvious that he wasn't following her. "What about them?" he asked.

Marlowe sighed. "Does Colton Oil even *have* a day care center?" She knew it didn't, but she was trying to make a point.

Payne looked at her blankly. "What?"

She did her best to patiently explain what she was thinking. "I feel awful that I never even *thought* about that until it suddenly affected me directly."

Her father scowled at what he felt was convoluted thinking. "Why should you?" he asked her. "I certainly didn't."

"That's just the problem, Dad," Marlowe insisted. Couldn't he see that?

It was obvious that Payne was losing his patience with this discussion. "Marlowe, maybe you *should* take a few more days off," her father told her. "You're not thinking clearly."

"No, Dad," Marlowe contradicted, "for the first time in a long time, I *am* thinking clearly. We need to set up a day care center right here on Colton Oil's premises."

Exasperated, Payne exchanged glances with Rafe. "So now you're saying we need child labor?" her father asked sarcastically.

Marlowe tried again. "No, Dad, I'm saying we need a day care center on the premises. If I want to be close to my baby, other mothers, other parents," she corrected herself, widening the circle to include fathers, too, "should have the same option, as well. How about it, Dad? Can we set one up here?"

Payne didn't like being put on the spot like this, especially since it wasn't his idea to begin with. "I'll think about it," he told her evasively.

But Marlowe shook her head. Her father's answer wasn't good enough to satisfy her.

"You need to do more than just *think* about it, Dad," she insisted. And then she looked at her brother. "Back me up here, Rafe."

Rafe said simply, "I think she's right, Dad."

"Oh, you do, do you?" Payne asked his adopted son in a mocking tone.

The tone was meant to make Rafe back off, but the latter surprised him by digging in. "Yes, I do."

Payne looked at him in disgust. "And just who is going to foot this bill?" he demanded.

"Oh, come on, Dad," Rafe answered in disbelief. "You're pinching pennies now? Having this day care center on the premises will buy you more goodwill than you can possibly imagine," Rafe assured the overbearing head of Colton Oil.

Payne frowned. He really hated to be forced to admit it, but he had to say that Marlowe and Rafe did have a valid point.

Although he wouldn't come right out and say it, he demonstrated his agreement by retreating.

"All right, you two handle it," he told the pair. "I'll underwrite the day care center. Now let's move on

to more pressing problems," he said authoritatively
to the duo.

Marlowe and Rafe both knew their father was talking about trying to locate the real Ace, as well as finding the one whom they had thought of as Ace for all
these years. There would be no peace until both of the
Aces were found and the mystery surrounding their
unorthodox switch was solved.

"I'm already looking into that, Dad," Rafe reminded his father. "I still think the idea of hiring a
private investigator is a good one. Think about it,"
he said before Payne could protest. "If it's our PI, we
get to control what news is released and what is kept
secret until such time as all the pieces of the puzzle
come together."

Marlowe nodded her agreement. "Rafe has a very
good point," she told her father.

Payne looked from his daughter to his son. "So
now the two of you are tag teaming me?"

Marlowe wasn't certain if her father had just made
a joke. But for the first time since she had entered her
office that day, she smiled at the larger-than-life man.

"Is it working?" she asked.

"Maybe," Payne answered evasively. And then he
finally conceded. "Yes," he said. "But don't let that
go to your heads. Odds are that you've got to be right
at least once in a while," Payne conceded.

"Thanks, Dad," Marlowe said. "Coming from you
those are glowing words of praise." His daughter was
only half kidding.

Payne looked at her for a long moment, thinking.

"Seriously," he began in a tone that was extremely
subdued from the one he usually used. "Did that bas-

tard hurt you? The stalker, I mean," he added in case he hadn't been clear.

"I know who you mean, Dad, and no, he didn't. Thanks to Bowie," she stressed, wanting Payne to acknowledge that she was here due to Bowie's efforts.

Payne frowned as he cleared his throat. "Yeah, well, tell the boy I said thanks," he mumbled.

"Wow. More praise," she marveled in surprise. "I'll pass that along, too," Marlowe told her father, clearly impressed by this magnanimous side he was displaying.

"Yeah, you do that," Payne said in a low, less-than-enthusiastic tone of voice.

It was clear that uttering kinder words like this made the older Colton completely uncomfortable. Payne was far more in his element when he was shouting at people and ordering them around than when he was dispensing any sort of praise, no matter how much the other party might deserve it.

"Well," Payne said, looking from one of his children to the other, waiting. "Anything else that we need to discuss?"

"Not that I can think of at the moment," Marlowe answered. She turned toward Rafe. "You?"

"Nope," Rafe answered. "I'll let you know how things are progressing once I've hired that PI. I've got a number of candidates I want to vet first."

Payne nodded, his thick salt-and-pepper hair falling into his eyes. He combed it back with his fingers out of habit.

"I expect nothing less," Payne informed his adopted son.

"I know," Rafe replied, well aware how his father operated.

"And you…" Payne turned toward his daughter, belatedly beginning to take on the role of a hands-on father, a role that wasn't exactly second nature for him and didn't suit him, either. But he was trying his best.

Surprised by her father's attention, she asked, "What about me?"

"Your doctor say that you're okay to go back to work?" he asked. "You and the baby?" Payne added after a beat.

Marlowe could only stare at her father. This was a first. A whole new side to her father that she had never seen before and she wasn't sure how to react. He had never been a concerned father unless there was something about a particular child's behavior that could be seen as reflecting badly on the company. Then he would make his displeasure known.

"Well?" Payne pressed. "I know you can talk, girl. You damn near can talk the ears off a brass monkey," he declared. "Why aren't you talking now?" Always one to anticipate the worst, Payne stared at his new CEO, waiting to hear the news. "The doctor say something bad?" he asked.

"No." At least that much she could say honestly, Marlowe thought.

"Then he said it was all right to come back to work right after what you went through?" Payne pressed, watching her face intently.

He was like a dog with a bone, Marlowe thought. Once he latched onto something, he was not about to let it go until he was good and ready to. When Marlowe said nothing, his eyes all but burrowed into her.

"Well? What did he say, girl?"

Marlowe had never lied to her father. She thought

of lies being in the same category as quicksand. Once she stepped into that territory, there was no getting out of it, and she didn't want to have to go through the ordeal if she could possibly avoid it. Because she knew in her soul that no matter how finely crafted the lie would be, somehow, some way, her father would find out that she had lied to him, and then all those years she had spent building up and cultivating his trust would be lost to her in a single second.

"Well?"

"She didn't say anything," she finally said. She was very aware that not only her father was looking at her but Rafe was, too. She really wished that lies could come rolling off her tongue with ease, the way they did whenever Selina talked. But she lacked that particular talent, and most of the time, that was all right with her.

The next second, she berated herself for wanting to be like Selina in any manner, shape or form.

"Why not?" her father asked.

"Because I didn't schedule an appointment with an ob-gyn yet," she answered in exasperation.

Her father looked surprised, then thought her answer over. "I appreciate you being tough, but this isn't just about you, it's about—the baby you're carrying," he forced himself to say, although she knew it wasn't easy, since the child in her belly was half Robertson. "You have a responsibility to it."

She never expected to hear her father say anything remotely like that. To acknowledge her condition and even be concerned about her state. Especially since he was aware of the fact that the baby was Bowie's— *and* the grandchild of his archenemy. A grandchild that would very possibly force the two families to come together.

"Point taken," she told her father.

"So finish whatever you have to do," he instructed, "And then call your doctor. Tell her what happened yesterday. Don't leave anything out," he said harshly. "And then do whatever she tells you to."

"And if the doctor tells me to stop working?" she challenged.

"We'll deal with that when the time comes. Now I've got a meeting to go to," he announced. Looking at Rafe, he said, "Let me know when you find a private investigator," he ordered.

And with that, Payne walked out, leaving his two children flabbergasted in his wake.

Chapter 23

"Mind if I walk you home?"

Marlowe looked up from the assessment estimate for the proposed day care center she had been working on for the last few hours. She was surprised to see Bowie standing in the doorway.

Belatedly, his unusual question registered in her tired brain, and she looked at him as if his words weren't computing.

He found her bewildered expression endearing. "What?" he asked innocently as he came in. And then he gave up his ruse. "Sorry, that's my impression of me the way I might have sounded as a teenager."

That cleared up nothing for her. "Why?"

"Well, since we didn't travel in the same circles back then, I thought I'd pretend to go back in time to see what it might have been like if we did the typical, universal things, you know, like my walking you home after school, things like that." Reaching Marlowe's desk, he bent over to brush his lips against hers.

She found the taste of his lips exceedingly arousing as well as comforting. Without thinking, she sighed with pleasure. And then she laughed softly, warning herself not to slip into that trap.

"You're crazy, you know that?" she asked Bowie.

He didn't bother pretending to take offense. Instead, he merely grinned at her. "Yeah, maybe a little. All right." He feigned thinking the matter over. "I'll drive you home instead of walking."

It didn't seem right to have him chauffeur her around, even though she could easily let that become a habit.

"My car's still parked here," she reminded him.

"And it'll still be here tomorrow," he answered. "I'm sure the parking structure attendant won't let anything happen to Ms. Colton's car if it stays here for another night." Bowie dealt any argument she was going to come up with a death blow by adding, "Your father will have his head."

Getting up out of her chair, Marlowe gathered her things together. "My father's not all that bad," she informed Bowie, feeling it was her obligation to come to her father's defense, especially after this morning.

Bowie just gave her a very dubious look. "Hey, legend has it that Payne Colton eats interns and new hires for breakfast."

"Bowie—" she warned as she picked up her briefcase.

Bowie relieved her of the case, taking her other hand in his.

"Okay, I'll stop," he conceded, leading the way toward her doorway. "But that means you have to let me take you home."

"Whose home?" Marlowe asked. "Yours or mine?"

He paused next to a coatrack, took the lone coat hanging there and slipped it onto her shoulders. Bowie kissed her again as he began to close her buttons for her. "Your choice."

"Seriously?" She thought he'd have had this all plotted out at this point.

"Hey, I'm just trying to be accommodating." Finished buttoning her coat, he picked up her briefcase again.

"Speaking of being accommodating," she said, thinking of what she had spent her afternoon working on. "Guess what my father agreed to do this morning?"

They began to head toward the elevator. "That was *not* where I thought this conversation was going to go," Bowie admitted playfully. There was no doubt about it. She brought out the lighter side of him. "Okay, I'll bite—what did your father agree to do this morning?"

Marlowe announced the news proudly. "To open up a day care center here for the employees who have very young children."

He saw the pleasure in her eyes. Bowie caught himself thinking that Marlowe could even make work seem adorable. "Let me guess—your idea?" he asked her. He held his hand up between the elevator doors to keep them from closing before they got on.

"Yes, but that doesn't matter," she said, waving that

part away. "He actually agreed to it. He wouldn't have a few months ago."

Bowie pressed for the ground floor. "A few months ago, he didn't have a daughter who was going to make him a grandfather," he pointed out.

"Be that as it may," she continued, "it doesn't change the fact that he's becoming more human, more sensitive to what people need."

Heralding Payne Colton didn't sit quite well with him. "Maybe he doesn't like falling behind and realizes that he needs to keep up with the times," Bowie told her. The elevator stopped and its door yawned open. He waited half a beat to allow her to get a step ahead of him.

"My father doesn't keep up with the times, he blazes trails," Marlowe informed him.

Leading her back to where he had parked his vehicle, Bowie took her words in stride. And then he smiled at her. "Maybe he should consider having you doing his PR for him."

About to say something curt, Marlowe realized that she was becoming unduly defensive. She curbed that. "I guess maybe I did come on strong," she admitted.

Reaching his car, Bowie opened the passenger door for her and waited for Marlowe to get in.

"Just a tad," he agreed. "But your loyalty is one of your more admirable qualities," he told her.

Closing the door again, he rounded the hood and got in on the driver's side. Buckling up, he asked, "So, have you decided?" Then, when Marlowe gave him a puzzled look, Bowie prompted. "You know, have you made your choice? Where you want me to drive you tonight?" he added.

"To your place," she answered.

"Good choice," Bowie said with approval. Starting up his car, he waited until he pulled out before asking, "So, how was your day?"

"I just told you the highlight," Marlowe said. "Otherwise, my day was filled with everyone stopping by, asking me how I was doing and if they could get me something." She shrugged, not comfortable about having everyone being so solicitous toward her. "But I suppose that is only to be expected, since I am the boss's daughter—and the new CEO—and this just might be their way of trying to butter me up."

"You're forgetting the most important part," Bowie told her. He could feel her looking at him, waiting for him to continue, so he explained, "You're a terrific person."

"Now who's doing the buttering up?" she asked, trying her best to suppress a grin.

"I can't give you a compliment without an ulterior motive?" he asked Marlowe innocently.

A smile played on her lips. "I don't know, can you?"

"Absolutely," Bowie told her.

Marlowe suppressed a sigh. He was making her feel things, want things.

Want him.

She knew she needed to change the subject before she went with her impulse and asked him to pull over to the side of the road so she could give in to those feelings. The overwhelming warmth she was experiencing was liable to make her do things she didn't want to be caught doing out in the open.

But it was getting harder and harder to bank down those feelings.

"How's Wallace doing?" she asked Bowie without any preamble.

That caught him by surprise. "Wallace?"

"Yes, you know, the man whose head was used as a football while he was doing his best to guard me?" she reminded Bowie.

"I know who Wallace is," he told her, "although I tend to think of him by his last name. I was just surprised that you're asking me about him out of the blue like this."

"Not out of the blue," she protested. "I've been thinking about him all day."

He slanted a glance in her direction. "Should I be jealous?"

"No, you idiot," she retorted, curbing the strong impulse to hit him, "you should be relieved that I'm not this self-centered woman whose only focus in life is herself."

He hadn't seen her in that light for weeks now. "I realized you weren't like that when we slept together at the conference."

His response surprised her. "I thought you said that you didn't remember anything about that night," Marlowe told him.

"Oh, but how could I have possibly forgotten you?" Bowie asked teasingly.

He pulled his car into a driveway and then turned off the engine.

For a moment, she thought he was reading her mind, then she realized that they were in front of a condominium. He had arrived at his home.

"Wallace is doing fine," he answered. "He's not here," he continued, anticipating her next question, "because I told him to take some more time. I thought with your stalker safely locked up in jail and out of the way, you didn't need a full-time bodyguard anymore. Just maybe a part-time one," he added, then flashed a smile at her. "I could fill that position," he told her. "Actually, I'd *like* to fill that position." He turned toward her. "Ready to come in?"

Marlowe looked at him uneasily, responding to his tone. "You make it sound like I should be bracing myself for something."

"Maybe," he allowed. And then, with what she could only term as an impish grin, he said, "I'll tell you a secret."

"A secret?" she echoed, a little bewildered. What kind of a secret could he possibly be sharing?

"Yes. I'm not exactly the world's neatest housekeeper," he told her, then confessed, "Actually, I'm pretty bad at it."

She laughed, relieved. From the nature of his tone, she had been expecting him to say something so much worse. "Nice to know you're not perfect. And that so-called vice of yours, well, it can easily be rectified with a cleaning crew coming in maybe once a month. Or maybe less," she added.

Bowie unlocked his front door, and she walked in ahead of him. She looked around at the opened room. "Or, maybe more," she amended.

It wasn't the last word in cluttered, she thought, but it was definitely close to it.

Bowie had never liked the idea of a stranger pawing through his things.

"I'll think about it," he told her. "But right now," he continued, closing the door behind them and then locking it. "But right now," he repeated with renewed energy, "I've got something more important than a cleaning crew on my mind."

Marlowe's breath caught in her throat as she looked up into his eyes.

"Funny, me, too," she told him just before she turned her mouth up to his and melted into his kiss.

The moment she did, she wrapped her arms around his neck and kissed him again.

And again.

In absolutely no time at all, he had her blood rushing and her heart pounding, going faster than a hummingbird's wings.

In less time than it took to think about it, Bowie was carrying her up the stairs and into his bedroom. Once there, they made slow, languid love the first time around. Then, catching their collective breath, they did it all over again, but faster and more intensely the second time.

Finally, when it was over, Bowie pulled himself up onto his elbow and looked at Marlowe. "You know, I think you could get to be very habit-forming."

He said the word *think*, but in reality, he already knew that she was. Deep down, his cautious nature wouldn't allow him to state the fact flatly because, more than anything, he didn't want to set himself up for rejection just in case she didn't feel the same way he did—or didn't *want* to feel the same way that he did.

"Could get to be, huh?" Marlowe said, repeating the words he had just used.

It just proved to her what she had feared all along. That Bowie was not the type of man to commit, even though he had promised to provide for their child. She didn't *need* him to provide for this baby; she could do that on her own and do it well. She didn't need his money, and she didn't need him, not if she had to twist his arm like this.

"Well, I wouldn't want you to get any bad habits on my account," she told him, her voice rising as she threw off the sheet and started to get up.

Seeing the way Marlowe had just thrown off the covers, he stared at her. "Where are you going?"

"I'm getting dressed, and then I'm going home. To *my* home," she emphasized.

But Bowie caught hold of her wrist, anchoring her in place. "Hold it—did I just say something to make you do a U-turn like this?"

"No, of course not," she answered sarcastically. "You didn't say anything. Anything," she emphasized with feeling.

Still holding her in place, his eyes looked into hers. "I'm sensing hostility," he told her.

"Very perceptive of you," she replied bitingly. "Now if you'll just let go of my wrist, I can get dressed and leave you to whatever it is you want to be left to."

"Marlowe, calm down," he told her sternly. "We need to talk."

"No, what I need to do is have my head examined for actually thinking that we—" Her phone rang just then, distracting her. "I need to have my head examined," she repeated, upbraiding herself for being so naive and stupid.

She got no further because her phone rang again.

Exasperated, Marlowe looked down at the screen. It was her mother.

Talk about bad timing, she thought.

"I have to take this," she snapped. "It's my mother, probably calling to make sure I haven't been abducted again." Blowing out a breath, she swiped her phone on and declared, "I'm fine, Mom," before her mother could say a word.

And then she realized that her mother wasn't able to say anything. Her usually composed parent was sobbing almost hysterically.

Feeling guilty, she said, "Mom, please, calm down. I'm fine, really. There's no reason for you to cry like that."

But Genevieve Colton didn't seem to be able to take any comfort from her daughter's assurance. For a moment, she couldn't speak at all. And then, still sobbing, her mother managed to get out a few words.

"Mar…lowe. You…you have…to…come…"

At a loss as how to deal with her mother's very obvious distress, Marlowe tried to figure out what her mother was trying to tell her.

"All right, Mother, if it means that much to you, I'll come home to the ranch."

"No…"

The words her mother was trying to say seemed to get caught in her throat.

That didn't make any sense to Marlowe. "Wait, you *don't* want me to come home?"

"Your father…" Genevieve gasped, trying desperately to catch her breath and be coherent.

Marlowe tried hard to fill in the blanks and guess

what her mother was trying to tell her. "My father's worried about me, too?"

"No!" her mother sobbed, frustrated.

"He's *not* worried about me?" Marlowe asked.

None of this made any sense to her. If her mother was this hysterical, she suspected that her father had to be involved in this somehow. Maybe her father had fed her mother details that the chief had given him and that was what had made her mother so beside herself like this.

"What is it?" Marlowe asked, desperately trying to unscramble what her mother was trying to tell her.

"Marlowe…your father… He's…he's been…shot," her mother finally managed to get out.

Marlowe was on her feet instantly, reaching for her scattered clothing, her outstretched hand trembling.

"How?" she demanded. "When? Is he… Is Dad…?" She couldn't get herself to ask the question, fearing the answer she would hear.

Listening to her end of the conversation, Bowie was already getting into his own clothes, throwing them on while never taking his eyes off Marlowe.

Ace was now on the phone, having taken it from his mother. "Marlowe, it's Ace. Dad's at Mustang Valley General Hospital. The police brought him here. The whole family's here, and we're not sure if he's going to pull through," Ace told her. He sounded totally shaken. "You need to get here as fast as you can."

"But what happened?" Marlowe cried urgently. "And where were you? When did you—"

Her questions went unanswered. Ace had ended the call.

Chapter 24

Marlowe was trying very hard to keep from being overwhelmed by the shock that vibrated through her. Still, the phone slipped from her fingers.

She looked in Bowie's direction, hardly seeing him. "My father's been shot," she cried, dazed.

Bowie bent down to pick up her phone and handed it back to her.

"I heard," he said gently. He couldn't imagine what she was going through right now. "Do they know who did it?"

Numbness all but saturated her, stealing away her very breath. Marlowe shook her head in response to his question. "I don't know."

More than anything, he wished he could take her pain away. "But he's still alive, right?"

He saw Marlowe's eyes fill up with tears. "For

now," she whispered. Looking around the room, trying to focus, she said, "I've got to get to the hospital."

"Get dressed," Bowie told her. "I'll drive you over there."

That was when Marlowe looked down and realized that she still hadn't put anything on. She was still nude.

"Oh. Right," she mumbled. Her brain felt as if it was stuck in first gear.

Moving quickly, Bowie picked up her scattered clothes and laid them out for her on the bed. His heart ached for Marlowe. She looked so stricken, so lost, it was as if she was moving through a fog, searching for her footing.

"Do you need any help getting dressed?" There was nothing sexual or seductive implied in his offer. All he wanted to do right now was somehow help her get through this.

"I can manage," Marlowe told him. She could barely squeeze the words out. They felt like shards scraping against her throat.

Bowie's eyes, full of sympathy, met hers. "I know you can," he said, doing his best to sound encouraging.

She was dressed in seconds.

"Ready?" he asked.

"Ready," she blurted out.

They were back in his car and on the road to the hospital in less than two minutes.

In response to the attempted homicide, the hospital corridor directly outside the OR was crowded with people, drawn there by concern. They were all keeping vigil.

A quick scan of the immediate area told Marlowe that, just as Ace had said, her whole family was already there, even Ace, who had been conspicuously missing ever since the flare-up had happened between him and their father.

Marlowe's siblings—even her older half brother Grayson, who didn't work at Colton Oil and was not close to their father—were all surrounding Genevieve Colton. Another brother, Rattlesnake Ridge Ranch foreman Asher, stood next to their mother, who looked frightened and terrifyingly frail and brittle. She gave every indication of a woman who was on the verge of falling apart.

Even Selina was there, hovering around along the perimeter. She gave Marlowe the impression of a vulture ready to pick the anticipated carcass clean the moment the last breath was drawn.

Deliberately ignoring her father's ex-wife, Marlowe crossed to her mother and threw her arms around Genevieve, hugging her.

"Oh, Mother, how is he? Does anyone know what happened?" she asked, embracing the woman.

A little more composed now than when she had called Marlowe, Payne's distraught wife gave their daughter what details she could, the same details that she had finally managed to give to the chief.

"The cleaning lady called me from your father's office," she said in a shaken voice. "She was the one who heard the shot."

"So someone did shoot him?" Marlowe questioned, wanting to get straight as many details as she could.

But just saying that sounded so incredible to her. *Someone had shot her father.*

Her mother pressed her lips together to keep from sobbing again. She wanted to get through this once and for all for Marlowe's sake without breaking down.

"Payne was working late again," she told her daughter. "The cleaning lady said she heard what she thought was a gunshot, followed by the sound of someone running away, and then a stairwell door being shoved open, then banging shut again. After that, she said there was nothing but silence. The brave woman ran toward the sound of the gunshot.

"Thank goodness she did," her mother continued with feeling. "because she found your father lying on the floor, bleeding profusely from the wound in his chest. She immediately called the police. If she hadn't done that, your father could have died without the proper medical attention." Her voice hitched, and she pressed her fisted hand to her mouth, stifling another sob. "He still might," she said, her voice breaking.

"Shh, don't think that way, Mom," Marlowe chided. "He's going to pull through. Dad's tough. He's going to be all right," she insisted.

Genevieve Colton was crying again. Marlowe could feel her mother's muffled sobs against her shoulder, seeping into her clothing.

"I'll take over, Marlowe," Callum offered quietly, drawing their mother away from his twin and over toward him.

"Does anyone have any idea who did this?" Marlowe asked, looking around at her siblings to see if *any* of them could give her more information.

Murmured voices blended together in what seemed

like non-answers. And then Ace's voice rose above the rest. "The police said they were checking the security footage to see if it caught anyone in the vicinity of Dad's office," he told her. "But so far, all they know was that Dad was shot twice in the chest."

"That's either revenge or the killer was a damn poor shot," Rafe said.

Marlowe closed her eyes. "Oh Lord, I thought once Bowie caught that disgusting stalker, everything was going to start going back to normal. But this is just too awful," she declared, her eyes filling up with tears again.

She felt strong arms going around her shoulders and knew that Bowie was trying his best to comfort her, literally offering her a shoulder to cry on.

Marlowe struggled to pull herself together, but for now, she just let him hold her and did her best to rally for her mother's sake, if not for her own.

Bowie remained with Marlowe and her family until Payne's surgeon, Dr. Jonathan Bohan, came out to tell them that the operation had been successful. The bullet had not hit any vital organs. Currently, he was in the recovery room.

"When can we see him and talk to him?" Ace asked.

"You can see him in an hour once they bring him to his room. Talking to him, however, is going to be another matter," Dr. Bohan told them.

Instantly suspicious, Ainsley asked, "Why do you say that?"

"Because," the doctor said heavily as he delivered the news, "Mr. Colton slipped into a coma."

"A coma?" Rafe questioned. "How long is that going to last?" he demanded. "When's our father going to wake up?"

"I'm afraid that is anyone's guess," the surgeon said. "It could be in the morning, could be in a few weeks."

Ace looked up sharply, disturbed by what he was hearing. "Or it could last forever?" he questioned.

"It could," the surgeon agreed matter-of-factly.

"In other words, anything is possible," Marlowe said, hating to even entertain that idea, but it seemed that was what they were being told.

The surgeon exhaled heavily. "I'm afraid so," Bohan answered.

"But he could wake up tomorrow," Bowie hypothesized, speaking up for Marlowe's benefit in order to give her something to hang on to.

Bohan nodded his head. "We can only hope that," the surgeon told the family members.

Somberness gripped the Coltons even tighter.

Bowie remained with Marlowe for a few more hours, doing what he could to bolster her morale. He congratulated himself on achieving moderate success with his efforts.

When Marlowe appeared to be doing a little better, he decided that he could leave her for a while in order to take care of something that had been preying on his mind. Watching this drama unfold before him the way that it had, having something so traumatic happening without any warning, convinced Bowie that he needed to square things with his own father.

This had shown him that there weren't endless opportunities in which to take care of things, to square them away and make them right. There was only now. Tomorrow might never come.

Time was mercurial and fleeting.

He almost hated to disturb her, but he knew he'd never forgive himself if he let this matter go and something happened to his father the way it just had to hers.

Leaning over toward Marlowe as they all sat in the waiting area, Bowie whispered in her ear, "You'll be okay for a while if I run an errand?"

Marlowe was touched that he actually cared enough about her to ask if he could leave her side for a while. "I'll be fine," she assured him. And then, because she wasn't sure if he was going to leave permanently, she asked, "You're coming back here?"

On his knees if he had to, Bowie thought. But he didn't want to crowd her at a time like this. "Unless you don't want me to," he qualified.

She hesitated, wanting to tell him that she didn't need him to stay with her, that she could get through this on her own. But then she thought, Who was she kidding? "Come back," she told him.

Bowie knew that took a lot for Marlowe to say. It was, in effect, exposing herself. "As fast as I can," he promised. "Call me if you need me to come back faster than that," he added, concerned.

"Go do whatever you have to do," she told him, sending him on his way.

The drive back to the Robertson Renewable Energy Company offices went by both quickly and slowly. Quickly because it was over before he was even aware of the trip taking place, and slowly because he kept reviewing and rehearsing what he was going to say to his father once he got him alone.

None of the words sounded right to him, but they were all he had.

And then he was there, and there was no more time to rehearse.

"Is he in?" Bowie asked Jeannie, his father's administrative assistant, as he quickly walked past the woman's desk.

"Yes, but he's on his way out," she warned, calling after him as she half rose from her desk.

"He's always on his way out to somewhere," Bowie answered. Reaching his father's office, he knocked on the door and opened it without waiting for Franklin to give him permission to enter.

His father was in the middle of packing his briefcase and he looked up, surprised. "Didn't think I'd see you today," Franklin commented. It was clear that his father was preoccupied and wasn't about to remain.

Crossing to his father's desk, Bowie put his hand on top of the papers, causing his father to stop putting the papers into the case.

His father looked at him quizzically.

"Dad, we need to talk," Bowie told him.

"Sure," Franklin's tone was carelessly dismissive. "When I get back."

"No, Dad. Now," Bowie insisted.

Stunned, Franklin looked his son. "What's this about, Bowie?"

"About a few years overdue," Bowie told his father quite honestly. He could see that his father didn't understand. He tried a different tact. "I want you to hear this from me, Dad."

"Hear what?" Franklin asked impatiently.

"You're going to be a grandfather," Bowie told him.

Several emotions seemed to sweep over the older Robertson's face. And then he said, "Well, I suppose you were bound to slip up sooner or later. Will the woman listen to reason?" he asked.

He knew that his father meant, Could she be bought off? He contained his temper. "I'm going to marry her, Dad," Bowie said.

Franklin's eyes opened wide. "Oh?"

Bowie couldn't quite read the expression on his father's face, but he pushed on. "It's Marlowe Colton."

"What?" Franklin shouted, stunned. "Payne Colton's daughter?" His face was red now. "What the hell were you thinking?"

"That Marlowe Colton is the woman I've been looking for all my life," Bowie answered simply.

"That's a bunch of horse manure!" Franklin declared. "You can't be serious," he insisted.

"Actually, Dad, I am *very* serious," Bowie told him. "So serious that I'm willing to walk away from the company I love and believe in because my priorities have totally changed. I intend to be the husband and father that Marlowe and this baby both deserve and are entitled to, and I'm not about to allow anything to get in the way of that."

Franklin stared at his son in disbelief. "You really mean that?"

"Yes, I do," Bowie told him. "I know I don't have an example to follow, but that wasn't your fault," he added quickly, absolving his father of any blame for being absent for all those years. "You were busy building the company for the family. However, I fully intend to be a good father and husband to the best of my ability. I'm sorry to be so blunt, and if I hurt you, Dad, I don't mean to, but—"

"No, you didn't hurt me, Bowie," his father was quick to assure him. And then he took him totally by surprise by adding, "I only wish that I had been half the man that you are. And, if you want to marry her, you have my blessings, Bowie. But please, don't leave the company," Franklin implored. "I need you, and I can't do this without you. RoCo needs you," he emphasized. "Stay. Whatever else you want to do is fine with me. I won't stand in your way, but please, stay."

Bowie hadn't expect this, not in a million years. He grinned at his father, relieved beyond belief. "I will, Dad."

"And tell the Colton girl she's a lucky woman," Franklin said, calling after his son as Bowie left his office.

Bowie knew his father meant that sincerely.

"I will. But I'm the one who's lucky, Dad," he said by way of parting.

Bowie found Marlowe just where he'd left her, still at the hospital, sitting in the waiting room. He came up behind her and gave her a quick hug.

Surprised, Marlowe turned around to look at him. "You came back," she said, smiling at him.

"I said I would." Rafe made room for him and Bowie sat down next to her. "How's your father doing?" he asked.

Marlowe smiled bravely. "The same, but at least

he's still breathing. Get your errand taken care of?" she asked, wanting to change the subject.

"Yes, I had to clear up something with my father," he confessed.

He hadn't mentioned that. "Your father?"

"Yes." He grinned. "I wanted to tell him that he was going to be a grandfather. And that I wanted to marry you," he added, his eyes now searching her face for a sign that he hadn't frightened her off. "If you'll have me."

She looked at him, stunned and almost speechless. "Wait, back up," she cried. "What?" She was certain she was hearing things.

"I said I want to marry you and be a father to our baby," he repeated as if it was an everyday occurrence.

The words still weren't sinking in for her. This was Bowie, the commitmentphobe. Was he actually saying what she thought she was hearing? It didn't seem possible.

"Seriously? You want to settle down? You, Mr. I Want To Be Free, is talking about putting down roots?" she asked incredulously.

"Suddenly being free isn't all that appealing anymore," he told her. "So, what do you say?"

Did he think she needed help? Was that why he was saying this? "This is the twenty-first century. Women don't need to get married to have a baby."

"I know that," he told her, "but I need to marry you."

She looked at him suspiciously. "Why?"

He laughed and shook his head. Leave it to her to over-examine this. "Because I love you, Marlowe

Colton, despite that sunny, easygoing personality of yours."

She started to laugh then. "Good answer," she said to him, beaming with approval.

"How about you?" he asked. "Do you love me?"

"I guess I could put up with you for a while." And then she laughed again, throwing her arms around his neck. "Yes, I love you, you big idiot."

He considered her response. "Not the most romantic answer," he decided, "but I guess it'll do." She finally realized that Bowie was a man of his word—he wouldn't leave, and they were going to be a family together.

"Well, it'll have to," she informed him just before she kissed him long and hard, with all the feeling she had been trying so hard to bury.

Bowie was not about to disagree.

Epilogue

Wrapping her fingers around Bowie's hand, Marlowe crossed over to where her mother was sitting in the waiting area with Callum.

"Mother," she spoke up, getting her mother's attention, "I know this is a very difficult time for all of us right now, but I have an announcement to make." Marlowe's eyes swept over the members of her family. All of them were still determined to keep vigil over her father for as long as they were able—or until such time as Payne Colton regained his consciousness and recovered.

"Now, Marlowe?" her mother questioned. It was hard to tell what Genevieve was thinking as the woman looked at Bowie intently.

Marlowe smiled at her mother. "I thought this might provide a little shelter in this storm we're enduring." At least that was her hope. "Bowie just asked me to marry him—" she glanced at Bowie "—and I said yes."

For a moment, the silence in the room was almost deafening, and then Callum rose to his feet and clapped Bowie on the back by way of congratulations.

"Well, it's about time!" her twin declared, moving on to Marlowe. He gave his sister a bear hug. Looking over toward their grim-faced mother, Callum said, "This is a good thing, Mother."

"I know," she replied. "I realize that. I just wish that this news came at a better time," she told her children sadly.

"It'll be better soon," Rafe promised, squeezing the older woman's hand before he moved on to shake Bowie's and hug Marlowe. "Congratulations," he whispered into Marlowe's ear, genuinely pleased for her.

Ace was just adding his own voice to the congratulations when Marlowe, facing the doorway, stiffened slightly. She saw a tall, slender woman entering the room where they were all gathered.

Marlowe had a bad feeling.

"Can I help you?" Bowie asked, stepping forward. This was not the time to bother Marlowe's family, he thought, acting as a buffer. He had noticed the uncomfortable look on Rafe's face when he saw the woman walking in.

The redhead walked over toward Bowie. "I'm Detective Kerry Wilder," she said, introducing herself. Next to her, Rafe noticeably stiffened. Marlowe wondered why.

Marlowe instantly reacted. "Do you have any information to tell us about my father?" she asked eagerly.

"No, not yet, I'm afraid. We're still looking into all the possibilities." She turned toward the men in the waiting area. "Which one of you is Ace Colton?" she asked.

Ace stepped forward, moving around Grayson. "I am," he told the detective.

She nodded, as if she already knew which of the men he was but wanted to see if he would volunteer the information.

"Would you come with me, please?" she requested.

"Where are you taking him?" Grayson asked, clearly ready to protect his older brother. Like Marlowe, he had never stopped thinking of Ace as that, no matter what his father had said about switched babies.

"To the police station," Kerry answered. "There are some questions that need clearing up."

It was apparently all that the detective was willing to say at this time. Putting her hand on Ace's arm, she began to usher him out of the room, leaving the others to exchange looks and wonder what was going on.

"Are you arresting him?" Ainsley asked.

But the detective didn't answer. That left everyone wondering: *Did* Ace shoot his father? Was this what Ace had meant when he'd told the older man that he would be sorry for having thrown him off the board?

Marlowe refused to entertain that thought, but it certainly looked that way.

She was determined to find out as soon as possible for everyone's sake—most of all for Ace's, even as she looked forward to her own future with Bowie and their child.

* * * * *

Don't miss book two in
The Coltons of Mustang Valley series,
Colton's Lethal Reunion *by Tara Taylor Quinn*
Available now wherever
Harlequin Romantic Suspense books are sold.

And check out book three—
Colton Family Bodyguard *by Jennifer Morey—*
and book four—
Colton First Responder *by Linda O. Johnston—*
Both available in February 2020!

WE HOPE YOU ENJOYED THIS BOOK!

HARLEQUIN®
™

ROMANTIC suspense

Experience the rush of thrilling adventure, captivating mystery and unexpected romance.

Discover four new books every month, available wherever books are sold!

Harlequin.com

COMING NEXT MONTH FROM

ⒽHARLEQUIN
ROMANTIC SUSPENSE

Available February 4, 2020

#2075 COLTON FAMILY BODYGUARD
The Coltons of Mustang Valley • by Jennifer Morey

After Hazel Hart's daughter witnesses a murder, former navy SEAL Callum Colton saves them from being run down by the murderer's car. But now that the three of them are on the run, Callum's demons are back to haunt him—and he'll have to focus on the present to stop a killer.

#2076 COLTON FIRST RESPONDER
The Coltons of Mustang Valley
by Linda O. Johnston

Savannah Oliver has been arrested for the murder of her ex-husband, Zane, after their ugly divorce—but she doesn't believe he is dead. Grayson Colton believes her, and as Mustang Valley recovers from an earthquake, the two of them have to clear Savannah's name.

#2077 COWBOY'S VOW TO PROTECT
Cowboys of Holiday Ranch • by Carla Cassidy

Flint McCay had no idea what he was getting into when he found Madison Taylor hiding in the hay in his barn. But now they're both in danger and Flint must protect both Madison and his own secrets in order for them to make it out alive...and in love.

#2078 HIS SOLDIER UNDER SIEGE
The Riley Code • by Regan Black

Someone is determined to break Major Grace Ann Riley. After Derek Sayer, a friend with benefits, helps her fight off the attacker, he's determined to help Grace Ann, no matter how independently she tries to handle it. But as their relationship deepens, the attacker is circling closer...

YOU CAN FIND MORE INFORMATION ON UPCOMING HARLEQUIN TITLES, FREE EXCERPTS AND MORE AT HARLEQUIN.COM.

HRSCNM0120

Get 4 FREE REWARDS!

We'll send you 2 FREE Books plus 2 FREE Mystery Gifts.

Harlequin® Romantic Suspense books feature heart-racing sensuality and the promise of a sweeping romance set against the backdrop of suspense.

FREE Value Over **$20**

YES! Please send me 2 FREE Harlequin® Romantic Suspense novels and my 2 FREE gifts (gifts are worth about $10 retail). After receiving them, if I don't wish to receive any more books, I can return the shipping statement marked "cancel." If I don't cancel, I will receive 4 brand-new novels every month and be billed just $4.99 per book in the U.S. or $5.74 per book in Canada. That's a savings of at least 12% off the cover price! It's quite a bargain! Shipping and handling is just 50¢ per book in the U.S. and $1.25 per book in Canada.* I understand that accepting the 2 free books and gifts places me under no obligation to buy anything. I can always return a shipment and cancel at any time. The free books and gifts are mine to keep no matter what I decide.

240/340 HDN GNMZ

Name (please print)

Address | Apt. #

City | State/Province | Zip/Postal Code

Mail to the **Reader Service:**
IN U.S.A.: P.O. Box 1341, Buffalo, NY 14240-8531
IN CANADA: P.O. Box 603, Fort Erie, Ontario L2A 5X3

Want to try 2 free books from another series? Call 1-800-873-8635 or visit www.ReaderService.com.

*Terms and prices subject to change without notice. Prices do not include sales taxes, which will be charged (if applicable) based on your state or country of residence. Canadian residents will be charged applicable taxes. Offer not valid in Quebec. This offer is limited to one order per household. Books received may not be as shown. Not valid for current subscribers to Harlequin® Romantic Suspense books. All orders subject to approval. Credit or debit balances in a customer's account(s) may be offset by any other outstanding balance owed by or to the customer. Please allow 4 to 6 weeks for delivery. Offer available while quantities last.

Your Privacy—The Reader Service is committed to protecting your privacy. Our Privacy Policy is available online at www.ReaderService.com or upon request from the Reader Service. We make a portion of our mailing list available to reputable third parties that offer products we believe may interest you. If you prefer that we not exchange your name with third parties, or if you wish to clarify or modify your communication preferences, please visit us at www.ReaderService.com/consumerschoice or write to us at Reader Service Preference Service, P.O. Box 9062, Buffalo, NY 14240-9062. Include your complete name and address.

HRS20

Love Harlequin romance?

DISCOVER.

Be the first to find out about promotions, news and exclusive content!

 Facebook.com/HarlequinBooks

 Twitter.com/HarlequinBooks

 Instagram.com/HarlequinBooks

 Pinterest.com/HarlequinBooks

ReaderService.com

EXPLORE.

Sign up for the Harlequin e-newsletter and download a free book from any series at **TryHarlequin.com.**

CONNECT.

Join our Harlequin community to share your thoughts and connect with other romance readers!
Facebook.com/groups/HarlequinConnection

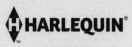

**ROMANCE WHEN
YOU NEED IT**

HSOCIAL2018